THE ONE *For* FOREVER

HANNAH SHIELD

The One for Forever (West Oaks Heroes Book 6)

Cover Photography: Wander Aguiar

Cover Design: Angela Haddon

Published by Diana Road Books

Edgewater, CO

Ebook ISBN 978-1-957982-22-9

THE ONE *For* FOREVER

PROLOGUE

Ten Years Ago

The cab driver pulled up to the curb, took one look at me, and his jaw dropped. His window buzzed down. "Are you Quinn?"

"Yep. That's me."

"You okay?"

"I'm…not great."

I imagined this moment from his perspective. We were in front of a swanky Ocean Lane hotel. I was wearing a tulle ballgown with my hair swept into an updo that had taken me two hours to perfect. And mascara had left black streaks down my cheeks. I'd seen in the bathroom when I'd been trying and failing to stop crying. Rookie mistake. Should've worn waterproof.

But I'd made a lot of rookie mistakes tonight.

"Prom night?" he asked.

"How'd you guess?"

I opened the back door of his Honda and stuffed myself and my tulle skirt inside. It wasn't easy. We'd taken a limo on the way here, me and my date and all my friends, and the skirt had seemed far more manageable then.

The driver eyed me in the rearview mirror. "You're not drunk, are you? Not going to make a mess of my upholstery?"

"One hundred percent sober." Every part of me was dry now, including my eyes. "Just wanna go home."

He drove away from the curb. "Night didn't go as you'd hoped?"

I huffed a laugh. "That's the understatement of my senior year."

I kept glancing at the automatic doors to the hotel lobby, wondering if one of my friends would dash out to join me. But they didn't know I'd left. And I'd been way too mortified to tell them what had happened. How stupid I'd been.

I was known for being an overachiever. But getting dumped by my date for another girl in the middle of prom? That had to be worthy of a superlative. *Most Clueless Prom Date. Most Likely to Never Have a Boyfriend.*

Halfway home, my phone started to ding. I pulled it from my tiny clutch purse. My friends had realized I'd disappeared and that Landon was dancing with someone else. Our group chat exploded with concerned messages.

Q where r u?

what happened with landon?

wtf whrd u go?

Long story. I'm okay.

Then Cliff broke out of the group and texted me separately.

Hey for real, r u ok? Do u want me to come home?

Ugh. The truth was, I kinda did want my best friend right now. But Cliff didn't deserve to have his prom night ruined, too. Plus, his girlfriend would've maimed me if I told Cliff to leave the dance.

I promise I'm fine! Just not feeling well! Have fun with Tori!!!!!

Cliff didn't call me on my excessive punctuation or my fake cheerfulness. He texted back that he'd see me tomorrow. I locked my screen, turned the volume to silent, and stuffed my phone back in my clutch.

I was over prom night. Over senior year, and over high school. I wanted my real life to start so everything could stop sucking.

The cabbie pulled up in front of my house. "Hope your night gets better," the driver said.

"Thanks. I hope so too." *Even though it won't.*

I pushed my skirt out of the backseat, getting tangled up in tulle before I managed to free myself. With a half-hearted wave, I walked up to my front porch, and the cab drove off. All the windows of my house were dark. My parents were away for the weekend. Yep, I was so trustworthy that they'd left me to my own devices on prom night. Thank goodness I hadn't mentioned that fact to Landon. He probably would've gotten even more gross ideas.

Cliff's house next door was dark, too, which meant his dad wasn't home. Our cul-de-sac was sad and lonely. Just like me. Instead of going inside, I sat on the porch.

I'd been looking forward to senior prom since… Well, freshman year basically. Who hadn't? I'd been on all the committees. I'd helped run the fundraisers. I'd even pitched in on decorating the hotel ballroom we'd rented for the event. It was supposed to be the capstone to our year.

But this year, anything good had been followed by absolute *crap*.

I was sitting on my porch step, mid-wallow, when headlights turned onto our street. A huge, black lifted truck. A vehicle I'd know anywhere. My head dipped, hoping he might not notice me. But I was a pale pink puffball. How could he *not* notice me?

His truck pulled into the driveway right next door, and the moment the engine cut off, Rex Easton was out and striding toward me across the lawn. "Quinn? What's wrong? What happened?"

"Oh, hey Mr. Easton." All casual, like we'd just run into each other in the frozen foods aisle. I tried rubbing my cheeks, but I was probably making the mascara streaks worse. "I'm okay. I was just heading in."

Rex frowned at me, crossing his muscular arms. He wore snug jeans, his usual scuffed boots, and a black T-shirt. He was a professional bodyguard. And way more handsome than an almost-forty-year-old dad had any right to be.

More handsome than my eighteen-year-old self should've been noticing.

"Quinn," he said sternly. "Why aren't you at prom?"

"I left early."

"Did your date drive you home?"

"No. I called a cab."

He didn't like that answer. The pulsing muscle in his jaw said so. "Why?"

I didn't answer. *Please let it go*, I begged silently. *Leave me to wallow alone*.

He didn't.

Rex walked over and sat on the bottom step of the porch,

a few feet away from me. "Are you hurt? Did your prom date do something?"

I shook my head, skin burning. "He didn't touch me. Nobody was molested."

He cleared his throat, eyes widening. "Hurt feelings count too. But something clearly happened. Because you're sitting here by yourself in your prom dress, and you've been crying."

"Would you believe if I said I've got allergies?"

"Not even close."

I rubbed my face again. "It was just general disappointment. Nothing to write home about."

"I don't believe that either." He clasped his hands together. "There's no shame in being sad. I'd be the biggest hypocrite in the world if I claimed otherwise. You've walked in on *me* crying."

My eyes filled with tears again, but I forced my gaze to meet his.

The Eastons had moved in next door a little less than a year ago, after Rex had retired from the Army. He'd been a Green Beret, running around saving the world in the most dramatic way possible. At least I assumed so, based on the googling I'd done, since he didn't talk much about his twenty years in the military.

His son Cliff and I had bonded instantly. We were both onlys, both runners. I couldn't imagine switching schools for senior year, but Cliff had acted like it was no big deal. He made friends easily. Lots of friends.

I was far more likely to stay in and binge *Criminal Minds* on a Friday night than go to a wild party. I had a bad habit of avoiding crowds and confrontation. There was a reason I'd chosen the track team over basketball or volleyball. Joining the debate club this year had helped me speak up more. But where I was shy and self-effacing, Cliff was breezy and outgoing and just a little ditzy.

We'd kissed once, and we'd both agreed never to repeat it. Zero romantic chemistry. But endless chemistry as best friends.

Yet even better had been spending time with the whole Easton family. They were the kind that had dinner together almost every night. Shared private jokes and kisses and hugs. Cliff's mom and dad had been high school sweethearts, but still deep in love. A stark contrast to my own parents, where half the time, one or both were traveling for business and they could barely stand each other.

The Eastons were the family I'd always wished I could have.

But then, only a few months after they'd moved in, Cliff's mom had died suddenly. A stroke. And their perfect world had shattered.

So yeah, I'd seen Cliff and his father both cry. I'd cried for them. After it happened, I had tried to be around for them as much as I could. Managing the food brought by well-meaning neighbors, helping Cliff clean the house. It had been rough. And so unfair.

"Sorry," I murmured. "I have no good reason to cry." Except an asshole prom date who thought he'd get laid tonight. I had let Landon know that would not be happening, and he'd complained about a bait and switch. Because *of course* the virginal good girl would want to punch her V card on prom night.

It had taken Landon all of five minutes to find a different girl to make out with on the dance floor. I'd meant to leave with my dignity intact, but instead, I'd taken a detour into the ladies' room so nobody would see me crying. Not because I was sad about Landon, per se, but because I'd really had my hopes up for a fun night. I'd gotten all dressed up for such a let down.

But no way was I going to tell Rex Easton any of that.

His chiseled, masculine features were going all soft and sympathetic. "Don't be sorry for how you feel. It's valid."

I shrugged.

After I was silent for a long time, Rex sighed. "What about your parents? They aren't home tonight?"

"Mom's at a conference in Phoenix. Dad has a meeting first thing Monday in Cleveland."

He muttered something like, *Of-freaking-course,* then spoke louder. "You should have someone here to take care of you."

"I'm almost nineteen." At least, I would be in September.

"That doesn't matter. We all need somebody sometimes."

"Isn't that from a song?"

His mouth quirked. "Why don't we call Cliff? You're his friend. He shouldn't have let you leave the dance alone."

"Cliff texted me when he realized I was gone. But I want everyone else to have fun tonight. It's not their fault my date was…" I shrugged. "A dick. I mean, um, a jerk."

"Will you tell me this dick kid's name?"

Rex's dark hair and eyes shone in the dim light. For a moment, he looked predatory. But I wasn't worried for myself. I was worried for Landon.

"Probably best if I don't do that. He's not worth it."

"He doesn't deserve *you,* if he disappointed you at your prom. You're a very special person, Quinn."

"Yeah, okay."

"It's true. You're beautiful and smart."

"Even with mascara all over my face?"

He didn't even flinch. "Yep. Because your beauty comes from inside. You deserve someone equally great. I'm sure you'll find him someday."

Ugh. I rolled my eyes because that felt like the appropriate response to those awkward statements. From the hot dad next door, no less. "Maybe next year in college."

"College. Sure. Maybe." Rex coughed, looking away from me as he stood up. "Hold on. I'll be right back."

He went over to his car and opened the door, grabbing something inside. I watched him, curious about what he was up to. Which gave me the excuse to stare.

Rex wasn't just handsome. He was *good*. He protected people for a living, and that was after fighting bad guys around the world for decades. I knew he and Cliff didn't always get along, and there'd been some distance between them since Mrs. Easton died. But to me, it was hard to imagine a better man than him.

Maybe, if I was lucky, that "special guy" I was destined for would be someone like him. That thought filled me with pleasant tingles.

A man like Rex with his strong arms around me… His mouth on me… *Quinn, you're beautiful.*

"I'll let you in on a secret," Rex said softly. His voice was deep, smooth yet raspy.

"What?" I looked up, my face flushed.

But whatever scandalous thought I'd been entertaining, this wasn't it. Rex was holding a bucket of fried chicken. "I picked this up on my way home, and I was probably going to eat it all myself, saturated fats and all. Want to share? Save me from consuming so many calories?"

"Uh, sure." I shook off my weird train of thought about his muscly arms and sexy voice.

He sat on the lowest porch step again and held out the bucket. I took a drumstick. "Sorry if it got cold sitting in your car," I said.

"Don't worry about that. I think it's better cold anyway." Then Rex held out some napkins with his other hand, and as I grabbed one, our fingers brushed.

Contact.

My throat was closing up. Heat raced through my insides.

My heart sped up to a hundred miles an hour. He'd turned away, calmly biting into a thigh piece. But I felt elated and sick all at once.

If one touch of his hand made me feel like that, what would the rest of him do?

Oh God. I really shouldn't think things like that.

Maybe Landon had been onto something. I was a good girl who wanted to be bad. But not with a high school boy.

Rex Easton was all man.

Right. As if Cliff's dad would ever look at me that way in a million years. In fact, it would've scared me if he *did.*

But that didn't stop me from imagining him leaning over. Kissing just under my ear, the scruff on his chin tickling my skin as our fingers tangled together…

"Should I put on some music?" I asked.

"Great idea."

"I've got a 90s playlist. So you'll probably know a lot of the songs."

He grinned. "Probably."

We didn't get up and dance, but we swayed in place and sang along to songs we both knew. We sat on my front porch until we were both yawning. Cliff was spending the night at the prom after-party, so he wasn't coming back. It was just Rex and me on the cul-de-sac. Of course, nothing was going to happen.

But inside my mind, my fantasies were in overdrive.

Rex said goodnight to me at the front door, reminding me to lock up and set the alarm. "Thanks," I said. "You saved my prom night." I wanted to make a quip about him being my hero, but everything that came to mind was way too cheesy.

"Just being a friend. Like you were to Cliff and me after Lydia passed. Don't forget what I said, Quinn. You deserve someone as special as you are." His smile was bittersweet. "Be safe."

"I will."

I went inside, watching through the window until he vanished from view. But I already knew I was doomed.

I had a full-blown crush on my best friend's dad.

My only hope was that I'd get over this quickly. And if not, I'd head off to college in a few months. It would be out of sight, out of mind. Even *I* wasn't hopeless enough to pine over a man I could never, ever have.

Please say I'm not that hopeless.

1

Quinn

Present Day

I step into the ballroom, smoothing my hands over my satiny, floor-length dress. This is the same Ocean Lane hotel that hosted my senior prom all those years ago. They've updated the decor, and tonight's event is crawling with high-powered lawyers instead of teenagers. But it's probably an equal level of maturity.

At least I've got a more subtle fashion sense these days. I even remembered my waterproof mascara. Though if I wind up crying tonight, something will have gone seriously wrong.

"There she is," Cliff says in a sing-song voice, striding over to me. Then he whistles, giving me a once-over. "Who are *you* trying to impress tonight?"

I smack him on the shoulder of his tuxedo jacket. "Shut up," I murmur. "You look like you should be serving champagne on tiny trays."

He leans into me. "I know, right? There *are* guys here in tuxedos serving champagne on tiny trays. This event is swanky. I can't believe they let us in."

I snort. "Me neither. Where's Lia?" After an endless string of girlfriends, Cliff's latest relationship finally seems serious.

"Gossiping with some of her SWAT friends."

We both survey the scene, grabbing two glasses of bubbly when a waiter passes by. The West Oaks Bar Association is putting on this gala to celebrate the Lawyer of the Year winner, Jane Holt. It's a mixed crowd tonight. Public and private lawyers. Prosecution and defense. And because Jane is married to Sean Holt, the chief of police, the place is crawling with cops too. Like my best friend, Cliff Easton.

We've both come a long way since high school, though we still bicker like siblings. I'm not that shy, quiet girl who struggled to stand up for herself. In fact, tonight is about the older, wiser, more independent me. A woman who splurges on a slinky, strapless gown for a black-tie event. The kind of woman who is *not* hung up on an unattainable man.

A certain man who might be here tonight.

I tug at the bustline of my gown and take a gulp of champagne. A picture of elegance, right here.

A finger brushes across my bare shoulder, and I turn around to find Derek Keller standing behind me, wearing a fancy custom tux and his signature smirk.

"Hands to yourself," I say.

"You had something on your arm."

Cliff narrows his eyes. "Sure she did."

Derek pointedly turns away from Cliff. He has a glass of champs too, and he holds it up to clink with mine. "Looking good, Ms. Ainsley. Didn't know you could clean up so well."

He's not flirting. Derek knows exactly what he's doing. Back when we were One Ls in law school, his little digs got under my skin. But not anymore.

"Thanks," I say. "You look nice too."

"I should. This is a Tom Ford." Derek takes a drink, flashing his cufflinks. Which I'm sure wasn't intentional.

Right. "Did you see the motion my office filed yesterday?" he asks.

On Friday afternoon, like they were hoping to ruin my weekend? "Yeah, I glanced at it. But we shouldn't talk work tonight. Neutral territory."

Derek just smirks. "You think a group of lawyers can resist talking about work? Especially with the celebrity trial of the decade coming up?"

Well, he has a point.

In about three weeks, Derek and I will be on opposite sides of the courtroom for the trial of Amber Printz. She's a former child star and model who rocketed into super-stardom after murdering her movie director husband. *Allegedly*. It's also my first big murder case as a West Oaks deputy district attorney. I'll be second chairing the trial with the district attorney herself. It's a huge deal for me. For our entire office.

And after the way the story has caught fire in the media? Pretty much the entire country will be watching. Criticizing everything we do. That *I* do. People have been showing up to picket our office with handmade signs. *Free Amber. Amber was framed.*

"But we're all friends tonight, right?" Derek says.

"And all of our bosses are here," Cliff cuts in, draping a protective arm around me. "Which means we're on our best behavior."

"True, can't have too much fun." Derek sips his champagne. "But that's rarely Quinn's problem."

Cliff steers me away from my former law-school classmate, which is a good thing, because I'm fresh out of witty zingers. "Asshole," Cliff mutters. "He's wrong. You're fun."

"I appreciate the best friend vote of confidence, but he's not that far off." I shake my head. "I mean, who cares about Derek Keller's idea of fun? But he's right that nobody expects anything but good behavior from me." My reputation hasn't changed much in the last decade. I'm not shy anymore, but I'm still the good girl who doesn't intimidate anyone, least of all opposing counsel. "But that was the old Quinn."

Cliff nods. "Ah, yes. The 'New and Improved Quinn' Project."

"The new Quinn is a formidable prosecutor. She eats snarky defense attorneys as happy hour snacks."

"And she lives by herself now instead of with her best friend and their awesome roommates."

"Because she's a grown up and can't afford to spend weeknights playing foosball and having video game tournaments."

He scoffs. "You hardly ever played anyway. You were always too busy studying or working."

"Exactly! I have other priorities. I need to focus."

"Ouch. That cuts close to home."

"I'm just saying what's best for me."

We've had this conversation before. Cliff was upset when I finally moved out of our shared rental six months ago. Up until that point, we'd had a great run together. But then our roommates Danny and Aiden moved out. They fell in love with amazing women, settled down into their real lives. Even Cliff has Lia.

I want to fall in love too.

Correction: I want to fall in love with a man who will *love me back*.

And I can't do that living in a house where Rex Easton shows up all the time.

Cliff gives me a one-armed hug. "Just don't go changing too much. Some people like the old Quinn a lot."

"Aw, I like you too. I miss seeing you in the hallway and cooking together. But don't accuse me of neglecting you. We still hang out all the time."

"Ew, you like me? Gross."

He reaches up to ruffle my hair, and I point a finger at him. "Mess up my hairstyle, and you die."

This is one thing I *don't* want to change. Cliff and me. Our friendship. And hopefully, it will never have to.

~

Cliff and I make the rounds, saying hello to people we know. I get pulled aside by some fellow DAs, and Cliff ends up in a circle of patrol officers.

My group gets quiet when our boss comes over. Lana smiles knowingly, rubbing circles over her pregnant belly. "Don't stop talking on my account. Unless you were talking about me."

"We were just complaining about Derek Keller," I say under my breath. "He keeps blinding people with his cufflinks."

Lana rolls her eyes. "I'm surprised he's not carrying around one of those 'Free Amber' posters." Then she winces. "Nobody repeat that. Sorry. I'm supposed to set a good example for you young people." Which makes us all laugh because she's in her thirties and not that much older than us.

But she's still my idol.

After chatting with the group for a few minutes, Lana grabs my wrist. "Quinn, can I steal you? There's something I wanted to chat about."

"Of course." Like I would say no. My colleagues watch in envy as Lana takes me to a secluded corner of the ballroom. When she spins around, she's got her game face on.

"What did Derek Keller say to you?" she asks. "Was he gloating about the motion his firm filed yesterday afternoon?"

Lana Marchetti is the youngest district attorney in West Oaks history. Despite her jokes, she's usually a great role model for getting along with the other side. Jane Holt, tonight's honored Lawyer of the Year, is the top defense lawyer in town and one of Lana's closest friends. Both Lana and Jane are moms, pillars of the community. And they each have adoring husbands who happen to be drop-dead gorgeous.

They have it all. The careers and beautiful families. Exactly what I want. But when Lana was twenty-nine, a year older than I am now, she was first-chairing a major murder trial. The previous DA was already grooming her as his replacement. She's gracious, but she's also a formidable litigator who doesn't take crap from anyone.

In short, she's amazing. And everything I want to be.

"Gloating might be a strong word," I say. "There was definitely smirking."

Lana taps her chin with a red fingernail. "They're moving to allow cameras in the courtroom. They want to turn this trial into a media sideshow."

"It's getting there already. Last I heard, #FreeAmber was trending on TikTok."

"Yes, but I'm afraid of it getting much worse. I don't want to worry you. Or put a damper on tonight. But this could be serious." Lana pulls me closer, whispering, "We've been receiving threats."

"*What?*"

Lana hushes me. "They were few and far between, all directed at me, until this morning. I've gotten plenty of vague threats before as DA. I've always passed them on to Max." Her husband, Max Bennett. The owner of Bennett Security. "He usually insists on investigating, and he brings in West Oaks PD if it seems warranted."

"But the one this morning?"

She chews her lower lip, a hand still making unconscious

circles over her baby bump. "The one today was about you and me both."

Chills slide under my skin. "Me?"

"It was a letter sent to our office, accusing us of being corrupt. That we're persecuting Amber because she's young and beautiful, and we're jealous of her."

I shake my head slowly. Lana and I are the only women on the trial team for the prosecution. The other two are men. "That's the most idiotic thing I've ever heard."

"And probably not the worst I've been accused of. But the threat against us was…more concerning. The letter had some choice words about what might happen to us if we don't leave Amber alone. How we might disappear and the world would be better for it."

"Crap."

A couple of years ago, a deputy DA from our office was attacked in the parking lot after a trial verdict. It took months for him to heal from the head injury. And everyone knew Lana had been targeted years ago during a major murder trial. She'd actually been kidnapped. Max had helped track her down.

If Lana is taking this threat seriously, then it's a very big deal.

I set my half-empty champagne glass on a nearby table. "What should I do?"

"You mean, what should *we* do. I'm not throwing you to the wolves, Quinn. I want you on this team because I think you're ready for it, and you deserve this opportunity. But I'm also going to see that you're protected."

"Protected how?"

"I promise having a bodyguard is not as bad as it sounds." Then her eyes lift, her attention drawn by something past my shoulder. Her worried expression smooths out, and her mouth curves in a smile. "Speak of the devil, and there he is. My protector in chief."

I'm stuck on a certain word she used. *Bodyguard*. My heart rate accelerates for entirely new reasons.

I turn around, following Lana's gaze. I see her husband first. Max always looks casual, even when he's dressed in a shiny tuxedo that makes Derek Keller's Tom Ford look off-the-rack. But my eyes quickly move past Max Bennett to the other man beside him.

I knew that Rex would probably be here tonight. But I still wasn't prepared to see him after the last several months I'd spent avoiding him.

Rex Easton might as well have a spotlight shining on him. That's how much he stands out to me. He cuts just as impressive a figure as he did the first time I saw him well over ten years ago. Broad shoulders, straight spine, an easy smile. His dark hair has turned salt-and-pepper, and gray streaks the stubble on his chin. There might be an extra line or two around his eyes. But if anything, he's gotten more handsome over the years.

Rex's muscular frame fills out his tux, which fits him like a tailored glove. If that's a thing. Even though he's a little rough around the edges, I wouldn't be surprised if someone mistook him for the billionaire owner of Bennett Security instead of Max. But I also know Rex has no interest in running companies. He's a full-time hero. Not just as a member of the Bennett Security bodyguard team, but as a volunteer when he heads to disaster-ravaged areas to help them rebuild with a nonprofit called Team Triumph.

He's also been the star of most of my fantasies since I was eighteen.

Yes, I am exactly that hopeless.

Rex turns, his dark eyes finding mine. They narrow appraisingly, then widen slightly, as if he's just now recog-

nizing me. I guess that makes sense, given the fact that I rarely dress up. Rex probably hasn't seen me in evening wear like this since...*ugh, senior prom night*.

"You know Rex Easton, don't you?" Lana asks. "You're friends with his son?"

"Yep," I manage to say.

She's waving them over. I'm trying to come up with an excuse to escape. Because apparently, New and Improved Quinn runs and hides just like Old Quinn did.

But it's too late. Rex and Max are already walking toward us.

2

Rex

"Why am I here again?" I murmur to my boss, just as we enter the hotel ballroom.

"Because it's a party, and you look decent in a tux." Max elbows me. "Almost as good as I do."

After all these years as a Bennett Security bodyguard, you'd think I'd be used to wearing a tuxedo by now. This is practically part of the uniform. But I don't feel anywhere near as comfortable in this getup as I used to in desert fatigues. Or better yet, my worn-in jeans and a white T-shirt.

I'm nowhere near the cocky SOB that Max Bennett is. And I say that with love.

Tonight's event honors Jane Holt, someone I know and respect, but I can't imagine that she or Sean Holt will notice if I'm here or not. I scan the crowd, hoping to spot Cliff. I texted my son earlier to ask if he'd attend, but he didn't get around to responding. Now, I'm regretting that I didn't call to demand an answer.

Because I can't stand fancy parties. I hate networking and schmoozing. I don't even like champagne.

Yeah, I said it.

"Quit it with that face," Max says.

"What face? This is my pleasant, approachable smile."

"No, it's your *I'm going to bounce as soon as Max isn't looking* smile."

"Stop reading my mind."

He pats my back. "I've known you for way too long. Sorry, not sorry."

I'm skilled enough at being social. I can fake my way through. But I tend to keep my real thoughts and feelings close to the vest, sharing them only with the people closest to me. At heart, I'm an anti-social hermit. Max is one of the few people who knows that. He's also one of the few people who can get away with calling me out on it. We've been solid since we were in the Army. Though never best friends because we've tended to be at different life stages. When I was happily married, he was still sowing his oats. After I became a widower, my hermit-like tendencies only got worse, while Max viewed the West Oaks social scene as yet another challenge to win.

But with Max, few things are purely social. These days, if the man isn't focused on his wife and family, then he's thinking about his business or running it. Something that I admire about him. There's a reason Max runs Bennett Security like a well-oiled machine, while I'm just muscle. Probably because I feel the same way about numbers as I do about champagne. I'll pass.

"Alright, you're not *only* here to look good," Max admits, and his tone turns serious. "Lana's received some threats related to that celebrity murder trial. The Amber Printz case. You know how I feel about my wife's security on any given day, but this comes with the territory now that she's DA."

Max is overprotective of his family, like most of the guys we call friends. He and Lana have a little girl they adopted a few years back, and now Lana's six months pregnant. His protective instincts are no doubt through the roof. But Lana also refuses to let the possibility of danger stop her. She's fierce. She can definitely handle herself, pregnant or not.

Which means this isn't the typical threat.

"But?" I prompt.

"But some creep sent a letter today that's more specifically concerning. It also mentioned one of her deputy DAs by name, and Lana doesn't want to take any risks. As she shouldn't. I'd like you to head the protection detail for her trial team."

"Why didn't you say so in the first place?" It's not like Max to hide the ball. Not from me.

"Because I've already got some of our guys on Lana, and her trial team is here right now, surrounded by dozens of lawyers and cops. They're fine for the moment. I can introduce you to Lana's team, and we'll make the arrangements for their extra security on Monday morning. I asked you to this event because I want you to *enjoy* yourself for once. You're more of a workaholic than I am."

"Not possible."

"Before I got together with Lana? Maybe. But now, I'm the picture of work-life balance."

"And you're spreading the gospel to all your employees?"

"Exactly. It's the new Bennett Security wellness program." He steps behind me, grabbing my shoulders and speaking into my ear like the demon on my shoulder. "Do you realize how many single women are here tonight? You must like smart, successful women. And they seem to *love* you, not that you give them any encouragement. Do you ever notice how many women's heads turn the moment you walk into a room? Take your damn pick, man. Wealthy clients and donors are here, too. Bag yourself an heiress or dowager or something."

"A *dowager*? I'm sensing a commentary on my advanced age."

Max chuckles. "Your age is pretty advanced."

"I'm not loving the new wellness program. In fact, it sucks and it's a clear HR violation." I try to walk away, but he grabs my shoulders again.

"C'mon, Rex. I'm trying to keep this lighthearted. But don't you think it's time?"

That makes me pause. I guess he's right. But it's still not easy to admit it.

Max and I met as fellow Green Berets. I had over a decade of experience on him, but he beat me to leaving the Army. He was a West Oaks native and returned home to start his security company. I stayed in for a few more years to finish out my twenty. Earned my pension. Then I followed my younger friend out here to California to join his startup.

All I wanted back then was to enjoy a new stage of my life with Lydia and Cliff. And continue serving my community, of course.

But fate had other plans for me.

"Who says I'm ready?" I ask Max.

He regards me with sympathetic yet unyielding eyes. "Lydia probably would."

Ouch. Hitting me right where it hurts.

In a few months, it'll be eleven years since Lydia passed. She was my high school sweetheart. The woman I was supposed to spend my best years with. And still, I've never loved any woman but her. I probably never will. But enough time has passed that I'm not eaten alive by grief. Not anymore. I can think back on our marriage with gratitude for everything we shared. For the son we raised together.

But it's another thing to imagine finding someone new.

I want to argue that I'm happy with my life. I like having an objective. A mission. I'm usually either focused on work, or on Cliff. Even though my kid isn't interested in being the focus of my attention, and he hasn't for a long time. As for work, it's great. I love that I get to help people, whether it's through Bennett Security or Team Triumph.

And even if I did want more, how the heck would I find it? I'm forty-nine years old. Next year I'll be...jeez, I can't even think about that. The thought of starting all over, of dating, is even scarier than the prospect of a hundred-page spreadsheet.

I glance over the room, hoping again that I'll spot Cliff. Maybe I can use my son as an excuse to avoid this conversation.

And that's when I spot her.

I see Lana first, cheeks glowing, a hand on her pregnant belly. But there's another woman talking to Lana, and that's where my gaze sticks. This woman is in a fitted blue dress, dark blond hair swept up off her shoulders. Her back is to me, so I can't see her face. Yet there's something familiar about her. Something that makes me pause. Linger.

I can't say what it is about her. If it's her smooth skin, or her hourglass shape, or the delicate bones of her shoulders. But I can't look away.

"Notice someone?"

I can hear the smirk in Max's voice, but I ignore it. "Who is she?" I ask.

"She works with Lana. One of the deputy district attorneys who Lana wants extra security for. I forget her name. Lana will introduce you."

I force myself to turn and face Max instead. "So she's the client."

Max is the first person to remind any bodyguard on our team never to touch a client. Even if he was *technically* protecting Lana when they got together.

"Okay, she's off limits. But you can at least flirt a little.

Get some practice in. I mean, look, she's definitely noticed *you.*"

When I turn back around, the blond is staring at me. My breath catches. She really is beautiful. A full, pink mouth. Button nose, eyes I can tell from here will be blue or green. Makeup accentuates her features, but she has the kind of beauty that shines through no matter what she does. My chest warms, tightens, overwhelmed again by that sense of familiarity. Comfort, even.

Then it dawns on me like a bucket of ice water splashing down onto my head.

"That's *Quinn,*" I blurt out.

"I thought you didn't know her."

"She looks different tonight. I didn't realize." *Didn't realize I was just ogling my son's best friend.*

"Even better. No need to break the ice." Max grips my shoulder, steering me toward the women. Quinn has an expression on her pretty face that I can't interpret. I can't sort out my thoughts, either.

Since when does little Quinn Ainsley look like *that*?

Then a flash a movement distracts me. Pulls my attention at some instinctual level. There's a guy walking toward Lana and Quinn, which shouldn't be anything remarkable. Plenty of people here tonight want to rub elbows with the district attorney. But this guy doesn't fit. His suit is okay, but the shoes are all wrong. Scuffed up and dirty the way no self-respecting lawyer or cop would wear to an event like this. His eyes are too intense. Too purposeful.

The guy reaches inside his blazer.

Fuck.

3

Rex

I feel Max tense beside me. He just spotted the guy too. But I'm already on the move.

"Hey," I shout, sprinting toward him. His hand withdraws from his blazer, and whatever he's holding glints in the light. He's trying to aim it at Quinn and Lana.

I crash into him, tackling him to the ground and wrenching whatever's in his hand away. The object slides across the granite ballroom floor. There are screams and commotion all around me. The guy tries to wiggle free, but I pin him down with my weight. "Stop moving," I order. He tries to spit at me, but that's hard to do facedown.

"Free Amber!" he screams. *"Free Amber!"*

When I glance up, dozens of police officers have their weapons drawn, all pointing at the guy. And, given my position, at me. But that doesn't raise my pulse. The thought of Quinn, though. Where is she? Is she okay?

"What the hell is this?" Sean Holt, chief of police, pushes through the phalanx of officers to reach me. Max comes up on my other side. "Are you two bringing trouble to my wife's event?" Sean asks quietly.

"Can't help ourselves," Max murmurs. They're keeping their voices down because, undoubtedly, cameras are pointed at us right now.

"The guy had a weapon. We need to find it." I scan the ground for the gun, but there are too many people crowding around, shouting and demanding to know what happened. An officer comes forward to cuff the intruder's arms behind his back, and all the while he's still screaming about *freeing Amber*.

"I've got it!" a feminine voice shouts. And the crowd parts.

There's Quinn, a stretch of her long leg peeking from the slit in her dress. She's got the pointed toe of her stiletto resting on something.

A perfume bottle.

Shit. *That's* what the guy was pulling from his jacket? He's lucky he isn't dead for pulling a stunt like that in a room with this many armed officers.

"Thanks, Rex." Sean pats my shoulder. "My people will take it from here."

"No problem." I stand and step back to give them room, but I can't tear my gaze from Quinn. That endless stretch of leg. The confident way she lifts her shoe to allow another officer to bag the perfume bottle as evidence. For several slow beats, the crowd swirls around us, but all I can see is her. And her pale blue eyes are locked on me.

I close the distance between us, barely aware of my feet moving. "Are you alright?"

"I was going to ask you the same thing."

Then time speeds up again as Cliff barrels toward us. "Quinn! *Dad*! What the heck happened?"

"We've got an audience," Lana says, nodding her head at the crowd.

Things start to settle, and our group moves off to the side.

Max and Lana, Cliff and Quinn. Me. Cliff's girlfriend, Lia, appears and says hello. We form a tight circle. "What's the deal with the perfume bottle?" Lia asks.

"It's called *Adore Me,*" Quinn says. "I recognized the shape of the bottle. Amber Printz was the spokesmodel for it a few years ago."

Of freaking course. That damn trial.

Max claps me on the arm. "Nice save, Rex. Lucky thing you got to the guy before somebody shot him. Would've caused a far bigger mess."

Quinn gives me a small smile, but too quickly, her eyes dart away.

Max kisses Lana on the forehead, wrapping his arm protectively around her middle. "I'm sorry, babe. That guy never should've gotten so close."

"No harm this time," Lana says. "Just a stupid publicity stunt. I'm sure the video is already being loaded to TikTok."

"But it could've been far worse." Max scowls in the direction of the intruder, who's being led out of the ballroom by uniformed officers. "I'm going to talk to Sean about their security for this event. I want to know how that guy got in, because I doubt he's a bar association member."

The event organizers are trying to calm everyone down, passing out more champagne flutes as fast as the servers can carry them. I keep trying to catch Quinn's eye again, but she seems to be looking anywhere but at me. Lia is whispering something to her.

I'm unsettled, but it's not the idiot who disrupted our night that's on my mind.

Seeing her tonight in that gown, hair styled in that sophisticated way, makeup accenting her features... It threw me off. And I don't like to be thrown off.

Quinn's grown up. *Really* grown up. She's twenty-eight, a

prosecutor. A woman with a career and her own apartment. Her own life. Probably a boyfriend. Or several.

How the heck did all of that happen without me noticing?

Maybe the real issue is, it reminds me of how old I am. That big birthday coming up next year. I cringe, thinking of the number. *Fifty*. Damned if that doesn't sound old. In my head, I'm still in my prime. But I guess all the gray in my hair and beard in the mirror should've been a clue. I've never been vain, but I've noticed sun damage from those years spent under the desert sun.

Is that what Quinn thinks when she looks at me? That I've gotten really freaking old, and I'm the only one who doesn't know it?

"That was *nuts*," Cliff says.

I turn my attention to my son. He's looking sharp in a rented tux. I give him a quick hug. With his light, straw-colored hair and freckles, he looks so much like Lydia. He doesn't like hearing that though. I've learned to keep those observations to myself.

"I was hoping you'd be here tonight, kid. You didn't answer my texts."

Cliff's mouth twists at the term of endearment. Whoops. It slipped. I know he hates when I call him "kid," but that habit is hard to break. "I meant to. Sorry. Got caught up helping Lia. Her dress was lost at the dry cleaner. It was a whole thing." He shrugs. "You want a drink?"

"Sure." The bar is crowded with people, probably eager to take the edge off after the excitement, but if we're stuck in line together we can chat and Cliff won't be able to run off. These days, those are the strategies I'm reduced to when it comes to getting time with my son.

But I need to keep an eye on Quinn, too. I might not technically be on duty tonight, but it's the kind of thing that doesn't need to be said. Max would want me to be vigilant.

I glance around, realizing with a start that Quinn and Lia have disappeared. *Crack bodyguard skills, Easton.* "What about the girls? Where'd they go?"

"I think they went to the bathroom."

"We should wait for them."

"Relax, Dad." He rolls his eyes a little. "I doubt you'll need to save them from any more perfume bottles. You can take five on the heroics."

Cliff starts toward the bar, and I follow.

I don't know what I said that was so problematic. But with my kid, it's usually something.

By the time we reach the bar, the line is three deep. And despite my prompting questions, Cliff is giving me nothing but one-word answers. Quinn and Lia haven't reappeared either. I've been keeping one eye on the exit, and they haven't left. Two of our guys from Bennett Security have taken up positions by the doors, which I'm glad to see.

"How are things on patrol?" I ask.

"Same."

"Great." I drum my fingers against my pant leg. "Chief Holt doing a good job? Better than the last chief, right?"

"Sure."

I'm the kind of guy who prides myself on competence in all things. But even when Cliff was little, we had trouble connecting. Lydia mediated between us. Smoothing over ruffled feathers. It always used to be the worst when I was deployed. Lydia and Cliff had support living on base, and I called them any spare moment that I could. I believed in quality time, even if that meant reading bedtime stories over a shitty connection from whatever undisclosed location I was operating from. But every call started the same. Cliff didn't want to talk to me, even though I *knew* he missed me, and Lydia would have to coax him.

After Lydia died, we lost that buffer. I was home then,

retired, yet somehow the barrier widened instead of narrowing. Cliff was a junior in high school, one foot already out the door. I didn't understand how he spent so many hours on video games and comics. He was a runner, track team, but he balked at any suggestion that he consider the military. And go with me to the shooting range at Bennett headquarters? Hell no. I was beyond shocked when he chose criminal justice as a major and applied to the police academy after getting his degree. But so damn proud, even if he remains reticent to tell me about his job.

The only other thing we've always agreed on? Quinn Ainsley.

After Lydia passed, Quinn was a welcome, warm presence in our too-quiet house. When they were teenagers, I assumed she and the kid were an item. I pulled him aside for a sex talk. It was just as awkward as you'd imagine. He assured me they were nothing more than friends. He wound up dating other girls. A *lot* of other girls. To my relief, he seemed to treat them well. At least he'd learned the right way to treat a woman, even without his mom around to set him straight.

Maybe Quinn had served that role for him. Like a surrogate sister.

But suddenly, thinking of her that way doesn't seem right either. I've never looked at her as my daughter. And tonight…

I most definitely wasn't looking at her in a fatherly way.

We reach the front of the line and order a couple of beers. "I had no idea Quinn was working on Lana's trial. Been a while since I saw her."

Cliff shifts his weight, then angles toward me. "To be honest, I'm nervous about this trial thing. All the stuff in the media about it? And that nut who showed up here tonight? It's messed up. Quinn really wants to impress DA Marchetti, and she's been working so hard. Quinn can get tunnel vision when she's really focused on something."

I lower my beer, trying to hide my amazement that he just shared all of that with me. "Bennett Security is going to provide protection for her and the trial team."

"You know Quinn's like a sister to me. If you're in charge of the trial team's security, I'm sure she'll be in good hands. If anyone will stay vigilant, it's you." He shrugs, looking into his beer bottle. He spoke begrudgingly, but hell, I'll take it. "And if you're protecting Quinn personally, she won't have some horny meathead panting after her twenty-four-seven. No offense, Dad, but I know the younger guys on the Bennett bodyguard team. She can do better." With that, Cliff nods at someone else he knows. "See you later, Dad."

He walks off, leaving me speechless.

A horny meathead? Nope. I don't like that thought one bit. I trust the guys on our team to make good choices, but Cliff has a point.

Because I don't want another man protecting Quinn either.

~

DURING DINNER, MY GAZE KEEPS SNEAKING OVER to Quinn at the next table. To the lithe bones of her arms in that strapless dress. She has tiny dimples in her shoulders, and I wonder how they'd feel if I pressed my thumbs against them.

Heat streaks down my spine, and I tear my eyes away.

What is wrong with me tonight? I blame Max. He got into my head with that nonsense about flirting and dating.

Chairs scrape the floor as everyone stands to give Jane Holt an ovation, including me. As Quinn joins in, she stands at an angle, but she still doesn't look over. And dammit, I'm disappointed.

When Quinn turns on her heel, weaving through the tables to leave before the applause is over, I follow. She makes a beeline straight for the bar. I catch up with her as the music strikes up again, and other attendees slowly fan out from the tables. Quinn orders something from the bartender, who steps away to grab it. I drop my elbow onto the bar counter beside her.

"Come here often?" I ask, and then force myself not to grimace. *What was that?*

"Ha, ha," she deadpans.

"Just trying to liven up the room. Jane's speech was great, but before that..."

"Yeah, pretty bad. We had some excitement tonight, but otherwise, these bar association things tend to be dull. You're lucky you don't usually have to come."

"Us bodyguards can deal with boredom, believe me. We do a lot of standing around. But when they put those budgetary spreadsheets on the big screen? Really?"

"Some people think numbers are sexy. Lawyers especially."

"Lawyers like you?"

Her eyes widen like she's surprised I asked that. "I'm a criminal lawyer," she reminds me. "The numbers I see are usually crime related. So no. Not very sexy." The bartender returns with a longneck beer for Quinn. He pops the top and hands it to her. But I take out my wallet and hand over a ten before she can pay.

"I'll have one of the same please." I don't tend to drink much, so I'll cut myself off after this. While the bartender grabs another beer, I say, "I would've thought you'd order a Cosmo or a martini."

"Why? Because I'm all dressed up? Don't be fooled. It's still just me."

"But you're clearly more sophisticated than your usual running shorts and T-shirt reveal. You look great."

"Thanks." She takes a slow sip of beer. I glance at her bare shoulders, and she's got goosebumps all over her skin. Her cheeks are flushed.

The bartender returns with the second beer. I pay and thank him, then move with Quinn off to the side. The lights in the ballroom have dimmed, and another room has been opened to reveal a dance floor. But neither of us make a move to head in that direction. We stand side by side, watching the crowd.

"I'll be honest," I say. "I didn't recognize you at first tonight. The last time I saw you dressed up in formal wear, it was your prom."

She groans. "Really? You had to bring that up?" But her pinched look quickly shifts to laughter. "I was thinking about that night too. Did you realize they actually held the prom *here*? At this hotel?"

"Seriously?"

As we chat, I think back to that night. Ten years ago. God, where did the time go? I'll never forget driving up and seeing her on the front porch, eyes red from crying, a picture of sadness and disappointment in her pale pink dress. I hadn't even known what happened in that moment, but I remember being furious. Whoever had been responsible, I wanted to punch the little asshole in the face. And I had *prayed* it wasn't Cliff.

Thank goodness my kid was better than that, even if I'd been annoyed that he let Quinn leave prom all by herself. But I'd been even more frustrated with Quinn's parents. The Ainsleys were away a lot for business, and I'm the last person to frown on them for that. I was away for plenty of Cliff's childhood. But where I sought out quality time, the Ainsleys didn't seem to make that effort. They left Quinn to her own devices. Abandoned her, practically. Yet she grew up sweet and generous. Maybe because she knew how much it meant to have someone around who cared.

I was so proud of her that night for sticking up for herself. Not letting her prom date talk her into something she wasn't ready for.

"Too bad they didn't have fried chicken for dinner tonight," she says. "Comfort food might've taken the edge off those boring speeches before it was Jane's turn. Wilted salad and dry pork medallions weren't cutting it."

"Is that why you didn't eat much of your food?"

"You noticed what I ate?"

Sure, because I was studying you like there would be a quiz later. "Noticing things is my job."

She seems to deflate. "Of course. It's what bodyguards do. I guess you'll be involved with our extra security during the Printz trial."

"I will. So you just let me know what you need. If that's threatening some punk football player for mistreating you, I'm here."

Her beer bottle freezes on the way to her mouth. "Wait. Did you actually do that? You threatened Landon?"

Whoops. Probably shouldn't have given that away.

Quinn looks incredulous. "That little shit apologized to me after prom night. And he was shaking like a leaf, like he was terrified of me. I thought Cliff said something to him! Landon avoided me for the rest of the school year. I mean, I was fine with that. But…that was *you*?"

I tuck a hand into my pants pocket, gesturing casually with the beer bottle. "*Threatening* is a strong word. I told Landon if he didn't say he was sorry, plus volunteer at the local homeless shelter for the next three Sundays, I'd inform his parents of his behavior." And, possibly, snap his femurs like twigs. The memory is fuzzy.

Quinn shakes her head like she can't believe me. I'm relieved when she barks a laugh, then clinks her beer bottle against mine. "Wow. I should be mad, but I'm not. Does Cliff know?"

"Not the exact details. But he's the one who told me Landon's name and where to find him. Cliff tries to look out for you. He cares a lot about you." I glance down at my beer. "So do I."

Her cheeks flush again. There's a lively song playing, and bright lights swirl over the dance floor. But this part of the ballroom is nearly empty. Quinn steps out of her heels and stretches her feet.

"Getting comfortable?" I ask.

"I love my heels, but dang, it feels good to take them off."

I decide to follow suit by taking off my jacket and slinging it over a nearby chair. "I haven't seen much of you lately. Why'd you stop coming to dinners with Cliff and me? I know you moved out of the Pink House, but you're still welcome."

"I've been trying something different. Being more independent and grown-up instead of holding on to things from my childhood."

"And how's that going?"

She takes a gulp of beer. "Harder than I thought it would be."

"You're always welcome with me and Cliff. You're family. Don't ever doubt that."

She opens her mouth, but she hesitates. It's like the words are there on her tongue. But she closes them off with a frown. She finishes her beer instead and sets it aside. "I think I'll call it a night."

"But we should talk about your security for the trial."

"Whatever Lana wants is fine. I'm just the junior attorney."

She's unhappy. I don't know why, but somehow, I said the exact wrong thing. "Wait."

I don't want Quinn to leave like this. Like I'm just one more person who's disappointed her. At the very least, I should ensure she gets home safely. Not only because I'm in charge of her personal security until the Printz trial ends—I really need to iron out those details with Max tomorrow—but because Cliff asked me to.

But most of all, I want to spend time with Quinn. I've missed her. I want to see her smiling, and that can't be a bad thing. The fact that she's grown into a gorgeous woman is… distracting. But it hardly matters. I'm here for her, *always*, and I need to make sure she knows it.

I hold out my hand. "Come with me. I know exactly what we both need."

"Where are we going?"

"Somewhere we'll be ridiculously overdressed. But I promise there will be no spreadsheets."

4

Quinn

I can handle this.

It doesn't matter that I'm walking toward some unknown destination with the handsomest, most irresistible man I've ever met. I am Sensible Quinn. A woman who doesn't get hung up on men she can never have.

It's a perfect West Oaks evening. Warm, a slight breeze, with the waves providing a calming backdrop to the sounds of nightlife. Ocean Lane bustles with locals and tourists out enjoying the weekend. We cross at a pedestrian walkway to reach the beachside path. By day, rollerbladers and power-walkers roam up and down this ribbon of concrete.

Rex has his bowtie slung around his neck, his jacket over one arm, the other hand tucked into his pocket. Like 007 on his day off. The Daniel Craig version, naturally.

We get a few curious glances at our formal wear as we walk, but most people take it in stride. West Oaks is a small town in some ways, but we're close enough to Los Angeles that we have new people constantly streaming in and out. Plus, a cadre of wealthy people with mansions in the hills.

My eyes linger as Rex undoes the top few buttons of his shirt. He glances over, and I face forward.

"We're not going far," he says. "Are your shoes bothering you?"

"Nah, I'm good." I had to put my heels back on, but the ache has dulled. Rex has always had that effect on me. Everything hurts less when he's around, being kind and attentive.

Of course, that usually causes a *different* sort of pain to throb in my chest. But I'm not thinking about that right now. That was Old Quinn.

I put a little extra strut into my walk, as if this is the kind of thing I do all the time. Just taking a stroll by the ocean in stilettos and a floor-length gown. The glamorous life of a criminal lawyer. *Ha.*

But this night has gotten surreal anyway. Might as well play it up.

It was bizarre enough for that guy to crash the event with his perfume bottle to shout about Amber Printz. I'm guessing he meant to spray Lana and me with that cloying scent. He probably wanted to get arrested in order to make some kind of statement about the justice system. Or just to impress Amber.

Don't get me wrong, it was unnerving, especially when Rex took the guy down like a linebacker and we had no idea what was happening.

But even with the anonymous threat Lana mentioned and the perfume guerrilla attack, I don't feel scared. Because I trust Rex to protect me. Like he said, it's his job. And I know he's good at it. He's protected me even when I didn't know. Even back in high school.

Which, let's face it, made me swoon so hard a few minutes ago I nearly lost my balance. If he'd noticed, I would've blamed these shoes.

What I don't trust is my stupid heart. I'm so sick of

falling for this man. I can't afford to get swept away in childish fantasies again. Yet here I am, walking by the beach with him, lights twinkling all around us. Like this is some perfect date out of a movie.

If he was ever going to notice me as a potential romantic interest, it would've happened by now. But I don't think Rex notices women much, period. In all the years since his wife passed, I've never seen him with a girlfriend. It would've torn my poor, hopeless heart to shreds if I had. But in a way, it was even worse that I'd never had the misfortune. Because that meant Rex didn't have anyone. He didn't want anyone else. Lydia was his lifelong love, someone who could never be replaced.

It would be romantic if it wasn't such a downer. I wanted him to be happy. Even if that would've meant seeing him with someone else. There's no way Rex realizes the effect he has on women. On me especially. He has no idea he leaves broken hearts in his wake. If he did, he'd be the villain in this story, and there's no way.

Rex Easton is one hundred percent hero.

We walk past a group of young men, and a guy in a neon orange jacket does a double-take when his eyes land on me. Rex shifts closer, glancing over his shoulder at the men as we pass.

"Do you know that guy? He's staring at you."

"No. Probably just what we're wearing."

"Could be."

It takes several more minutes, but finally Rex's shoulders relax. I look around as we walk, trying to predict where we're heading. I know Ocean Lane up and down. I grew up in West Oaks, and the police department headquarters isn't far. The district attorney's office is just a couple of blocks further on from there. But my mind is coming up empty.

"Can you give me a hint of our destination?" I ask. "The mystery is killing me."

He smiles, all dazzling white teeth. "We're almost there."

"Um, the surfboard rental? Even if that made sense, it's closed for the night."

"Nah, our destination is just past it. Tucked away. You'll see."

If Rex was anyone else, I'd think he was up to something. But no. We round the surfboard shop, and there's a tiny food stand. It's hidden from the view of the road. There's no sign. We join the line of people waiting. Clearly, Rex isn't the only local who knows about this place.

Rex leans in. "That's Eddie running the fryer. He makes fish and chips. That's the whole menu. Vinegar and tartar sauce optional."

The smell of sizzling oil already has my stomach rumbling. Rex was right that I didn't eat much of my food at dinner. Too much on my mind. "But is it as good as fast-food fried chicken?"

He laughs. "Better. I promise. Well worth the calorie splurge."

Like he has to worry about that. If anything, Rex is in trimmer shape now than ten years ago.

We step up to the front. "Hey Eddie," Rex says. "Two please."

"Good to see you, Rex." Eddie nods a greeting, not pausing in his work. He doesn't even blink at our fancy clothes. "Brought a lady friend this time?"

"Yeah. I try to be tight-lipped about this place because I don't want the line to get longer. But this is someone special."

My heart thumps out of rhythm.

Eddie grins. "I won't give her the dregs, then." He has a teenaged assistant, maybe a grandson or nephew, who takes our money and gives change. I offer to pay this time, since Rex got my drink earlier, but he's having none of it.

Eddie hands over two cones, fries on the bottom and fish on top. Rex adds vinegar and sauce, but I skip both. We take our food over to a picnic table in the sand. I have to slide off my heels and carry them in my free hand.

We sit across from each other, and I select a piece of fish. The batter is crunchy, just rich enough without being greasy. The fish is pure white and fluffy. So good. I moan as I chew. "This is incredible. Why haven't I heard of Eddie? I've lived in West Oaks a lot longer than you. My whole life. This place should be famous."

Rex finishes off his first piece of fish in two bites. "I agree, but I'm glad it's not. Eddie doesn't publicize because he doesn't want it to turn into a scene. He's only open at night, and only on the weekends. I know about it because I sometimes run on the beach at night. Just happened to stumble upon it."

"But you decided to let me in on the secret?"

"I figured I could trust you. Like I told Eddie, you're someone special."

"Thanks," I say lamely. I focus on my French fries.

"I knew you'd appreciate it. Remember those fish tacos Cliff used to drag us all the way to Ventura for? You always tried to talk him into something closer, but I saw your face when you bit into one. You're a seafood fan."

"You got me." Yet another thing Rex noticed about me. But not the way I'd *wanted* him to notice me.

"Should we take Cliff here next time?"

"Next time?"

"When it's family dinner night. Or will you keep avoiding those?"

I shake my head. Rex has a gentle way about him, but he's never hesitated to call it like he sees it. "Maybe. We'll see. For more of Eddie's fish, I could make room in my schedule."

"I hope you do."

My heart thumps again. I should get that checked out. Twenty-eight is too young for an irregular heartbeat.

I've missed those dinners with Rex and Cliff, but it didn't occur to me that Rex would miss *my* presence. I'm Cliff's friend, and he's Cliff's dad. The only other time we've hung out one-on-one was my prom night.

I'm honestly surprised Cliff has never picked up on it. I guess I've hidden my feelings well, considering Rex doesn't know. I hope to God he doesn't know. But at some point, Cliff will figure it out. Or more likely, his girlfriend Lia Perez will. That woman is sharp. And if Cliff finds out, it'll be weird.

Growing up, Cliff felt like Rex put too much pressure on him to be perfect. Their relationship is better now, but I'd hate to be the reason for a new source of father-son tension.

We finish our food and crumple up the trash, tossing it into a nearby can. "Walk with me?" Rex asks.

We go closer to the water, both carrying our shoes. Rex rolls up his tux pants to keep the sand and water off them. I inhale the salt-scented air, tasting it along with French fries when I lick my lips.

It's probably what Rex's lips would taste like if I kissed him.

Bad Quinn. I need to get myself back on track and my mind out of date mode. This is *not* a date. Even though it would be a perfect one.

Six months away from him wasn't enough time. Not near enough.

"Since you'll be doing security for the Printz trial, I could give you the rundown," I say.

"Please. I'll conference with Max and our team tomorrow,

but I'd love to get started. And I'm sure nobody knows the case better than you do."

"That's possible." As the DA, Lana has far more to think about than a single case, even one this big. I've got several others on my plate as well, but with the Printz case so close to trial, I've been thinking of little else at work. "I'm sure you've heard a lot about the murder on the news."

"But what they say in the news doesn't give the real picture. Why don't you start at the beginning? Give me the People's case. Tell me how it happened. I'll need the full background to understand the threats you're facing now."

"It all begins with Amber."

Amber Printz started out in modeling. She managed to get some magazine and runway gigs, but her big break was becoming the face of that perfume, *Adore Me*. The ad campaign gave her enough recognition that she had access to the upper echelon of parties and charity events when she moved to Hollywood. Which was ideal, because what Amber had always wanted was to be an actress. A movie star.

Enter the famous director, Thompson Hayworth. He had the Hollywood pedigree. Son of classic movie actors, graduate of a prestigious film program.

"The two of them met at a charity event in Beverly Hills," I say. During the prep for this trial, I've learned far more than I ever needed about Amber and Thompson's romance. "Thompson wasn't the type to go after younger women before Amber. He genuinely seemed smitten. She told him a whole backstory about overcoming poverty and abuse and moving to New York City on her own as a teenager to pursue modeling. Of course, none of it was true."

We've confirmed that by speaking to Amber's family and former friends from her hometown in Arizona. Yet in her public statements, she's always managed to hedge enough that her legions of fans don't seem to mind the discrepancies.

"People hear what they want to hear," Rex remarks.

"Thompson certainly did. He bought Amber a five-karat diamond and eloped with no prenup."

Rex whistles. "I guess he was a romantic."

"So they say. His son, who runs Hayworth Productions, was furious. And then, from what I've learned, the industry elites in LA weren't nice to Amber either. She convinced Thompson to move here. To West Oaks."

Rex nods. "I've seen their house. The one overlooking that bluff? Gorgeous."

"A picturesque backdrop for a gruesome murder."

"Is that line going to be in your opening statement?"

"Lana will do the opening, and she's more diplomatic than me. She's a politician now. She has to be."

"But if it were up to you?"

I think of the first day I saw the evidence at the homicide staffing meeting, and shiver. "I would just try to tell the truth. Which is…tragic. And brutal."

Rex studies me for a few moments, keeping quiet. As if he understands that I need to settle my nerves.

I resume the story. "Now that Amber had Thompson to herself, she started pestering him about his next Oscar-bait movie. Of course, he agreed to cast her in the starring role. But once filming started and the producers saw her acting chops, they told him Amber had to go. She was okay, but not Oscar caliber. Thompson was stuck. And by then, he suspected his young model wife wasn't the ideal angel he'd believed. There were rumors of cheating, of her siphoning his money. It was enough that he called his lawyer to schedule a meeting. Wanted to discuss his will and potential divorce proceedings. Their marriage was about to blow up. Amber was about to lose it all. A week later, Thompson was dead. Murdered in their home. The scene was staged to look like a home invasion."

"Awful," Rex says. "When did the police suspect Amber?"

"Not right away. She had an alibi for the day of the murder, but it's flimsy. The detectives started digging and found a wealth of circumstantial evidence. A big clue was her internet search history. She'd tried to delete it, so we got a warrant and the search engine turned over the info. She'd done dozens of searches on burglary crime scenes, reading up on forensics. Different methods of murder like poisoning and blunt force trauma. Claimed it was for a movie role."

Rex curses under his breath. "Do you think Amber did the deed herself? Or did she hire someone else?"

"There was no unusual DNA or physical evidence suggesting a stranger at the house. Only Thompson, Amber, and a few other staff members who had airtight alibis. Amber's fingerprints and DNA were on the murder weapon. It was her. You'd think it would take rage to do something so vicious, but the planning suggests she was cold as ice. She smashed her husband over the head with a sculpture while he was napping. It was—" I shake my head, trying to banish the memory of the crime scene photos. The blood. "Sorry. We were having a nice time. I didn't mean to turn our conversation so dark."

"I've seen plenty of darkness and violence. Wish the world wasn't like that, but it is." He touches my arm. "And I *really* wish you didn't have to see it."

My first instinct is to argue that it's my job. I'm not fragile. But Rex still thinks of me as the girl on prom night he wanted to protect, and that isn't going to change.

"Anyway," I say, "Amber is out on bail, living in her West Oaks mansion, posting videos to social media claiming she loved Thompson and would never hurt him. She went from a mediocre actress to a household name with millions of followers. Playing up that damsel-in-distress persona. Falsely accused by the evil West Oaks DA's Office because we couldn't find the real—"

I stop mid-sentence, mid-step.

"Quinn? You okay?"

"I don't have my purse." I pat my dress, though of course it's not hiding in the slinky fabric. No pockets here. *Crap.* "My phone and wallet are in there. I must've left it at the picnic table."

Rex frowns. "I glanced over the table as we left. It was empty. When's the last time you had it?"

"I don't remember. I...maybe I set it down at the food counter."

"It's okay. We'll head straight back. Maybe Eddie's nephew saw it on the counter and grabbed it."

My throat swells with embarrassment. Smooth move, Quinn. Way to be that responsible, mature adult.

If I've lost my wallet, I'll have to spend all day tomorrow canceling credit cards and replacing things. I'll have to get a new phone. But the thought of looking like an idiot in front of Rex is far worse.

I feel like I'm that teenager again, making a mess and needing Rex to help dig me out of it.

We hurry back in the direction we came from. The path curves, weaving through palm trees, and I spot Eddie's booth. There's still a line, even though it's getting late. Ocean Lane is lined with streetlights, but over here near the water, the spots of darkness are wider. The shadows stretch.

I gasp as someone steps into the path, blocking our way. Even in the dimness, his neon orange jacket stands out.

It's the same guy we passed earlier, an hour ago at least, who was staring at me.

Rex holds out his arm to keep me behind him. "You need to move, son."

"She's Quinn Ainsley," Orange Jacket says. "Isn't she?"

Fear prickles my skin with goosebumps. "None of your business," I snap. Rex is still in front of me, a wall of muscle in a tuxedo. His stance is loose, but I can read the tension in his frame. He drops his jacket to the path. Clenches his fists.

"Last time I'm asking," Rex says. "*Move*."

Orange Jacket shouts, "It's her!"

Then someone else darts out from behind a palm tree. One of the guys Orange Jacket was with earlier. He's holding something in his hand like he's ready to throw it.

But just as quick, the guy disappears from view as Rex grabs me, spinning us both. Putting himself between me and whatever that guy was throwing. Rex's arms clutch me tightly against him. Suddenly all I can focus on is warm, solid muscle, the deep, spicy scent of his cologne. My feet don't touch the ground. But we're moving.

The next thing I know, Rex sets me on the sidewalk. We're beneath a bright streetlight, and the two others—Orange Jacket and his friend—have vanished. I'm breathing fast.

"What just happened?" I ask. "Are you okay?" The street scene comes back into focus. A view bystanders are watching with mild curiosity.

"I'm just fine," Rex says softly. "Did any of that hit you?"

"Any of *what*?"

He doesn't answer that. He pulls me against him again, head swiveling to glance around us. "The little assholes took off. Typical. This dry-cleaning bill isn't going to be pretty."

"Rex, what *happened*? What did that guy throw?"

He lifts his arm, turning slightly, though he doesn't let go of me. There's something pale brown splattered all over his white tuxedo shirt. "It seems I saved you from a perfume bottle and now a chocolate milkshake. I'm in rare form tonight."

I would laugh if this whole situation wasn't so frustrating.

Who does that? Throws a milkshake at someone? At *me*? And Rex stepped in front of it. Hustled me away like the guy had been aiming a bullet at me instead.

This is because of the Amber Printz case. Has to be. That guy just now recognized me, knew my name.

Oh my God. What if it really is a bullet next time, some random nut job deciding to defend Amber's honor? Just how bad could this get?

Rex tucks me into his side, coaxing me back toward the path. "Come on. Let's find your purse."

~

We grab his coat and my shoes from where we dropped them on the path.

My clutch is exactly where Rex thought it might be. Safely behind the counter at Eddie's. His nephew turns it over, and Rex tucks an extra twenty into the tip jar.

Rex puts on his coat over his ruined shirt. We head back to the hotel, where he parked. I spot his truck a block away. He still drives the same lifted model. I always thought that was interesting, because Rex is an understated guy in many ways, and his truck is anything but.

However, after seeing how ferocious he got when defending me from Orange Jacket and his friend?

Somehow, the giant truck fits. It says, *Don't even fucking think about it*.

"I'll give you a ride," he says.

I nod, in no mood to argue. I don't feel like calling a Lyft and facing some stranger. I've had more than enough of strangers tonight.

We get into the truck, and now that we're separated, I realize Rex and I were touching the entire walk back. Either his hand had been on my shoulder, my arm, or my waist. It had felt nice.

And when he'd swept me into his arms to carry me to safety?

I shift in my seat. I'm going to be thinking about that moment for many nights to come. I guarantee it.

I have never in my life touched Rex Easton as much as I have tonight. And I'd better not make a habit of it, because I'm already getting hooked.

Rex locks the doors and starts the engine, but he doesn't put the truck in gear. Instead, he's doing something on his phone. Then he taps his fingers against the gear shifter. "How you doing?" he asks.

"Aside from annoyed at myself for losing my purse and beyond sick of Amber Printz's groupies? I'm actually pretty good. Thanks for everything tonight. I'm ready to crawl into bed and sleep this off."

He drums his fingers on the gear shifter. "Quinn, I don't think it's wise to take you back to your place."

I sit forward in my seat. "What? You don't think my apartment is safe?"

"Hear me out. I just texted Max and Chief Holt about what happened. Holt is going to send a unit to your place, just in case. But I don't think that's enough. You're being targeted, and we don't understand yet who's doing it, or why." He holds up his hand. "We *think* it's Amber Printz, but that's just it. I can't develop a plan for your safety if I have no idea what's going on and how serious a threat we could be facing. Max agrees."

I bite my lip, considering. "Then where am I supposed to go?"

"For tonight, I could take you back to my place. I've got plenty of room."

"No."

I spit out the word so quickly that we're both taken aback. But I *can't*. I cannot go back to Rex's house and spend the night in Cliff's old room and act like it's no big deal. After all the touching and the saving and the general amazingness Rex has been displaying all night?

Not happening. My mental health, my sanity, demands otherwise.

"I'll stay with Danny and Lark," I say breezily, taking my phone from my clutch. "I'm sure they won't mind. They're great friends." Danny is my ex-roommate, a West Oaks firefighter, and Lark is his girlfriend. They're some of my favorite people. And Lark in particular will understand the predicament I'm in.

Rex pauses a beat, then nods. He puts the truck in gear. "Sounds good. Just give me their address, and I'll take you there. Then I could swing by your apartment to pick up a few—"

"Nope, no need. I can borrow what I need from Lark and figure out the rest tomorrow."

"If you're sure?"

I study the view outside the windshield. "Absolutely."

On the way, I confirm with Lark that I can crash on their couch. When we reach their row house, I go to unbuckle my seatbelt, but Rex stops me with a hand on my wrist.

"If anything comes up, let me know. I'll stop by tomorrow, and we can start putting a security plan in place."

"Got it." I grab my purse. "Thanks again."

I feel his eyes on me as I rush to Lark and Danny's front door. Lark opens it before I can knock, her expression tight with concern. But Rex doesn't drive away until I'm inside.

I can still feel the warmth of his fingers on my wrist.

5

Quinn

I blink and sit up. Morning sun shines through the blinds. Botanical prints decorate the walls, and I've got a chunky hand-knit blanket slipping off my shoulders.

For a moment, I can't remember why I'm in Lark and Danny's living room. Then it comes to me.

Right.

The strangest night ever. With Rex.

I stand up and stretch as I yawn. I'm wearing some of Lark's clothes. Baggy shorts, a concert T-shirt, slouchy socks.

Giggling comes from the nearby bedroom. The subtle squeak of a mattress shifting. So I'm not the only one who's up.

Smiling, I head to the bathroom, then the kitchen to make coffee. If they're getting frisky in there, hopefully the sounds of the coffee maker will cover the noise. For the sake of their privacy, not because I'm jealous.

Well, not *that* jealous.

I search the cabinets until I spot the coffee and filters, humming to myself. There's a stack of knitted potholders on the counter. Lark's new hobby. Danny's a firefighter, so he works long hours, and she took up knitting to keep herself busy during his nights at the station. She made Danny an awful, lopsided sweater, and of course he wears it every time the temps dip below sixty. Which isn't much given that this is Southern California. But I give the guy credit for trying.

It's wonderful to witness Lark and Danny's epic happily ever after, given everything they've been through in the past. Lark especially. They're such a perfect match for each other. Yet it can be hard to be around all that lovey-doveyness sometimes.

My perfect match must be out there somewhere too. After this stupid murder trial is over, I might have a chance to get out there and find him.

Preferably with some distance restored between me and Rex.

The bedroom door opens, and Lark steps out. Her long black hair is disheveled, and I think I spy a hickey peeking from the neckline of her oversized West Oaks FD shirt. She pads into the kitchen, tattooed arms only half visible.

"Morning. Oh, you got the coffee started? Thank you."

"You know me. Usually up early."

"To run. I know." She sticks out her tongue. "Danny's tried to get me into the running cult. No thank you. Nothing but carbs and caffeine in the a.m. for me."

"And a sexy quickie?" I nod at her neck.

Laughing, Lark pulls a sleeve of bagels from the fridge. "Wasn't going to go there. But yeah. Of course."

When Lark and I first met, she was hesitant around me. Especially after Cliff and his big mouth spilled that Danny and I had hooked up in the past. But I'd promised Lark that it hadn't been a thing. I'd been in law school, starved for touch and with no time to date between hours of class time, reading case law, and issue-spotting. And back then, Danny was fairly free with his affections. If you know what I mean.

But Danny and I were never more than friends with a few benefits, mostly cuddling and kissing. I've never spelled that out to Lark, because there's no way she wants the details on me and Danny. But the truth is, I've never been that into sex. I lost my virginity to a college boyfriend, and it was fine. Not bad. Same with my few hookups. But there were no fireworks. I've been waiting for that special spark of passion that other people talk about, and I haven't found it yet.

Except, of course, for someone who obviously isn't a candidate.

I haven't *constantly* pined for Rex. I've been too busy for that. I had other crushes here and there. But my feelings for him have never gone below a simmer, always ready to flare up at the least encouragement.

I pour Lark a cup of coffee, then one for me. She leans against the counter, warming her hands on her mug. "So, what exactly happened last night?"

I groan. "Craziness." When she and Danny heard I needed a place to stay, they just said to come over. They didn't push me for a bunch of explanations. It had been late, and I'd been exhausted. "It's about a murder trial we have coming up. Some vague threats." Lark's brows shoot up, and I add, "It's nothing very serious yet. Our trial team is going to have extra security as a precaution. I'm sure it'll be a pain."

Lark gets a knowing smirk. "And is a certain handsome bodyguard the one who's been assigned to protect you? Don't deny it. I saw him drop you off."

"It's…true. Yeah." I glance at the bedroom door, which remains closed. "Rex was with me last night when some creep tried to accost me with a milkshake. He took the hit. Ruined his tuxedo shirt."

"No way! Who throws a milkshake?"

"My thought exactly. It's a waste of good chocolate. But anyway. I managed to avoid him for six months before last night, and then he turned up, being all chivalrous and kind and protective." I drop my voice to a whisper. "He told me he'd missed me."

She gasps. "How dare he? What a monster."

"I know, right?"

Lark knows all about my sad tale. That was how we first bonded. Over confessions and tequila shots. She and Danny don't have secrets from one another, but she's told me this is *my* secret, not hers. If Danny found out, he'd probably spill it to Cliff in five seconds.

She tops up our coffees. "I saw you in that gown last night. You looked hot. Rex would be an idiot if he didn't notice how amazing you are, and he's no idiot. Are you sure there's no chance?"

"Don't get in my head with that kind of reasoning. I've known the man for too many years. It's hopeless."

"But for a lot of those years, you were too young. Now you're practically thirty." She squints at me. "Is that a wrinkle?"

"Hey, watch it."

Lark snickers. "I'm just saying you shouldn't give up entirely. I saw him watching you walk up to our door, and I swear there was longing in those dark eyes. And if you're worried about Cliff's reaction, I bet he'd roll with it. That's the kind of guy he is."

I groan. "Lark. Stop. Don't do this to me."

"Why? I'm as cynical as they come, but love finds a way." She shrugs. "Danny showed me that. He turned me mushier than an overripe peach."

There's a twinge in my chest. I know Lark isn't trying to be hurtful. She's trying to do the exact opposite. Be a good friend. But I can't let myself get all misty-eyed and dreamy over Rex. Not again. I can't bear it.

I want what Lark and Danny have. Someone to go home to at night. Who can't wait to see me as much as I can't wait to see him. To ever have that, I *have* to move on.

Danny emerges from the bedroom soon after, bleary-eyed and eager for coffee. He's shirtless, showing off his many tattoos, even more than Lark has. I glance away at their good morning kisses, as if they didn't wake up beside one another a little while ago.

I catch Danny up on what happened the night before. The threats related to the Amber Printz trial.

"Stay as long as you need," Danny says. "I'm sure Lark would love the company when I'm on my twenty-four-hour shifts."

She nods. "I'll teach you to knit!"

I sputter, almost spitting out my coffee. "That's a tempting offer. I just might take you up on that, Lark." She winks at me, likely already knowing I will *not* be doing that. "But I'm hoping to go home today. I'll have to see what the security expert says."

Danny grins. "Either way, it's no trouble at all. Once a roomie, always a roomie."

I'm about ready to get myself cleaned up when there's a knock at the door. Lark makes it there first and peers through the peephole. Then she spins and smirks. "Quinn, someone's here for you."

Before I can react, she opens the door, revealing Rex on the doorstep. He's dressed in jeans and an olive-green tee. His short hair is styled, scruff trimmed. He has a messenger bag over his shoulder, and a brown paper bag in his hand. "Brought breakfast. If anyone's hungry?"

Danny waves him in. "Hell, yes. Anyone bringing food

has a permanent invite. How are you, Rex?" He ushers the older man into the kitchen.

Never mind that I'm standing here in PJs with no bra, my hair a mess.

"Better this morning. Last night had more surprises than I usually prefer. I like being prepared." Rex smiles at me. "Had to run by the dry cleaner that's open on Sundays, and they have a great bakery next door, so I picked up some pastries. Oh, and Quinn. This is for you." He holds out the messenger bag. "I thought you might need some of your things. Cliff told me he had your spare key, so I had Lia run by your place."

"Oh. Thank you." I accept the bag, checking inside. It's got my favorite jeans, fresh underwear, a bra, a sweatshirt, and a few toiletries. I'll have to thank Lia. I told Rex I could get by with borrowing from Lark, but I'll admit this is better. I love the woman, but I don't need to share her undies.

"Very thoughtful." Lark gives me one of her patented knowing looks.

Shut it, Lark, I try to telegraph silently back.

"It was no trouble," Rex says. "I'll take you by your place later, if that sounds good. We can discuss your security plan."

We have more coffee and enjoy the chocolate croissants Rex brought. Half an hour later, I'm dressed in my own clothing, and I've carefully stowed my gown, clutch, and heels in the messenger bag. The gown needs to be cleaned anyway.

I thank Danny and Lark, telling them I'll see them later. We go out to Rex's truck, and I climb into the passenger seat. "I already conferenced with Max this morning," Rex says as we drive toward my apartment.

"Never a day off for a bodyguard, huh?"

"Not when I'm on duty. Especially when it's family we're talking about. Max has been on a tear since this involves Lana, and you're…" He gestures. "You."

Whatever that means. It doesn't mean what I wish it did.

"Did something else happen with Lana?" I would check my messages on my phone, but I haven't heard anything. Aside from a million texts from Cliff checking on me. I've already written him back that I'm fine. And it sounds like Rex was in touch with Cliff anyway, given that he saw Lia earlier.

"No, nothing with Lana," Rex says. "But we want to make sure nothing does happen. We conferenced in Chief Holt this morning, and Holt told us they interrogated the intruder from the gala last night. The guy with the perfume bottle? The perp said he was acting alone and had wanted to impress Amber Printz. But he swears he's had no direct contact with her."

"Figures." That's what I expected.

"Since there was no damage, and it was a misdemeanor trespassing charge, the perp had to be released. But we'll be keeping tabs on the guy. Lana has given Max the official go-ahead to handle all security for your trial team, and we'll have two-man teams working in shifts outside the DA building, as well as on call for the other deputy district attorneys as needed. But for you and Lana, we're adding another layer of protection."

"Because we're the only attorneys who've been threatened by name?"

Rex nods matter-of-factly. He's been using his official voice with me, and I appreciate that. His businesslike demeanor actually makes this feel less…personal. "Max will see to Lana's protection. And I'm now formally assigned to you."

I gulp. "Okay."

A glance. "Will that work for you?"

"Why wouldn't it?"

"I'll be with you as much as possible, which includes escorting you to and from work and to the courtroom."

"But…at night…"

His mouth curves. "At night, I'll be off duty unless there's a pressing need."

"Pressing need," I repeat. "Got it." *Stop thinking about pressing needs.* "I'd prefer going back to my own place soon. My own bed. Do you think it'll be safe to do that?"

He considers. "I'll have my guys assess whether your apartment is going to be safe enough. I know that's not a firm answer, but it's the best I have at this point. Let's get to your place, and we'll take a look."

"Thanks again. For everything."

"No problem. You don't have to keep thanking me."

"Because it's your job," I say, reminding myself.

"And because you're family," he says firmly.

"That too."

I can do this. I'll have to. Because there's no more avoiding Rex Easton.

My phone buzzes, and I take it out to check the notification. Lark just texted.

Any longing glances yet?

Go away.

Whatever. You love me. And you'll really love me when I turn out to be right about Mr. Distinguished Bodyguard.

"What's that?" Rex asks.

I almost fumble the phone as I cover the screen. "What?"

"That piece of paper." We stop at a red light, and Rex reaches over. He grabs something on my phone and tugs at it. A tiny piece of paper pulls free. "It was stuck in the case," Rex says.

I take the paper and unfold it. "What the heck?"

It says, *I have information on the Hayworth murder. Please contact me*. And then a phone number.

A car honks behind us, and Rex drives forward before pulling over quickly to the side. "Can I see that?"

I hand him the note. He lifts an eyebrow. "How mysterious."

He's being all cool and calm about this, but I can't help getting excited. "Wait, do you think someone put this in my phone case last night when my purse was missing?" The possibilities are swirling in my head. This is the kind of intrigue that only happens on TV. And for that reason, I should be cautious.

But come on. A secret witness?

Why would they decide to contact *me*?

"It's possible," he says. "Which suggests you didn't leave your purse behind. Whoever left this note might have taken it. Which means they were following you."

That's all true, but I can't imagine it was that orange jacket guy or his friend. Nothing was taken from my purse. Whoever left this note only took my clutch for that purpose. There's no way it was the same guy who accosted us, or his buddy who threw the milkshake. Those guys had zero subtlety.

This person managed to get my purse without me or even Rex noticing.

"It might be legit," Rex says, "or it might not be. But either way, I want to check it out. The timing alone makes me nervous. A secret witness turning up just as you're getting more attention for your part in the trial."

"That could be the very reason this witness decided to get in touch. I need to tell Lana. See what she thinks. There's no harm in seeing what the guy has to say."

Rex looks over at me, and I'll admit, I look for some sign of something in his eyes. I blame Lark.

He does look concerned. But there's also a twinkle of interest. And excitement. In the possibilities for our case, of course. Nothing else.

"If you want to show this to Lana right now," Rex says, "I know exactly where she is. Are you up for a detour?

"Are you kidding?" My Sunday just got a lot more intriguing. "Let's go."

I've never been inside Bennett Security headquarters. But I've seen the place from the outside. It's hard to miss.

We head toward the ocean, then follow the coastline to the north side of West Oaks. A huge brick building is perched right on the water, with waves crashing dramatically into the rocky beach below.

Rex pulls his truck into a driveway, swiping a key card that lets us into the underground parking.

While Bennett Security is known for providing protection to West Oaks elite and visiting celebrities, they also frequently work with law enforcement. And because Lana is married to the CEO, the company has a special relationship with the West Oaks DA's Office. Max has offered his company's investigative resources on numerous cases. And when it's made sense and there hasn't been a conflict of interest, Max has done the same for criminal defendants too.

Makes me wonder if Amber Printz tried to hire them at any point. Obviously, that's out of the question now, especially with Lana's safety at risk.

Chief Holt and West Oaks PD have done a great job giving us the support we've needed on a daily basis, and we have great investigators at the DA's office of our own.

But am I happy that Bennett Security is involved in this

case? That they'll be ensuring my personal safety? I'd be a fool not to recognize the benefits of that.

I mean, just look at this place. The West Oaks County legal complex is sleek and modern, a testament to all those tax dollars at work. But Max Bennett's bat cave puts the county's public buildings to shame. Not because its architecture is more flashy, but because of its seamless blend of high-tech and high style.

There's the retinal scanner as we walk in through the employee entrance and take the elevator. The banks of state-of-the-art computer terminals. Screens adorn one wall with a constant stream of statistics, camera feeds from around the city, and bodyguard assignments. Yet the exposed brick, artwork, and plush rugs keep the bustling work floor inviting.

But the crowning jewel of the huge, open workspace is the glass-walled office above, accessible from an open-riser staircase.

"That's Max's domain up there," Rex says, nodding.

"I figured."

He smiles. "Yeah, Bennett can be over-the-top sometimes. He's a great boss, though. A very good friend. You'll rarely meet anyone as loyal."

From our vantage point below, we can see Lana sitting on a couch near Max's desk. He brings her a cup of what looks like tea. "Not a lot of privacy up there," I comment.

"Those walls turn opaque at the push of a button. But we're one big family here." Rex touches my arm, ushering me forward. "Come on. Let's show them what you found."

What we found, I almost correct. But we're not a *we*.

They see us coming. Max meets us at the door, while Lana looks on from her spot on the couch. "Quinn, what are you doing here? Is something wrong?" She already knows what had happened last night, so I quickly explain the latest developments.

Lana holds out her hand. "Can I see this note?"

I pass it over to her. I briefly wondered about forensic evidence, but I already covered it in my own fingerprints in the car. Lana shares a glance with Max, who's examining the note over his wife's shoulder. "Seems too good to be true," Max comments.

Lana just says, "Quinn, let's chat. Let the guys see to themselves for a few minutes."

Max laughs. "Does that mean I'm dismissed, DA Marchetti?"

She winks at him. "Thanks. I'll let you know when I need you."

Max and Rex head downstairs. And just like that, she kicks the CEO out of his own office.

See why she's my idol?

"Max is right," Lana says. "The possibility of a secret, last-minute witness is probably too good to be true. But it's too juicy to pass up. Which means we have no choice but to follow up on it." She frowns. "I don't like that this person played games with you, though. Stealing your purse? It's way too cute. And frankly, rude. They could've just called our main phone line. I'm sorry this case is causing you so much unwanted attention."

"I can handle it," I rush to say.

"Clearly. You're not afraid to work hard, and you give any case you're involved in your all. That's why I wanted you on this team. You're passionate and ambitious. Some people don't like those traits in a woman, but that's not the case in my office. You remind me of myself at your age."

"*Wow*. Thank you."

"That makes me sound ancient, and I'm not *that* much older

than you. But I think it's less about age, and more about stages of life, you know? Not that long ago, I was single and in love with Max, who I thought would never love me back. And here I am, our second child on the way and more crazy about our family every day. I can't believe I'm so lucky." Lana has fierce energy when it comes to work, but right now, her smile is soft and glowing. "Listen to me, so sappy. I blame pregnancy hormones."

It seems we have more in common than I even knew. It's a trippy thought. "No, that's amazing. I hope to have the same someday." Not with Rex, because I'm done hoping where he's concerned. But there must be someone else out there for me. "For the moment, I am extremely single."

"You'll find the right one when you're ready. Now, who do you think this anonymous witness could be? I want to know your theories."

I sit down on the couch beside her. As we talk, brainstorming about the case and these latest developments, Lana rubs her belly.

"Is he kicking?" I ask.

Lana nods. "He's been a tiny little acrobat late—" She grimaces suddenly, and I shoot up to standing.

"Are you okay?"

"Just Braxton Hicks contractions. They stink."

"Should I get Max?"

"No, sweetie," she says tightly. "I'm fine. Could you grab me a glass of water?"

I get up to pour a glass from the carafe near Max's desk. I pass it over to her, and she takes several swallows.

"Thanks. It's passing. But I need a few minutes."

"Of course. No problem."

"You can head home if you have things to do."

Lana doesn't like overworking us on weekends. But I'm not going anywhere. "We've got a mystery to solve, and maybe some new evidence to dig up. You think I'd miss that?"

"Woman after my own heart. Give me half an hour. We'll gather some of Max's best people. See what we can find out. We've got Bennett Security at our disposal, and I intend to make use of them."

"Sounds good. Should I hang out downstairs? Or..."

"Try the basement. That's where the bodyguards work out if they're not on assignment." She winks. "Best view in the house, if you ask me."

Laughing, I head to the door. If Rex is getting all sweaty, I should probably steer clear.

But...a girl needs *something* to occupy herself.

I've usually been good at keeping myself out of trouble. But the last couple of days, trouble keeps on finding *me*.

6

Rex

"Come on, old man," Devon Whitestone says. "You can do better than that."

"Really? Seems to me, you're the one in a headlock."

"Not for long."

I can't help smiling. I remember when Devon was fresh from the Army Rangers, too strait-laced and uptight to talk shit to his elders. Now he's married with kids, the co-captain of our bodyguard team, and full of bravado.

I left Quinn upstairs a little while ago and came down here to get a workout in. I have just enough time to show him I can still whoop his ass.

Devon makes his move. He's trying to take me down with some fancy footwork. But I'm ready for him. Within seconds, I've tossed him over my shoulder, and I've got him pinned on the ground. He taps out.

"You were saying?" I ask.

I get up and hold out my hand to help him stand. Devon's gracious, despite his trash-talking, so he accepts my help with a grin. "Guess you've still got it. On occasion."

Tanner Reid steps over, smacking Devon on the shoulder.

He's Devon's co-captain, a giant of a man and a former Navy SEAL. "Or you're just out of shape, Whitestone. Is Aurora pregnant again? You do have a tendency to put on sympathy weight."

Devon's eyes bug. "Don't put that energy in the universe, man. I'm not ready for another one yet."

There are laughs all around. We've gathered an audience. Some of these guys don't have an assignment today, and others just decided to drop by. Tanner continues to rib his co-captain, in typical style.

But I head to the water cooler for a drink. Shit-talking isn't my thing. Never has been. Lydia used to call me stoic and reliable, saying I had a calming way about me. I think that was a kind way of pointing out how I don't compete for attention. I'm happy to fade into the background and let my teammates take the spotlight. That's why I never accepted Max's offers to lead our bodyguard team, though I've got the most military and security experience of any of them. I never wanted to be a full-time bodyguard.

When I'm on a Bennett Security assignment, I'll work twenty-four-seven if that's what the job requires. But I also take weeks off to volunteer for Team Triumph, a nonprofit disaster-response group. That's always been part of my contract with Bennett Security. I'm able to split my time equally between bodyguard gigs and helping communities around the country recover after hurricanes, fires, mudslides, you name it.

When I left the Army, giving back was important to me. And after Lydia died, I was more than happy to dive into helping others so I could keep the focus away from myself. But Bennett Security has become my family just as much as Cliff. Even if I hadn't come in today with Quinn, I probably would've come in to train. That's the kind of work environment we have here. I've seen these guys grow up.

I've spent over eleven years doing this, and until recently, I would've balked at changing that.

Devon was kidding when he called me "old man." But I have been feeling my age more. I mean, a lot of the guys on our team now are younger than my son. To them, I really am old. I guess when I was their age, forty-nine seemed old to me too.

I've got more aches and pains than I used to. I can't recover as quickly. I've got a sore shoulder I can't shake and more grinding in my joints than before. But I don't have a problem keeping up with these twenty- and thirty-year-olds.

Case in point—I think I held my own last night protecting Quinn. Maybe it was only against a perfume bottle and a milkshake this time. But no matter what came at us, I would've stood in the way of danger. I know my abilities and my strengths.

The question is whether I *want* to keep up with these young guys forever. Is this what I want for the rest of my life?

That's the thing about getting older. You realize that nothing is ever truly *settled*. I've had more than one career. I married the love of my life and raised a son. I can still bench press almost as much as Tanner, and he holds the record for our team. I've got a lot to be proud of.

But can't I still do more? Be more? Answering that question isn't as simple as finding a girlfriend, no matter what Max thinks. But he was onto something. I've got an itch for a new chapter. If only I knew what that would look like or where I might find it. Since last night, that's been on my mind.

Devon and Tanner start an impromptu clinic with the other guys on grappling. We're always trying to keep our skills fresh. But I need to get cleaned up and check on Quinn. I left her to talk with Lana about their secret witness. Her protection for the Printz trial could pose some unique challenges.

And for some reason, my mind conjures up the image of her in that strapless dress last night. The dimples in her bare shoulders. I've already worked up a sweat while sparring, and a fresh wave of heat rolls across my skin.

I banish those thoughts. So she looked stunning last night. It surprised me. So what? I need to get over it and focus on my job. I might be debating my future as a bodyguard, but I have an assignment right now. A damned important one.

The fact that Quinn Ainsley grew into a breathtaking vision of womanhood shouldn't matter.

Why is my throat so dry again?

While I'm refilling my water cup, I hear the door to the gym open, and a different murmur starts up among the bodyguards. Spines straighten. Chests puff out. It's a visceral mood change that I've experienced plenty of times over the years as a guy working with young, testosterone-driven men. A shift in the air that can only mean one thing.

A woman just walked into the gym, and she's not one of our co-workers.

I turn to look at who's getting so much attention. I catch a glimpse of blond hair. Bright, intelligent eyes, which scan the gym.

It's Quinn.

I down the rest of my water and toss the paper cup in the trash.

Tanner and Devon spare Quinn only a glance, but several others seem to have set their sights on her. Leon Kozinski reaches her first. He's someone I partner with a lot. Probably because I'm supposed to impart some wisdom and maturity on the kid. If you'd asked me yesterday how I feel about him,

I would've had nice things to say about his growth and improvement.

But watching that predatory gleam in his eyes right now as he approaches Quinn?

Nice is the last thing I'm feeling about Leon.

My jaw clenches as I make my way across the gym. By the time I reach her, Quinn's head is tilted in amusement and she's got her arms crossed over her sweatshirt. "I promise I'm not lost," she says.

"I'd still be happy to take you on a tour," my junior colleague offers. "I'm Leon."

"I've got this." I reach them and aim a glare at him. "As you were."

Leon lifts his hands, backing away. "Message received, Foxy. She's all yours." He's smirking, and he quickly turns to lope back to the practice mats. Several other people are watching me, but they avert their eyes when I frown.

I'm not known for being grumpy. But I'll gladly make exceptions when it means protecting my charges. That's the only reason I'm getting territorial.

Touching her lower back, I steer her toward the door.

"Foxy?" Quinn asks. "What's that about? I'm intrigued."

"It's a bodyguard thing. Never mind."

I'm lying through my teeth. *Foxy* is an idiotic nickname Leon gave me after our last assignment together. Short for *Silver Fox*, because our female client seemed to have a crush on me and kept commenting on how "distinguished" I look.

"Did you finish up with Lana?" I ask when we reach the hall. "I was about to head back upstairs to check on you, but I didn't want to rush you."

"She needed to take a break."

"Oh? Everything all right?" I remember when Lydia was pregnant with Cliff. She was exhausted by six months.

Quinn waves my question away. "You can ask Lana when

you see her. Actually, I came down here on a mission. But I didn't mean to..." She gestures at my clothes, her eyes darting over me and then away. "Interrupt."

I smooth a hand down my shirt over my stomach. "Just killing some time. Tell me what you need."

"Lana said something about gathering Max's best people and making use of the resources here to unmask our secret witness. I'm eager to get started. I hoped you could show me around and introduce me to whoever I need to know." Her shy smile turns sly. "Or I could ask Leon. He was friendly."

I clench my jaw as a low sound rumbles in my chest. Almost a growl. "I'll take care of you."

Her eyes linger on mine. Then, as always seems to happen, she glances away. "I'd appreciate that. Thanks."

"Just let me swing by the locker room. Then I'll take you on the grand tour." I can't stop myself from adding, "A much better one than Leon could manage, rubbing together those two brain cells of his."

"Never suspected you were so vicious, Rex. First my poor prom date, now Leon." Her laughter sings like music up and down my spine. "I'll be careful not to get on your bad side."

A grin tugs at my lips. "Not much risk of that happening. I've got a soft spot when it comes to you."

I probably shouldn't be admitting that. But since the moment I saw her in that ballroom last night, my reactions to Quinn keep surprising me.

~

AFTER A LIGHTNING FAST SHOWER, I TAKE QUINN on an insider's tour of the Bennett Security facilities, as promised. The server room, the infirmary, the shooting range. I don't take her inside the weapons room, because we don't take non-employees in there. But I point out the sights from the large, bulletproof window.

"You should come in to shoot at the range sometime," I say. "Lana comes in for practice about once a month. When she's not pregnant."

Quinn shrugs noncommittally. "I've been to a range with Cliff a time or two. I don't usually carry."

I make a note of that. When I'm guarding someone, I want to know where all weapons are at all times. Often, I don't want my client carrying because they might make a poor decision that'll lead to the client or my team getting hurt. But on the other hand, I want Quinn to have every possible means of protection.

"I'd like you to at least have basic proficiency with a gun," I say. "We also offer self-defense lessons to our clients. It's a failsafe in case everything else goes wrong."

"Are you saying you're fallible?" There's sarcasm in her tone, but the question is a fair one.

"Always. We're not superheroes. I will take a bullet for you, but if that happens, you have to be ready to do your part in getting away. A helpless client is a vulnerable one."

She winces. "Nobody will be taking any bullets."

"I hope not, but we have to be prepared. We don't know yet how serious these threats are. Or what your 'secret witness' really intends."

Her easy smile has vanished. I want to put it back in place. I don't want to scare her. But I also don't want Quinn to underestimate the realities of my job or the danger she could face with a target on her back.

I always have to plan for the worst. Because too often in my experience, the worst will happen. The natural disaster will hit. You'll lose the person you love.

Shit, now I'm making *myself* feel down.

"But that's why you're here today." I rest my hand on her

elbow. "To start finding out what's really going on. The whole point of this is to make you feel safer. And to make sure you really *are* safe as well."

Her long lashes flutter as she blinks. "I've always felt safe around you. That's a given."

There's a tug low in my stomach. My hand stays on her arm, not ready to give up that warmth and connection. "Good. Let's head upstairs. When I need to run background for a case, there's only one person I go to, and that's Sylvie Trousseau."

As we wait for the elevator, I keep our point of contact. But as soon as the doors slide closed and we're alone inside, Quinn side-steps just enough that my hand drops from her arm. I can't tell if it was on purpose or not. But if I'm being honest, I miss it. I like comforting Quinn. I like taking care of her.

It's important for a bodyguard to stay objective. That's rarely been a problem for me. I'm not the kind to let emotions interfere with my job. I'm not completely objective with Quinn, yet I've already dismissed the idea of turning over her protection to someone else.

So, I'll just have to make sure I'm vigilant. Nothing will go wrong if I don't let it.

7

Rex

Back on the main floor, we cross the open workspace, nodding hello to techs at computer terminals as we pass. We're heading toward the back corner, but trust me, this is where the heart and soul of Bennett Security lies. Not in Max's shiny office in the sky, and not downstairs where my fellow bodyguards hang out and pump iron.

"This way," I say to Quinn.

We reach an alcove, where curving computer screens form a barrier between this corner and the rest of the massive room. I hear fingers tapping like mad over a keyboard. "Knock, knock," I say. "Anybody home?"

A small head pops up. A blunt bob haircut, chunky glasses, big eyes, and pursed pink lips.

"For you, always." Sylvie steps out from behind her screens. She's petite, but don't let that fool you. As usual, she's wearing an all-black ensemble and combat boots. Tattoos decorate her arms and shoulders, visible beneath her cropped tank top.

Our dress code is flexible here. But even if it wasn't,

Sylvie can get away with anything she wants. Max's name might be on our logo, but she's the one keeping us running.

"Quinn, this is Sylvie Trousseau. She's our head of research, communications, computers. You name it, and Sylvie probably has a hand in it. We couldn't survive around here without her." She's got a legion of underlings now, but when I need the best, I always go to the source.

"No need for flattery, Foxy. I already love you." Sylvie shakes Quinn's hand. "Great to meet you, Quinn."

"That's the second time I heard someone call him 'Foxy.' What is that about?"

Ugh, that dumb nickname again. I try to signal with my eyes for Sylvie to take mercy on me, but she's having too much fun. "Can't you guess? Look at the man. 'Foxy' is self-explanatory."

Both women are staring, but it's Quinn's attention that has me heating up once again.

"And even better, it makes our dear Rex uncomfortable to be in the spotlight," Sylvie adds. "He prefers to be the strong, silent sentinel. He's so cute when he's flustered, which doesn't happen often."

"Enough," I rumble. "We're here to work."

Sylvie rolls her eyes. "Likely story." She stretches her arms over her head. "Okay, lay it on me. How can I help?"

A few minutes later, we've taken over a conference room. Quinn gives Sylvie a primer on the Printz trial, the increasing threats against their trial team, and the mysterious note left in Quinn's purse about the so-called witness. Sylvie examines the piece of paper when Quinn hands it over.

"A nice little puzzle, isn't it?" Sylvie muses. "If it's okay with you, Quinn, I'll start by doing a reverse lookup on this phone number."

"I tried that this morning," Quinn says. "Couldn't find anything."

"I expect not." Sylvie opens the laptop she brought into the conference room. "But my methods are a bit more thorough."

Quinn gets up to watch over her shoulder. "We have to keep this by the book. If this person really ends up being a trial witness, we may have to turn over all our info on them to defense counsel and the judge."

"Don't worry, honey. Not my first time consulting on a case for the DA. I know how Lana likes to do things."

At that same moment, the DA herself walks into the room. "How do I like to do it? Is this about what Max and I may or may not have done on his desk last weekend?"

The three women crack up. Quinn's face is turning red. I clear my throat, just in case they forgot I was in the room.

"Oh, hi Rex," Lana adds with a smile.

Thankfully, the ladies get their minds out of the gutters and onto the case at hand. It's not that I have a problem with a dirty joke here and there. I've told my share. But regardless of our history and close friendship, Max is still my boss, and Lana is his wife.

And Quinn is…not someone I should be thinking those kinds of thoughts around.

"The number is a burner," Sylvie says. "Unregistered. But I've got the serial number of the device, and I can trace it back to where it was sold." She taps on her laptop a bit longer, then announces, "Our witness's burner phone was purchased at a convenience store in West Los Angeles."

"Where exactly?" Quinn asks.

"On Olympic." Sylvie pulls up a map on her computer. Quinn and Lana study it, then exchange a glance.

"That's just a couple of blocks from Hayworth Productions in Century City," Quinn comments. "The production company that our murder victim founded. Same company that was making his last movie before he died."

So, very much *not* a coincidence. I have no doubt Sylvie's team will track down the convenience store's security cameras and credit card receipts. But very likely those won't be helpful if the person was careful.

Sylvie leans back in her seat. "All right. Our anonymous witness could be connected to Hayworth Productions. But if this person has more info on Amber Printz, why wouldn't they have come forward before?"

Quinn nods. "Exactly what I'm wondering. Maybe this person wants some extra guarantee or protection. Maybe they're incriminated in Thompson's murder or the coverup, and that's why they've kept this quiet until now. But there's only one way to find out." She gets up from her seat, and I'm impressed by the way she's got us all hanging on her words. I knew Quinn was smart, but she's confident in her abilities too. It's a good look on her.

A *damn* good look.

"The witness wanted me to make contact," Quinn says. "So I'll give him what he wants. I'll write and see what he has to say. If you're okay with that, Lana. You're the boss."

Lana shrugs. "I suppose I am, according to the last election. But as far as I'm concerned, you're in charge of investigating our new mystery witness. You've got free rein."

Quinn looks thrilled by her boss's vote of confidence. But I don't like this. My instincts are screaming that we should put on the brakes.

"Hold on," I say. "Just because the witness wants *you*, Quinn, that doesn't mean you should deliver. Let Sylvie and her team handle this. They can make contact first. Test the waters and learn more. Then, if this witness seems legit and isn't triggering any warning bells, you and Lana can consider talking to him."

I've conveyed all this in a reasonable, calm tone. Even though *my* warning bells are already chiming. But Quinn aims a scowl my way. "If the witness is really connected to the Printz case, it's likely he—or she—has already met me. He might have a sense of how I'd talk. The wording I would use. There's a reason he chose to contact *me*, and I don't want to scare him away by handing the contact off to someone else."

"Exactly why I'd advise caution." When I think of this person watching Quinn, singling her out, my insides twist. If this is truly a reluctant witness, then it makes sense he'd gravitate toward Quinn. I imagine she's great at putting witnesses at ease. But if this person has more nefarious intentions? "We don't know what this person is really planning. We can't be impulsive about this. I'm in charge of your security for this trial, and my advice is to let Sylvie's team go in first."

"I appreciate the input," Quinn says. "And I acknowledge everything you're saying, Rex. But you're overruled."

I'm sorry. *What*?

I glance at Sylvie, expecting her to back me up here, but she just shrugs. "Like Lana said. Quinn's in charge. And we're just talking about a text conversation. Right? I can set up a burner device for Quinn to use to make contact. That way, we can squeeze every bit of info out of their dialogue. And Quinn won't be compromising her own phone."

"Very helpful of you," I deadpan.

With a knowing grin, Sylvie dashes off to get the burner. But I can't stay annoyed for long. Quinn's excitement and optimism are contagious as she strategizes with Lana. She's leaning with her hands against the conference table, strands of blond hair trailing across her cheek. Her eyes glitter as she thinks. And I can't help but watch her in her element.

It's another of those moments that my brain seems to get stuck. Just marveling at how different she is from that girl next door. How much she's changed without me realizing it.

Until now. Am I less observant than I always believed? Are my skills getting rusty in my advanced age?

No, fuck that. My skills otherwise are as sharp as ever. It must be something about Quinn. As if I had a blindspot in the exact shape of *her*.

But I'm seeing her now. I'm definitely seeing.

And for some reason, a hint of discomfort slides down my spine. I shift in my seat and take a sip of water from the glass in front of me. I'm probably just unsettled about Quinn's security.

With that in mind, I text a bit with Max, updating him on our investigation into the mystery witness, as well as my plans for the trial team's security at the courthouse. He's handling some other matters, but he assures me he trusts me to take care of this. Good thing *he* trusts me, at least. Since Quinn seems to have no issue ignoring my advice.

It doesn't take long for Sylvie to get the burner set up. She returns to the conference room and hands Quinn the device. "This might look like a regular iPhone, but it's loaded up with software by yours truly. Completely untraceable to any outsider, but it's connected in real time to our Bennett Security network. Every single call and text gets uploaded to us, along with any data we can pull about the sender. "

"But they can't do the same to me," Quinn says. "Perfect." Her thumbs move over the keyboard on her device, and the image of her screen projects onto the larger flatscreen on the wall.

Text bubbles appear.

> This is Quinn Ainsley. I got a note with this number last night. Are you the one who left it?

A couple of tense minutes pass. I find myself getting up to pace across the length of the conference room. But just as

Quinn opens her mouth to say something to the rest of us, three dots appear. We all go quiet, waiting until the reply comes in.

Yes. Thanks for writing me. I was worried you might not.

Who are you?

Can't say yet. I know the cloak and dagger is dramatic, but it's necessary.

I can assure you any communication between us will remain confidential for now. But I need to know who I'm speaking with.

I understand. But this could be dangerous. For both of us.

What kind of danger?

I think you've already seen hints of it. But it could get far worse.

What the hell is that supposed to mean? It sounds like he's implying a threat. "Sylvie," I say, "are you getting anything to pin down this person's identity or location?"

Sylvie frowns at her laptop. "Unfortunately, no. It seems our witness has some protection of his own. VPN and a wicked firewall. But keep going, Quinn. My programs are running in the background. Don't worry about that."

Quinn nods and goes back to typing.

I never doubt Sylvie's abilities. But it still makes me anxious for this person to have a direct line to Quinn. Even if it's purely through text messages at this point.

Do you mean the threats my office has received? Or the people who accosted me last night?

All of the above. Amber has put the word out to her minions, through indirect channels of course, to target you.

Why me?

Because you're young and beautiful and full of promise. Like Amber used to be. Your district attorney knows it too. You're going to be her secret weapon at trial. When Amber testifies, you can get up there and ask the hard questions. Get under Amber's skin. And the jury will eat up every moment. Isn't that how it works?

"The guy is trying to manipulate me," Quinn says.

Lana tilts her head. "That's probably true. But he's not wrong about your role in the trial." We all glance over at Lana, and she shrugs. "Anyone who sees Quinn in the courtroom knows she's a force to be reckoned with."

"But I think Quinn's also right that he's angling for something," I say. "What does he really want?"

Quinn thinks for a moment, and then types again.

I'm just doing my job. Which includes searching for the truth. You said you have evidence for us. If you don't give me something, I'll have to assume you're not serious.

Damn right, I think. I'm proud of her for not being distracted or swayed by flattery. Even though it's well deserved in Quinn's case. I have no doubt she'll be fantastic at trial.

I keep pacing and then pause beside her, watching as she awaits the source's response. I feel the need to stay close. Even if this person can't reach through the phone and touch her, he could still harm her. It's my job to keep that from happening. I hate the thought that I might not be able to.

Quinn looks up at me. "Wish he'd hurry up," she murmurs.

"Means you're keeping him on his toes. Well done."

She doesn't acknowledge the compliment, but the extra color above her cheekbones suggests she's pleased by it.

> I'm talking about eyewitness evidence that Amber wasn't where she claimed to be on the day of the murder.

Quinn sucks in a breath, while Lana sits up straighter. The tension in the room has just dialed up to eleven.

"I'm guessing that's what you were hoping to hear?" Sylvie asks.

"And then some," Quinn says. "On the day of the murder, Amber was at a hair salon and spa for most of the day. It's her alibi. She posted on social about her appointment. Made sure that a dozen people saw her arrive that morning. But there was a stretch of time, about three hours, that she was entirely unaccounted for. She claimed to be in the sauna and locker room where there are, conveniently, no cameras. No witnesses either. Our theory is that she left the spa, killed her husband, and sneaked back into the locker room before her pedicure appointment. The physical evidence supports it."

"But it's one of the weaker aspects of our case," Lana admits. "If we had an eyewitness putting Amber at the murder scene during the key time period, that would be the finishing touch on the case we're building."

I cross my arms. "All the more reason for suspicion. This supposed witness is dangling exactly what you need."

"Exactly why we can't afford to disregard it," Quinn points out. Immediately, she starts typing again.

What's this evidence? We need a proffer.

I don't have it yet. But I can get it to you. If...

If you think the DA pays for evidence, you'd be wrong.

That's not what I want. Not money or anything like that. But I will need assurances.

Such as?

I'll let you know. I'll be in touch.

Wait, what's your name? I need to know this is legit. How do I know you're not wasting my time?

Hello?

But the source doesn't reply. Quinn curses, setting the phone roughly on the conference table.

Meanwhile, I raise an eyebrow at Sylvie in a silent question. She shakes her head. *Nope*. We got nothing on the source's identity or location. At least not yet. I clench my hand into a fist, then release it. I've learned to be patient, but I wish I had more for Quinn right now. I hate that she's disappointed.

Lana sits at the head of the conference table, tapping her nails on its surface. "The ball is in our witness's court now. Probably just what he wanted. Unless this witness agrees to testify or leads us to verifiable evidence we can authenticate and use, it doesn't matter anyway. All we can do is wait."

Quinn gets up, as if she's too full of nervous energy to sit still. It's what I was feeling during that entire text exchange. Yet now that the witness has vanished, I don't feel much better. *What was that really about?* My gut says the so-called "witness" is full of it. This person has some kind of agenda. I intend to find out what it is.

"Sylvie, your team will keep looking into the witness's burner phone and location?" Quinn asks.

"Absolutely, hon. I'll make it a priority. I'll pass anything I find on to Foxy for you." Sylvie gives me a wink.

Quinn's frown turns into a soft smile as her gaze meets mine. "Sounds good."

"We'll sort this out," I assure her and Lana. "I'll coordinate with everyone here at Bennett and keep you both informed."

"Just what I want to hear," the district attorney says with a sigh. "This baby is demanding enough of my attention. I've got all I can handle as it is." She gets up. "I'm going to find Max. Rex, you'll see Quinn safely home?"

"Absolutely. My team is checking out her apartment building as we speak."

Lana grips my shoulder on her way out. Sylvie is gathering up her computers and equipment. But Quinn is chewing her lower lip, as if she's holding back something more that she wants to say. I'm sure she has a lot on her mind.

I just hope she's not cooking up some kind of plan to find the witness on her own. The Quinn I knew before was cautious and practical. But this grownup version of her? I can't quite predict what she might do.

And that idea is just as exciting as it is dismaying.

8

Rex

"You handled that well," I say.

I glance over at Quinn in the passenger seat. We're heading back to her apartment building. My guys have finished assessing the security at her place, noting the exits and potential vulnerabilities. I'm confident that she's safe to return home. But she's gazing out the window at the palm trees flying past, still pensive after the afternoon at Bennett Security headquarters.

"You think so? You were against the idea of me contacting the witness at first."

"True, I had reservations. But I couldn't have scripted your side of the conversation any better myself. You showed him you're not a pushover, and you're not naive. If he doesn't put up soon, then he'll have to shut up."

She slumps against the seat with a sigh. "But in the end, the guy didn't give us anything yet. He could still be stringing us along. There might be no secret evidence at all."

"He gave away plenty." I know Quinn is disappointed that our witness stopped texting. But from my perspective, we got a lot today. Though it certainly didn't reassure me.

She perks up slightly. "Like what?"

"We've confirmed that both the witness and Amber Printz are focused on *you*. And we have a better sense of why. Before, we were just guessing."

"Right." She scoffs. "Because I'm *young* and *beautiful* and Lana's secret weapon in the courtroom." Her voice drips with sarcasm.

"Is that so hard to believe?"

"Not necessarily. I can accept a compliment. But really, it's just sensible trial strategy on Lana's part. Amber Printz is around my age. We're both blond and blue-eyed. She and her attorneys are going to do everything in their power to make her look like the innocent ingenue. So, I'll be there as her counterpart on the other side. I can ask Amber the tough questions when she's on the stand without looking like I'm a bully, beating up on her unfairly."

"All valid. But Lana clearly has faith in your abilities. Your skill and intelligence. That has nothing to do with how you look. Although." I can't resist the excuse to glance away from the road and study her. The sun is setting over the ocean, and the rich colors briefly breakthrough the buildings, setting off the pale aqua color of her eyes. Like fire and ice. "Beautiful is an understatement when it comes to you."

Quinn takes a slow breath in, eyes widening slightly. And there's a light, fizzy sensation lifting my chest. At some point today, she pulled her hair back into a messy bun secured by a ballpoint pen. A few pieces have fallen, and I feel the urge to brush them back into place. Let my fingers trail along her neck…

I face the road, gripping the steering wheel a little too hard and making the leather creak. "How important is this evidence the witness is teasing? How essential is it to your case?" Lana mentioned it would help them, but I need Quinn to level with me.

She drums her fingers on her cheek thoughtfully. "As DA, Lana wouldn't have brought the case to trial if we didn't have the evidence to back up the charges. But it's almost entirely circumstantial. Each piece might have an innocent explanation taken alone, but added up, it's significant. We've got Amber's motive to get rid of Thompson. The strain in their marriage, and the fact that he was about to fire her from the movie. The money she stands to inherit. The suspicious internet searches and those missing hours at the spa when nobody can confirm where Amber was. And our expert testimony that the murder scene was staged to look like a break-in. But the defense will try to explain each and every piece away. Our case would be so much stronger with irrefutable evidence that she left the spa. If we had that, all their efforts to make Amber look like a sweet, angelic victim wouldn't matter." Her fist tightens, and her eyes narrow. "We'd have her."

"Wow. No wonder Lana values you and Amber is afraid of you. You're relentless when you put your mind to something."

She smiles and laughs. "When it's my career, maybe. My personal life? That's a mess. But I'm trying to let go of things that weren't working for me before." Quinn shrugs.

"I'm the same. My career has always been the easy part. At least, knowing the right direction to take. With Lydia, the personal stuff came pretty easily too. But since losing her, it's been uphill every step of the way. Especially with dating." *Or the lack thereof,* I add silently.

Quinn is quiet, and I wonder if I've said too much. Maybe she doesn't want to hear such personal info about her best friend's father.

Change of subject needed. *Stat.*

"Well," I say. "I'd prefer that you let Sylvie and me investigate this anonymous witness. But I have the feeling you're going to get impatient. So I'll make you a deal. If you have any brilliant ideas to track down the source or the evidence he promised, share them with me. I'll do whatever I can to help you. Don't try to tackle this alone."

"You won't go all *overprotective bodyguard* and shut me down?"

"Nah, that sounds more like Max Bennett than me. Not my style. I'll do my best to persuade you. Gotta be honest, I'm usually convincing. I tend to get my way."

"But I make arguments for a living."

I laugh. "Indeed. I have no doubt you'll keep me on my toes. If you overrule me, as you have a tendency to do, I'll work out a compromise with you."

"Good to know."

"My goal is to keep you as secure and protected as possible, while fulfilling all of your needs."

Her gaze flies away to the window as she makes a small, choked sound.

"You okay?" I ask.

"Uh, yeah. Itch in my throat." She coughs a few times. "All good."

I pull up in front of Quinn's apartment building. There's already a discreet SUV in the parking lot, manned by two bodyguards from our team. I wave at them, noticing with satisfaction that neither one is Leon, my younger coworker who wanted to give Quinn a tour earlier today. I might have dropped a request with our scheduler to prioritize Leon for a different assignment.

Maybe I should feel bad about that, but I don't. It seems I'm especially protective of this particular client. Quinn deserves the very best.

"The guys will be here tonight, keeping an eye out. They'll have a shift change around midnight. You have the main

Bennett Security numbers to use if you have any issues, and they'll connect you to the car on duty." I suppress the urge to ask her to call me directly. If she's in danger, she should call the main line. Our operators will ensure the fastest response, and that likely wouldn't be me if I'm off duty.

"Right. Sylvie's assistant explained everything."

"Excellent." I shift the truck into Park. "I'll see you in the morning, then." I'll be driving her to and from the courthouse, as well as providing her personal protection while she's at work during the day. It's pretty much what we discussed this morning, with some refinements that we made with Max and Lana this afternoon.

"Thanks."

Quinn reaches for the door handle. Our conversation is finished. But for some reason I ask, "Is there anything else I can do for you?"

"Nope. You've touched all the bases. I mean," she stammers, "made all the arrangements. Uh. I'll see you tomorrow. Goodnight, Rex." She's out of the door and halfway to her building before I can respond.

I'm not sure what that was. That odd spike of tension there.

But I find myself wishing I had some excuse to stick around longer. Quinn's heading into an empty apartment, and I'm about to head home to an empty house.

Hell, maybe I do need a girlfriend. Or a hobby or a pet or something. Because my mind has been in a strange, restless place the last couple of days.

~

THAT NIGHT, I MAKE MYSELF A DINNER OF SEARED skirt steak over salad greens. And against my better judgment, I download a dating app and scroll through the questionnaire as I'm eating.

"Am I looking for hookups, casual dating, or do I want to find *the one?*" I ask myself aloud. I'm sitting at the kitchen counter with a glass of Malbec beside me. One of my favorite jazz albums plays low in the background. It's my comfort zone.

But damn, it's quiet.

All right. It's *lonely*. I can admit that. And Max's words at the gala have stuck with me. It's time for me to try finding someone new. If only so that I'm not alone in this big house, night after night. Like I have been since Cliff went off to college.

On my app profile, I select dating, since hookups aren't me and a long-term relationship feels like too big a step since I'm just dipping my toes in. I haven't dated in, what, thirty years? Jeez. Just thinking that number could give me hives.

Back when Lydia and I got together, we didn't exactly date. It was high school. We just hung out in our group of friends and talked on the phone at night until I got up the nerve to kiss her. It was all pretty straightforward.

This isn't straightforward. The elaborate quiz I'm supposed to fill out. Then coming up with profile pictures and pithy remarks to convey the right impression.

I am so out of my element.

It's not like I've had no sex at all since Lydia died. I've had partners here and there. But the truth is, I can survive without getting naked with another person. Even when I was with my wife, the flame between us was more smoldering than a wildfire. But my dynamic with Lydia was wonderful. I remember waking up and smiling at each other. Morning kisses. Bringing her coffee. Just caring for her, checking on her throughout the day. Even when I was deployed, I tried not to let a day go by without reminding her in some small way that I loved her. It wasn't always possible, but the intention was there. She did the same for me.

That's what I miss the most. Having someone to share my life with. I don't expect to find another great love. That seems like a once in a lifetime kind of thing. But the companionship? The sex, sure, but also the cuddling and daily affection. I guess I *am* ready for it.

If I can just get through this stupid quiz.

Taking a bite of steak, I scroll through the questions. My personality, my likes and dislikes. *What age range am I looking for?* That gives me pause for a moment. Twenty is way too young. What would I have in common with a twenty-year-old?

Twenty-five is a little better. But still a bit young.

Quinn is twenty-eight.

I jump slightly at that voice in my head, wondering where that thought came from. But…I guess it's a relevant guidepost. Quinn and I get along well. Right? She's making strides in her career. She's old enough to know what she wants.

A buzzy feeling spreads through me as I consider all the ways Quinn has grown up. As I've been doing way too much lately. I can't seem to get my mind off her, even when I'm off duty.

Back to the quiz, I tell myself. I settle on marking twenty-seven to fifty years old, then move on.

After setting up a half-assed profile, I swipe through my matches. Many of these women look nice. Some of their profiles are snarky, others earnest. There's nothing wrong with any of them on the surface. Some, I think I could enjoy having dinner with. Hopefully an intelligent conversation. But nobody sparks more than a passing interest. Am I too picky? Am I not as ready as I thought?

Frustrated, I exit out of the app, tossing my phone onto the counter by my plate.

My phone makes a noise, and I have a brief flare of nausea when I think it's a notification from the dating app. But my anticipation surges when I realize it's a text from Quinn.

Thanks again for all your help today. Could you come a few minutes early in the morning? If you don't mind. It's my day to bring donuts for the office. There's a chocolate glazed in it for you, plus coffee. My treat.

Sounds great. Westside Donuts right? Are their apple fritters still your favorite?

Always and forever [apple emoji][smile emoji]

It's on my way, so I'll pick them up before I get you. A dozen assorted?

Yep. You don't know the meaning of MY TREAT, but thank you Rex. Night.

Goodnight. Sleep tight.

I've got a huge smile on my face as I settle in for bed.

I walk along the beach, hand in hand with a curvy blond. It's sunset, and a breeze blows her hair around her face. One moment she's wearing a strapless blue sundress. And the next, it's a fluffy pink ball gown. In the distance, there's a surreal landscape where the skyline of Los Angeles towers over a rainforest canopy.

Okay, I know this is a dream. I dream less and less as I get older, and more often than not, the dreams are partially lucid. Of course, that doesn't mean the dreams make sense. But I don't mind. The blond in my arms is stunning, and the vibes are smooth as silk.

I pull her closer to watch the sunset.

This is beautiful, she says.

Not as beautiful as you. The line is a bit corny. But it's true. And it seems I've said just the right thing, because she looks up at me adoringly. Pale blue eyes. A heart-shaped face that's both familiar and breathtaking, like the sunset itself. She licks her lower lip and gazes at me seductively.

What do you need? I whisper. *I'll give it to you. Anything.*

All my needs, huh?

Yes, gorgeous, I answer after a kiss, and she shivers. *Name it.*

I need you. Need you to fill me up.

Oh. I like where this is going.

The scene shifts, and we're suddenly in the living room of my house instead of on the beach. We're kissing. She unbuttons my shirt, because I'm now wearing a tuxedo. I tug the straps down on her dress, freeing her breasts. I hold one in each hand, thumbs flicking her nipples, my tongue thrusting into her mouth. The blond's fingers shake as she opens my fly and grips my hard cock. Her fingers are cool against my heated flesh. They squeeze slightly, and my shaft throbs.

I want you, she says.

I nibble at the skin just below her ear. *You sure, gorgeous?*

Please, she moans. *I always feel safe with you, Rex. Always and forever.*

When I jolt awake, my bedroom is dark. I'm breathing hard, barely aware of what's happening.

My hand is in my pajama pants, fisting my erection.

I squeeze the base of my shaft, then slowly drag my grip upward. My fist rotates, tugging my foreskin over the head, then down again to expose the tip. Precome smears down my length. I repeat the same motion. My other hand ventures lower to cup my sac.

"Ungh," I groan. Usually, I jerk off a couple days a week to take the edge off. But it's not like this. Right now, I'm filled with an urgent, aching need. I shimmy my pants down for better access.

It was that dream. The sexy blond in my arms.

As I stroke, images come back to me like a slideshow. Her sweet face, gazing up at me. Her striking blue eyes. The feeling of her tongue in my mouth, and the weight of her breasts in my hands. I imagine it's her hand on my cock. Up and down. Increasing the pace and pressure. Tension curls at the base of my spine.

Then she whispers, *I always feel safe with you, Rex.*

My eyes fly open.

Holy shit. That was *Quinn*.

At the same moment that I make the connection, the orgasm hits. Pleasure jolts through my body. My release splashes onto my bare stomach and my hand, which keeps on stroking, drawing out every last drop. My thoughts are scattered for a few long, blissful moments.

Then I realize what I just did.

Fuck.

I just got myself off to thoughts of my son's best friend. My current client. A girl I've known since she was a teenager.

But I *wasn't* thinking about the girl. I was picturing the sexy, sophisticated woman.

And God, is she sexy.

I grab for a discarded T-shirt on the ground to clean myself up. Then I sit on the edge of my bed, staring into the dark.

But all I see is Quinn.

In that strapless gown at the gala, delicate shoulder bones on display. What is it about those shoulder bones that does me in? Yet she's equally beautiful in a sweatshirt and jeans, hair up in a messy bun. Her intelligent eyes when she's analyzing, teeth pressing into her plush lower lip as she thinks.

My imagination shifts to a scene from my dream. Quinn, with all her womanly curves and full lips, telling me she wants me. Her soft, velvety mouth opening up to my tongue, her hand reaching into my pants to stroke my cock.

Even though I just came, my dick twitches again with interest.

"Nope," I say aloud, jumping up to pace my bedroom. "This is not going to be a thing."

But it is. *It is* a thing.

I want her.

This isn't the first time my body has betrayed me, especially since I've entered the other side of forty.

I try to push the thoughts and images away, wearing a path in the rug from how long I'm pacing. But my mind is in full rebellion, spinning away from me.

Quinn on her knees for me. Quinn naked and riding me. Quinn gasping as she spreads her legs and begs for my cock.

After a shockingly short time, I'm hard again.

I brace myself against my bedroom wall with one hand, the other wrapped around my erection. Jacking myself rough and fast. Maybe one more orgasm will sate this desire. Because I *can't* have Quinn. She's the very definition of off limits for me. These are fantasies I won't ever be acting out.

But now that I've got those images in my head, I can't unsee them. I can't erase that head rush I experienced when I climaxed to thoughts of her. Sweet, beautiful, intelligent Quinn.

My son's best friend.

9

Quinn

Something is up with Rex.

It's been two weeks since the day we spent at Bennett Security texting with the anonymous witness. The source hasn't surfaced again yet. I've been back to trial prep, plus working on my other cases. In many ways, Rex has been his usual self. Superhero-level handsome and charming. He opens the door for me on our way into the office in the morning or into the courtroom if I have an afternoon hearing. He's a stalwart presence by my side. As reliable as ever. Even if having him around me all day, every day is unusual in itself.

But underneath, there's something different about him. It's not just the fact that he's my bodyguard now. It's in the way I feel him studying me when he thinks I'm not looking. The intense, inscrutable glances he gives me when we're alone together. The darkly flirtatious tone in his deep voice. The way his hand seems to twitch toward me as we're saying goodnight at the end of the day.

And whenever I look back at him after he drops me off at

my building, I swear there's a hint of hunger in his dark gray irises.

It's enough to make my poor, lovesick heart hopeful.

But that was the old Quinn. I'm not that starry-eyed girl anymore, obsessed with her friend's father. I've been handling his proximity pretty well, if I say so myself. It's like exposure therapy. The more he's around, the stronger my defenses.

So, whatever the explanation for Rex's moods lately, I'm not letting it affect me. I'm certainly not going to imagine that it means more than it does. I will not succumb to foolish dreams that won't come true.

I'm finally getting over him, and it feels *so good*.

Instead of wasting my time pining for unattainable men, I've been focused on my work. That's how I find myself staring at my laptop, lost in thought, when a knock comes at my office door.

I look up, expecting to see Rex. But it's Derek Keller, defense counsel for the upcoming Printz trial and my former law school classmate. Except for a couple of hearings in the courtroom, I haven't seen him since the night of the gala. Certainly wasn't looking for him, either.

I paste on a smile. "Derek. What are you doing wandering the halls of the DA's office? Not spying on our work product, are you?"

His grin is equally fake. "I just finished a meeting with the DA. Surprised she didn't invite you."

"I've got plenty of other things to keep me busy."

"I can imagine. Busy work is a drag."

I know he's just trying to provoke me. To make me jealous that he's leading the defense while I'm second-chair. It's not going to work.

But I'd be lying if I said Derek's presence didn't irk me. Simply because he's a reminder that we've made no progress on finding that anonymous witness, or the evidence our mystery person promised.

The online threats against me have died down for the moment. I know Sylvie and her team have continued to investigate. They've succeeded in identifying some of the ringleaders posting nasty things about me online, but the culprits have all been random fans of Amber Printz. Nobody with the kind of inside access to make them our mystery witness.

Sylvie's efforts to learn more about the burner phone and who bought it haven't led anywhere. She sent an investigator to the convenience store where it was purchased, but the person had paid cash and the surveillance footage had already been recorded over.

If I want that evidence before the trial begins, I can't wait for Sylvie to dig up a lead. I have to make a move of my own.

Derek makes a show of glancing left and right. "Where's the guard dog? I thought you didn't go anywhere without him."

"You mean Rex? I assume he's getting lunch. He doesn't spend every second with me." Though I'm sure there's a Bennett Security car keeping an eye on our building entrance. They're a permanent fixture lately.

"Could've fooled me. Are you that afraid of public criticism?"

"Not at all, but I don't appreciate threats and harassment."

He snorts. "A thrown milkshake is hardly a pattern of harassment, Quinn."

I stand up from my desk. I won't let him bait me. But ugh, it's hard not to respond. "Don't you have better places to be?"

"Yes, I do." But instead of leaving, Derek takes a step into my office. His eyes rove over my desktop. I snap my laptop shut. "Is this really what you envisioned when you graduated?" he asks. "A low-level job upholding the system? You're better than this."

Wow. He's got more of an attitude than usual today. I'm opening my mouth to tell him off when a shadow looms in the doorway. Rex has just returned carrying a bag of takeout. His expression is as dark and stormy as the rain clouds that rarely grace our Southern California skies.

"Is this gentleman bothering you, Ms. Ainsley?" Rex asks. Playing up the bodyguard role to the max.

I suppress a grin as Derek whirls around to face Rex. My rival covers his shock well, but I can tell his bravado is a facade. Can't blame him. Rex is kinda scary when he's like this. "Oh. The guard dog is back. I was just leaving anyway."

Derek slinks by Rex, who moves from the doorway just enough to let him pass. Then, at the last second, he leans over Derek and whispers, "*Woof.*"

I can't hold in my laughter this time.

Derek scurries away, and Rex comes into my office, closing the door most of the way behind him.

"Thank you," I say. "I needed that."

"It was fun for me too." The corner of Rex's mouth lifts in a satisfied smirk. "If you want, I'll find out which BMW in the parking lot is his. I can let the air out of his tires. Just say the word."

I snort. "Don't tempt me. I'm trying to be more mature than that."

"Are you saying I'm a bad influence?" he teases.

And there it is. That dark intensity in his gaze that I never saw before two weeks ago. The kind that I have no idea how to interpret. It's almost…*wicked.*

I ignore the fluttery feeling in my stomach, because I am over that crush, and focus on the takeout bags in his hand. "Did you grab lunch?"

He sets the bags on the desk. "I did. I got Thai for us. Hope that's all right. You were so focused on your work, so I didn't want to interrupt you. But I intend to make sure you eat something. Yesterday you skipped lunch."

The flutters get worse. This is another thing Rex has made a habit of lately. Bringing me food, coffee, afternoon treats. Like he's determined to anticipate my every whim. I remember what he said to me before. *My goal is to keep you as secure and protected as possible, while fulfilling all of your needs.* Spoken in that deep, late-night sex operator voice of his.

Gah. My panties were damp after I heard those words. Could anybody blame me? Of course, Rex had no clue. He's never had any idea of the effect he has on me.

Had on me, I correct. That's all in the past.

He unpacks the takeout containers. I stick a fork into the drunken noodles. "No wonder Bennett Security is so successful," I say. "Your customer service is next level."

"I don't do this for every client."

"Right. It's because I'm family."

His fork pauses on the way to his lips. "Yep. Family." Briefly, a hint of something like dismay crosses his features. "What did defense counsel want?"

"Oh, Derek?" I finish chewing my bite of noodles. "I'm sure he had some ulterior motive for that visit. Not just to annoy me. He's fishing for something."

"Do you think he knows about the potential witness who contacted you?"

That occurred to me. I know Rex is still skeptical about whether the witness is legit, and so am I. For all we know, Derek was behind that gambit. But if that were true, why did I have the sense that Derek was sniffing around for info today?

"I'm not sure," I say. "But what I do know is that I have to track down the witness. If that evidence exists, I have to find it before it's too late." I push my lunch aside and grab my laptop. "We know that it's likely someone connected to Hayworth Productions. I've been narrowing down a list of potential suspects. I want to talk to each one in person. You said if I had ideas about the witness's identity, you'd be willing to help me."

"Absolutely. Let's do it."

"You—wait, you're already agreeing?"

I thought I would have to talk him into it. But Rex is nodding along with me. "I didn't want you to rush off and do something reckless to find this person. But you've taken two weeks to plan your next move. I'm sure you've put a lot of thought into it."

My mouth hangs open for a second. "I have. Yeah. That's what I've been working so hard on for the last few days."

"I figured. Lana gave you clearance to investigate this witness with Bennett Security's help. So, I'm in. Tell me where we're going, and you can give me the details on the way." Then he points at my uneaten food. "*After* you've finished lunch."

I grab the takeout box, rolling my eyes. But I don't mind the order. In fact, I like it. It's nice being the focus of Rex Easton's attention. I could probably get addicted to it.

I'd better make sure that I don't.

10

Quinn

I decide to clear my afternoon for this excursion. We're heading into Los Angeles to the main offices of Hayworth Productions. Which means a nice long drive through stop-and-go traffic, just Rex and me.

Good thing I'm now immune to his many charms.

"I've got three people on my list of potential IDs for the secret witness," I say. "Suspect number one, Thompson Hayworth's son. Christian. He took over as head of Hayworth Productions about two years ago. While Thompson directed Oscar-worthy pictures, Christian managed the business side of things. He's the wheeler and dealer."

When we pause to wait in traffic, I show Rex a candid shot of Christian. He looks more like a Wall Street trader than a filmmaker. He's in a slick tailored suit, his hair just slightly too long. No smile.

"He's actually the one who introduced Amber to Thompson at that charity event. But Christian didn't appreciate Amber getting her hooks into Thompson and using him to advance her acting career."

Rex's eyes return to the road as we move forward, slowly

making progress on the freeway. "What about the age gap between Thompson and Amber? I assume his son didn't like that much either."

Rex's eyes slide sideways, and mine do the same, our gazes meeting.

I shrug. "It's Hollywood. Hardly the first director to marry a younger actress. Besides, age isn't the defining feature of a person. Right? Personality is more important. Compatibility, likes and dislikes, sense of humor..." I trail off, aware that this topic is a little close to home for me.

Rex doesn't seem that comfortable with it either, even though he's the one who brought it up. He changes the subject.

"You said you have three people on your list. Who are the other two?"

"There's Thompson's assistant. She had a hand in pretty much all of Thompson's day-to-day affairs. She wasn't at his house on the day of the murder, but maybe she discovered some evidence against Amber somewhere else, and is afraid to speak up. My last possibility is Thompson's chauffeur. He drove Amber to the spa on the day of the murder. Camera footage on Ocean Lane confirms he didn't go anywhere else except a lunch spot a block away. But given his level of access to Amber and Thompson, the driver had to see plenty, and I doubt he's told us half of it."

"Both the driver and assistant might keep their mouths shut because they're afraid no other big Hollywood types will hire them if they aren't discreet."

"That's what I thought too."

Rex taps his thumb against the steering wheel. "I see the reasoning behind each of the three possibilities. Nice work. All three were close to the victim. All three should want his murderer punished. But for some significant reason, this witness is holding back. You would think the murder of their father or boss would be enough to get them to talk."

"Exactly why this person is coming forward now. They want to see justice done. At least, we can hope so." Then I shake my head. "That probably sounds naive of me."

He smiles fondly. "Nothing wrong with thinking the best of people, so long as you temper it with some healthy suspicion. Don't forget, we still don't know this person's true motives."

I haven't forgotten that fact for one moment. Yet I still have to pursue this, given the chance of finding the evidence we need. I appreciate that Rex sees that too.

Finally, we make it into Century City. We follow Avenue of the Stars to a sleek office building of steel and glass. Rex parks in a garage, both of us appalled at the rates they're charging per hour, but that's LA.

Up on the top floor, we walk into a lobby with a view of West LA, stretching all the way to the Pacific Ocean. "Have you been here before?" Rex asks quietly. Our footsteps echo against the shiny granite floor.

"Nope. Christian came to West Oaks for his initial interviews. Since then, Lana and I have spoken to him over the phone. But I figure surprise is the best tactic for this. If we catch the witness off guard, maybe he or she will give something away."

A receptionist looks up as we approach. She smiles politely, but her expression is carefully guarded. I might not be the security expert, but even I can spot the numerous cameras and locked barriers between the public and the inner domain of Hayworth Productions.

"I'm here to see Christian Hayworth," I say.

"Do you have an appointment?"

"Nope. But it's about his father's murder and the upcoming trial of Amber Printz."

Her placid expression betrays a few cracks. "Ah. One moment." The receptionist picks up a phone and speaks into it.

Rex and I step back from the desk. "Why not ask for the assistant first?" he murmurs.

I smirk. "A hunch. I think Christian will be a little more... receptive to seeing me."

"You mean, he's got a thing for you?" Rex's frown is so deep it might be visible from space.

"He may have flirted. A little."

Rex edges closer to me. "What else?"

"And he asked me to have a drink with him after his interview."

"Did you say yes?"

"That would hardly have been appropriate."

"But did you *want* to say yes?"

I have no idea why Rex cares so much, unless he thinks this is relevant to my security. From the way he's angling his body and glancing around, all gruff and menacing, you would think I'm in imminent danger.

But I don't get the chance to answer him. Because Christian Hayworth appears, emerging from a hidden door at one end of the lobby.

"Miss Ainsley," Christian says. "Always a pleasure. But you should have let me know you were coming." His eyes flick to Rex, though he doesn't ask for an introduction. "I don't have much time, but you can walk with me to grab a coffee."

"That works," I'm quick to say. "This is Rex Easton. From Bennett Security."

Christian nods in the barest acknowledgment. "You need a bodyguard because of that bullshit with Amber's rabid fans? Bunch of psychopaths. You're right. We do need to talk. I've got fifteen minutes." He barrels straight for the elevator.

Okay then.

I have to hurry to catch up. Rex follows a couple of steps behind, and I can almost feel the annoyance rolling off of him in waves. I cast an apologetic glance over my shoulder. But he's wearing a professionally distant expression, all muscly and intimidating in his suit. Playing the silent bodyguard role to a T.

I shouldn't enjoy that as much as I do.

Christian leads us into a private elevator that seems to be reserved for him. He pushes back his French cuff to check his watch. "What's happening with the trial preparations?" he barks. Like I work for him. I don't. As a deputy district attorney, I represent the People as a whole, not the victim or victim's family.

But from what I've seen, this is what Christian Hayworth is like all the time. He has a tendency to bark orders like he's used to them being followed. DA Marchetti was not a fan of that. But then Christian can do a one-eighty and turn on the charm. He's a good-looking man in his early fifties, fit and well-dressed, and he doesn't want anyone to forget it.

He's a lot.

But what he *doesn't* seem like is a man who's torn up over the death of his father. West Oaks PD thought that was suspicious until they confirmed that Christian was in London at some film festival when Thompson was murdered. Christian flew home immediately after he got word.

Does that mean he's hiding something? Does Christian have more evidence against Amber, but he's holding it back because it's sensitive, or because he could be implicated somehow? It's hard to imagine Christian Hayworth being afraid of anything or anyone, but I guess it's possible.

Unfortunately, I can't come right out and ask him if he's my secret witness. I can't risk giving away the source's existence.

"Preparations are moving forward," I say, keeping it as vague as possible. "But I had some additional questions for you."

I go over a few things about Amber and her relationship with his father. This is ground we've covered before, but I pay close attention to his answers, trying to assess if there might be anything extra that he's hinting at. Any clue that he's holding back evidence. Yet he gives little away.

We reach the coffee kiosk on the first floor of the building, and the barista hands Christian an iced latte as soon as he walks up. I'm guessing it's his daily order. I order two drip coffees, handing one to Rex, who gives me a wink and a small smile. Ignoring those stupid flutters in my belly, I turn back to Christian.

"Have you ever suspected that Amber had an accomplice?"

His eyebrows shoot toward the ceiling. "An accomplice? Have you discovered evidence of that?"

"Not specifically." I haven't seen anything to suggest that Amber had an accomplice. Everything the detectives found points to Amber as the sole assailant. She snuck into the home she shared with Thompson, hit him over the head with that marble sculpture, and tossed around their belongings to make it look like a burglar had done it.

But I'm pushing some buttons, hoping that I hit the right one that'll open Christian up.

"I'm just trying to anticipate anything that we might have missed. That's why we're going back over all the evidence." I take a sip of coffee. "If anyone did help Amber in some way, or knows more information that they're afraid to share, the DA would consider an immunity deal."

Christian laughs, but his eyes are shrewd. "Now you're worrying me. Do you think your case is weak? Because I've offered District Attorney Marchetti the services of my lawyers."

"Not at all. Just being thorough."

"Thoroughness is an admirable quality." His smile turns as dazzling as a toothpaste commercial. "Why don't we set up a dinner? I'd be happy to devote an evening to you to discuss the trial. For the sake of thoroughness."

"Do lines like that usually work for you, Mr. Hayworth?"

"Usually, yes."

"Please take a step back from Miss Ainsley," comes a deep voice behind me, laced with warning. I can't see Rex, yet I just know he's looming over my shoulder.

Christian chuckles like we're sharing an inside joke. "Your bodyguard is getting testy. He's acting like you're the heir to the throne or something."

"Just don't call me princess," I quip.

"I've probably got a joke somewhere about what else I could call you, but I have the feeling your bodyguard wouldn't see the humor." Christian smirks at Rex, but he also puts a few feet of distance back between us. "I'm willing to help the prosecution however I can. That's all I meant."

"Which is appreciated. We don't want surprises at trial. If anyone did hold back evidence, and the DA found out, I have no doubt she would prosecute."

"Understandable. What I want is that gold digger Amber Printz nailed to the wall." He says that like being a gold digger is her worst crime. Not murder. "Let me know if you need anything else."

"Is Thompson's former assistant in the office? Kendall Simms? I had a few items I needed to review with her as well."

There's a flicker of something like concern in his face before he covers it up. He tosses the rest of his iced latte into the trash. "I'm afraid our fifteen minutes are up, Miss Ainsley. Hope we can do it again. But call first next time, will you?" He lowers his voice. "And feel free to leave the bodyguard in West Oaks."

With one last smirk, Christian nearly sprints to the elevator.

One moment, he was cozying up to me. The next, he was gone. What does it add up to?

Rex steps up beside me, sipping his coffee. "What do you think?" he asks.

"The man's hiding something. But I still have no idea if he's the secret witness." I tap my chin. "Maybe I should've had dinner with him like he asked. He might've wanted to let me in on his secrets, but you scared him off."

"Not happening, princess."

I know he's joking. But something in his tone reminds me of that long-ago prom night. When Rex stepped in as my protector because I had no one else. But he didn't see me as an equal. Why would he see me as one now?

To Rex, I'll always be untouchable. Exactly why I'm supposed to be over this crush.

Yet those flutters inside me have turned to a profound ache.

"You all right?" Rex asks softly.

"Excuse me," a young woman interrupts. And I'm grateful for it. I blink away the sting in my eyes and focus on her.

It's the receptionist from Hayworth Productions.

"You're the lawyer from West Oaks, right?"

"Yes."

She tilts her head, pulling us to a shadowed part of the lobby, sheltered from the view of the elevator bank. "I overheard you ask about Kendall," she whispers. "Thompson's personal assistant. You're looking for her?"

"I am. I wanted to speak to her about the Printz trial coming up. I hoped to catch her at work today."

She shakes her head. "No chance of that. Because Christian fired her. It's so shitty. She worked for Thompson for years, and then his son just kicked her to the curb. Don't tell anyone I said that. But it's true."

I share a glance with Rex. "Do you know why Christian fired her?" Rex asks.

"She finally had enough of his crap and told him so. Braver than the rest of us. But now she's unemployed. Probably won't work in the industry again." The receptionist hands me a Hayworth Productions business card with a number scrawled on the back. "That's Kendall's new cell. Trust me, she's got plenty of time to talk to you. Maybe she can help you with whatever you're looking for."

I SLIDE INTO THE BOOTH ACROSS FROM KENDALL Simms. "Thanks for meeting me on such short notice."

"Not like I have anything better to do. I already sent out my daily batch of resumes, and I doubt I'll hear anything back."

We're in a cozy, old-school diner near the 405 freeway. When I called Kendall's number, she was eager to meet. Rex is sitting in another booth, keeping watch. We both agreed that Kendall might feel more comfortable talking to just me. Rex can be intimidating. And after the meeting with Christian Hayworth, Rex's protectiveness seems to be turned up to max.

Get your mind off the man, I tell myself. I focus on the young woman in front of me. She's in jeans and a stained tee, a stark contrast to the business wear and designer fashion on display around Century City. Kendall is an unassuming woman. Light brown hair, a pretty face, and a mousy demeanor. From the redness in her eyes, I'd guess she hasn't been sleeping.

We order cups of iced tea and slices of pie.

"I was so sorry to hear how you left Hayworth Productions."

"It's okay. You can say I was fired. Or maybe shit-canned is more accurate, given the scene in Christian's office." She grimaces. "Not my finest moment."

"You worked for Thompson a long time, right?" I ask.

"Since I graduated film school. Twelve years." She sighs. "He was like a father to me. Officially I was his assistant, but I was more like his apprentice. He was always so kind to me. Which is rare in this town. Truly a gem."

I remember she said similar things when we interviewed her before. But I understand she needs to share again. For some witnesses, the prosecutor becomes their confidante about the deceased. Someone they can show their true emotions to when they otherwise keep those feelings bottled up inside.

"I'm sorry," I say again, resting my hand over hers.

"Thanks. I don't mean to dump my problems on you. You've got enough to deal with, considering Amber's trial is coming up. And her ridiculous social media campaigning. The way her followers are painting your office as the bad guys."

"You heard about that?"

"Hasn't everyone? If there's anything I can do to ensure she's convicted, anything whatsoever, I'll do it. What did you need to talk about?"

I study her, wondering if Kendall could be my secret witness. But it's hard to imagine her holding back evidence against Amber. Especially now. In fact, if she volunteered new, uncorroborated evidence, the defense would tear her apart on cross-examination. They'd claim she had enough bias against Amber to make things up.

I shouldn't be too quick to cross her off my list. But I'm leaning that way.

"Do you mind me asking what happened with Christian Hayworth first?" I ask.

Our food arrives, and she digs her fork into the layers of pie crust and apples. "I got fed up with the way he's so callous about Thompson's memory. They've scrapped a lot of the projects he was working on. They're taking Hayworth Productions in a totally different direction, and I had an issue with that."

"But Christian has been in charge for a while."

"Sure, because Thompson turned over the reins to his son so he could focus on directing." She frowns. "And on Amber, of course. She demanded as much of his attention as possible. Thompson was an auteur, but he wasn't that great with the business side. People could take advantage. He decided to turn over his production company to his son in lieu of any other inheritance. Amber was named sole beneficiary in his will instead. And you know how that turned out. The fact that his wife murdered him is bad enough. But to watch his son tear apart his legacy, too? It was too much for me. I had to speak up. Big mistake. So, here I am. Blacklisted. I can't get a job as an extra, much less a position working for another director." She takes a slow bite of pie. "And I'm not the only person who was close to his father that Christian has gotten rid of. Like Pete Diamond."

I perk up. Pete Diamond was Thompson and Amber's driver. Number three on my list of possibilities for the witness's identity. "What do you mean?"

"Christian sent Pete off to some remote filming location in Nevada to shuttle around the C-list cast. I felt bad for Pete at first. But now I'm kinda jealous. At least he still has a job."

I chew my lip. Pete is supposed to testify at Amber's trial. Yet he said nothing to our office about leaving town.

It's interesting that Christian didn't fire Pete, as he did to Kendall. Not only that, Christian sent Pete away from Southern California, despite the impending trial. And failed to mention it to me today, despite claiming he wanted to do everything possible to help the prosecution.

I have no idea what to make of it. But I have all the more reason to chat with Pete Diamond.

11

Quinn

"Any other stops while we're here in LA?" Rex asks as I leave the diner.

"No. It'll be rush hour soon, and I want to get back to West Oaks so I can write up the interviews today. Plus think about what Christian and Kendall said." We spent hours on this trip today, and I'm not much closer to answers. Just endlessly multiplying questions.

When we get back to his truck, I fill in Rex on everything Kendall shared with me as he steers us toward the freeway.

"Do you think either of them could be the anonymous witness who contacted you?" he asks.

"They both say they believe Amber is guilty and want to help the prosecution. If they have evidence, why not just hand it over to me? Clearly, they've got their own agendas and motives at play. Wish I could see the full picture. But my hunch is that neither one is my source."

"That leaves you with the chauffeur. Diamond."

"There's still the possibility that my so-called source was lying. That there's no hidden evidence at all, and Amber Printz or her rabid fans are trying to mess with me."

"But I have no doubt you'll get to the bottom of it," Rex says.

"Thanks for the vote of confidence."

"Why don't we use this time to call Sylvie and update her. She can start researching Pete Diamond. Find out exactly where he is and what he's up to."

"Great idea." I take out my phone. "I've got her cell number."

Rex shakes his head. "No, use my phone. She has more than one number, and I've got the super-priority one saved in my contacts."

"Ah, because she loves you. Thanks for getting me on the inside track."

Rex points to his phone, which is sitting in the center console. He recites his passcode.

"You sure you trust me with all this sensitive info? First Sylvie's top-secret cell number, and now your passcode?"

"You're hardly a stranger."

We're family, I remind myself. Ugh. It's even worse than being friend zoned.

I unlock Rex's phone. The screen opens on some sort of texting app. There's a conversation visible. And I don't mean to look, I swear. But the words just jump out and into my brain.

Then I promptly choke on my tongue.

Some woman named Denise texted him. *I hope this isn't too forward, but I'd love to meet you in person. Are you free tomorrow night? I keep staring at your photos, and I can't wait to see if you've got that six-pack in person. We can meet up at my place.*

I throw the phone into the cupholder like it's a poisonous snake. "Oh my God. I'm...um..."

Rex's head turns sharply toward me, then back to the road. Then to me again. "What is it? What happened?"

"I didn't mean to read it. I'm so sorry. "

Keeping his eyes on the road, Rex grabs the phone. He glances at it long enough to check the screen. Then he drops it again, his expression almost as mortified as the one that must be on my face.

"I didn't realize I'd left the app open."

"It's okay." It is nowhere near okay, but I'm not going to say that. "It's none of my business anyway. If you're planning a hookup or whatever. Totally cool."

Crap, why can't I stop talking?

Rex is coughing, which started around the time I mentioned the word hookup. "It's nothing. Just a stupid app I downloaded. I was thinking about how it's been eleven years almost since Lydia died, and I've barely dated at all. Seemed like maybe it was time."

Chills cascade across my skin like the beginnings of a fever. Nausea crawls up my throat. "That's great. You should."

He frowns at the windshield. "I don't know. The app was a bad idea. I've barely even looked at it."

"But you were texting with her," I pointed out. "She wants to meet up."

"I have no intention of meeting her."

"Why not?"

"Because I'm…not so sure I'm interested."

"Oh. Fair enough. I'm sure there are tons of women on the app. So many to choose from. You might get a better offer." I force my mouth shut so I'll stop spewing verbal garbage. Also so I won't throw up from the thought of Rex going to that woman's house and showing her his six-pack.

He has a six-pack?

"What about you? Are you…seeing anyone?" Rex asks, shifting the subject away from him. Though the odd tone in his voice suggests he doesn't really want to know.

"Not me. I am perpetually single. But maybe I'll download an app, too. See what kind of options are out there."

He makes a low grumbling sound, his knuckles going white as he chokes the steering wheel.

The cabin of his truck goes quiet after that. Neither one of us mentions calling Sylvie. I slump in my seat, praying that now is the moment that my superpowers of invisibility kick in.

I knew this day would come eventually. It took him a long time to be ready to date after losing the love of his life. But it had to happen. A man like Rex has no business being alone in life.

Yet that rational knowledge doesn't dull the sharp ache in my chest.

I just want it to stop. For this painful longing to *go away*. I'm so frustrated with myself, so fed up with my ridiculous heart, that I want to scream.

But I have to sit there in silence, pretending I'm not about to crack down the middle.

The miles inch by until we're finally back in West Oaks, and he's pulling into the parking lot of the district attorney building. We head inside. The halls are busy with people leaving for the day. I'm often one of the last ones to leave, and today will be no exception.

We reach my office, but instead of saying goodbye, Rex follows me inside the small room.

"Quinn," he says. "I think I should explain. What you saw on my phone..."

"No need. What's there to explain?"

He's looking at me with that intense expression again. The one I just can't figure out. And I've finally, *finally*, had enough. There's only one way I'll ever be able to let go of this obsession and move on. I have to yank out this knife, no matter how much it hurts, so I can start to heal.

I need to break my heart the rest of the way.

"You know, you really should get together with Denise. In fact, we could make it a group thing. Invite Cliff and Leah."

His mouth presses into a thin, flat line. "I don't think so."

"Oh come on, it'll be *great*," I say, unable to keep a hint of sarcasm from darkening my words. "I'll bring a date too."

Rex's glower is getting more stormy by the second. "I'd rather you didn't."

"Why? I'm not eighteen anymore. I'm a grown woman who dates men. In case you didn't notice."

"I—"

"What about that bodyguard guy you work with? Leon? Do you know if he's taken?"

"*Quinn*."

"No, you're right, not Leon. He's kind of young." I barely even know what I'm saying at this point. My brain is going off the rails. "I've never told you this before, but I like older men. Silver foxes are *definitely* my jam. It's been way too long since I had a night out." I pull my phone from my pocket. "What's the name of that app you're using? I'm going to download it right now. Unless you can set me up with a friend of yours. A sexy divorced single dad who's looking for a good time? I'm down for it. If you get my meaning. DTF."

He plucks my phone from my fingers and throws it. The device goes sailing across my office, landing on the carpet. I stare after it with my mouth open.

Then I look back at him. And my eyes meet two pools of pure dark fire. Rex advances until I'm crowded up against my desk. The sheer masculine energy he's giving off stops my crazy train in its tracks.

"I don't want to hear about you with other men."

"*Other* men?" I repeat, just because his words won't compute in my head.

Rex grits his teeth as a wicked, low sound rumbles out of

him. He lifts his hand and presses his thumb against my lips to stop me from talking.

What is happening right now?

"*Quinn,*" he says again, and I have never heard my name drenched in so much emotion. Like he's speaking volumes, dredged up from his very soul, with that one word. His thumb moves to caress my cheekbone. The gesture is so tender. It must short-circuit something in my brain.

Because the next thing I know, I'm stretching onto my toes and pressing my lips to his.

Just a quick brush. But it's enough to shake me all the way down to my toes.

Rex tilts back and looks down at me. "Did you just kiss me?"

I don't know where this sudden, wild bravery is coming from, but I say, "Yeah. Are you going to kiss me back?"

"Fuck, yes."

His hand goes to the back of my neck, holding me there, and his mouth seems to melt against mine. Our lips fit perfectly together. The scruff on his chin gently scratches me, and I grab for the lapels of his suit jacket. The kiss is sweet and slow, the heat between us gradually building.

Then Rex's tongue brushes my lips. I gasp, mouth opening, and the tip of his tongue slips inside.

His tongue is in my mouth. How is this happening?

I don't care. I don't want to do anything to break this moment. I never want this to stop.

My tongue gets in on the action, stroking against his. Rex groans, his hands traveling down my back to my hips. He spins us both so he's sitting against my desk, bringing him lower and his mouth even with mine. No more strain on my neck. I stand between his spread knees and wiggle closer to him. Basking in his heat. The scent of his cologne. He deepens the kiss and sucks my tongue into his mouth.

Rex, Rex, Rex, my heart beats. I feel like a flower that's been closed up tight. And now, I'm blooming beneath the warmth of his touch. Like he's my personal sun.

"Please," I hear myself murmur. I can't even string two words together.

"What can I do for you?" he asks, voice scratchy, like he's as blissed-out as I am. His mouth trails to my neck. Sucking gently. Nipping at my skin.

"Anything. Just want you. Please."

He lifts his head and looks at me. Eyes of dark, smoldering fire. Burning me up from the inside out.

Rex stands suddenly. Reaches behind to sweep a neat stack of paper off my desk, right onto the floor. Papers scatter everywhere.

It's kind of unhinged, and I love it.

He picks me up and turns to set me on the desk surface. Lays me back. Then he's tearing at his tie. His jacket. Both wind up on the floor with my paperwork. He leans over me, and I reach for the buttons on his shirt. Is it necessary for bodyguards to wear so many layers of clothing?

He seems to have the same thought, because he gives up and bends over the desk to kiss me again. Like he can't wait a moment longer. We make out shamelessly, hands roving. My fingers find his belt buckle and try to work it open, which is made far more difficult because our chests and stomachs are pressed together as he pins me to the desk.

And then with a growl he brings his hips against mine. A slight shift, but suddenly I feel him. Long and stiff against my thigh.

"Oh, shit," I whisper.

"You like that?" He rocks his hips into me again. I gasp.

Rex Easton's cock is hard for me, I realize. What world am I living in?

The sound of a door slamming breaks me from my trance.

My gaze flies to the door of my office, which I realize is wide open. There are footsteps heading down the hallway. The quiet whistle of one of my coworkers leaving for the day.

And Rex has me splayed out on my desk, his shirt-half unbuttoned and my lips swollen from his kisses.

Hell.

He moves quicker than I do. He jumps upright and closes my office door. Then braces his hands against the wood, head bowing between his shoulders. His back moves up and down as he catches his breath. Same as me.

My mind is swimming. I'm lightheaded. I'm in shock at what just happened.

But it was *amazing*.

"I am so sorry." Rex hasn't moved. He's still facing the door.

"Sorry? Why?"

"I should not have done that. I lost control. It was..."

Perfect? Incredible? Volcano hot? I'd happily grab my thesaurus for all the ways to describe how great that was. But the realization is quickly sinking in that Rex doesn't share my elation.

"It was wrong," he finishes. "I need to go."

He's buttoning up his shirt in a hurry. Fixing his belt. He won't look at me. "The guys on the night shift are outside. Call the main Bennett Security line when you're ready to leave." He grabs his jacket from the floor, horror on his face when he surveys the mess of papers.

"But..."

"I am so sorry, Quinn."

He rushes to the door. While I sit on my desk and stare after him, not saying a damn thing.

Five minutes later, I'm still staring at my dark laptop screen, wondering what the heck just happened.

My stomach is twisting into knots. I can't decide whether to cry or throw up.

I jump to standing, grab my phone, and call Lark. She's the only person in the world who knows how I feel about Rex. The only person I can talk to about this.

Well. Now Rex knows my secret too. Right?

Nausea rears into my throat as Lark answers. "Hey, just the lady I was thinking of," she says. "I was about to call you. Danny is on-shift and I could really use an ice cream fix to soothe my sorrows. You in?"

"I kissed Rex."

A pause. "Oh. Wow. Okay. And—"

I pace across my office, ignoring the fallen papers. "He kissed me back."

"That's great! But why do you sound like that's the worst thing ever?"

"Because things got heated, we got carried away, and then he freaked out! He regrets it. He couldn't even look at me afterward." I squeeze my eyes closed. "What did I do?" I moan. "I think he hates me."

"There's no way he hates you."

"Then he hates himself for kissing me back. Maybe that's worse."

Either way, I screwed up.

For those few wonderful minutes that we were kissing, it felt like all my dreams were coming true. It didn't make sense that Rex suddenly wanted me back, but it didn't matter. I was flying.

And now, I've crashed and burned. I'm a heap of wreckage, my hopes and dreams hollowed out. And it hurts. It's a black hole of hurting, big enough to suck the rest of me down inside it. I'm eighteen again, the sad girl on prom night, but times a thousand.

Rex isn't going to swoop in and comfort me this time. I'd be shocked if he ever wants to see me again. Unless he wants to act like it didn't happen. I don't think I can do that.

"Lark," I whisper. "Please say something. I'm spiraling."

"I'm coming over there. Are you home? Or at your office?"

"My office, but don't come yet. I need to calm down first."

"Then tell me exactly what happened. Start at the beginning."

So I do. I put on my lawyer hat and tell the story, as if it's my opening statement and I'm reciting the facts for the jury. The strange looks Rex has been giving me for the last two weeks, and the way he acted today. Like he was jealous of the thought of me with anyone else.

I don't want to hear about you with other men.

"He actually said that?" Lark breathes. "That is romantic. And hot. Seriously, I'm fanning myself over here."

"Not really helping, babe. I made a fool of myself. I told him I'm into older men! Basically confessing my crush on him. And then I kissed him and practically ordered him to kiss me back."

"You hardly forced him. If Rex kissed you, it's because he wanted to. And you said it got heated?"

"Very. He had me on my back on my desk. I felt his erection."

"Nice."

"No! It's not nice, because we heard someone coming down the hall, and it was like a switch flipped. He'd been caught up in the moment. But as soon as he stopped and thought about it, about the fact that it was *me*, he was horrified. Then he started apologizing. He said it was *wrong*. And then he left. He couldn't escape fast enough." I slide down to the floor, wrapping my arms around my knees. "I kissed Cliff's dad. It was the best kiss of my entire life, and he wishes it never happened. I am such a fool."

Lark sighs. "I'm going to swing by the store, buy out their supply of Ben & Jerry's, and then I'm coming to pick you up. You can stay at my place and watch terrible comedies with me all night. And I promise, Quinn. It's going to be okay. You are going to be okay."

A tear slips down my cheek. "I don't feel like it."

"I know how that is, trust me. But you're strong. You can make it through anything. Stay there. I'll be at your office in half an hour."

"Okay." We end the call. I'm so thankful for Lark. She didn't tell me I was being overdramatic or that what I felt was wrong. She knows I need to wallow. I know it's not like ending a relationship, because Rex and I were never together. I never even thought I had a chance with him.

Maybe that's what is killing me about this. For those few minutes, I *did* have him. Today, I finally got a glimpse of what it was like for Rex to return my feelings. And it was better than I'd ever imagined. A dream come to life.

I knew I needed to break my heart in order to finally get over Rex. I guess that's what happened. Just didn't realize it would hurt this freaking much.

I've been sitting here for a while. "You're going to be okay," I murmur to myself. Repeating what Lark told me. She threw me a lifeline, and I need to grasp onto it. "Clean up first. Then get ready to go."

I stand up, brushing myself off. I go to bend over and scoop up my scattered papers.

Then I freeze.

There was just an odd sound right outside my office door. Could it be Lark? No, that wouldn't make sense. It's only been ten minutes or so since we ended the call. And she couldn't get inside my building without a key card.

I hear it again. It's the strangest noise, and I can't place it. The rest of the office has cleared out by now. And if there were any other stragglers, they'd just walk past my closed door. Whoever's out there is lingering.

Could it be the cleaning crew? But Jeff, the janitor, never makes it to my office before nine. I've been here late enough plenty of times to get to know him.

Tonight, of all nights, I don't have the patience for this mystery. I get up, walk to the door, and yank it open. "Can I help you with..." I start to say, but the words die on my tongue.

There's a person right outside wearing a Halloween-style mask, which is alarming in itself. But a glance at the outside of my door reveals streaks of bright red paint. *Lying Slut*, it says in messy letters.

This asshole was just spraying that on my office door. And he's holding up his phone, aiming it at me.

I think he's filming this.

Maybe I should be scared, but instead I'm furious. "Are you *kidding me*? Do you have any idea what a shitty night I'm having?"

The guy drops his can of spray paint, palms his phone, and runs. But no. I'm not letting him get away with this. Enough with anonymous stalkers coming after me, sending me notes, dangling promises. I want to see this guy's face and demand some answers.

"Stop!" I dash after him. Reaching out, I snag his black hoodie and yank him back. He stumbles. I grab at his mask, trying to pull it off. He grunts and pushes me. We struggle for a moment. The mask inches up. His face is exposed, but I don't recognize him. He's another random creeper.

"Amber was framed!" he yells at me.

"The hallway cameras already recorded your face, dumbass," I yell back. I go for my phone in my pants pocket. "You're the one who's going to jail."

For a split second, I'm distracted by unlocking my phone. I don't see it coming when he charges and slams me hard into the wall.

And then, I don't see anything at all.

12

Rex

Hell is knowing exactly what you want, what you crave, what you *need,* while also knowing for certain you can never have it.

But even worse? Taking something that's not yours. That can never be yours.

What have I done?

I slump in the driver's seat of my truck, wiping my hands down my face. It doesn't matter that Quinn kissed me first. I'm supposed to be protecting her. She's not just a client, she's my son's friend. And I just shoved my tongue in her mouth and rubbed my crotch on her.

Max Bennett would probably give me a pass, even though a bodyguard shouldn't fraternize with a protectee. But I never should've given in to temptation.

If Cliff finds out about this, I don't think he'll ever forgive me.

For the last two weeks, since that soul-scorching sex dream I had about her, I've been trying to stop lusting after Quinn. And failing. It's like I unlocked some hidden door in my brain, and now that it's open, there's no stopping me. I want her.

That's why I finally messaged that woman Denise on the dating app. I'd ignored a couple of *Hey, how's it going?* prompts from her. But then I figured, why not give it a try? Denise is thirty-eight, divorced, a mom of two. Attractive and successful in her career. A perfectly nice woman. An appropriate choice.

But after chatting with her a bit, I just wasn't interested. I let our conversations naturally trail off. Then she messaged me again today. While Quinn was chatting with Kendall at the diner, I responded politely to Denise with a last-ditch hope that I'd feel some spark of interest.

But there was still nothing.

The only woman occupying my thoughts is the one who should absolutely be off-limits. And seeing Christian Hayworth flirt with her today made the craving even worse.

That was why the app was open on my phone. Of course, I hadn't realized it. I never would've wanted Quinn to see my texts with Denise, much less that last one about meeting at her place.

I'm not going to meet up with Denise. *Especially not now.* After I practically molested the woman I'm supposed to protect with my life.

Okay, very bad choice of words. Quinn is a grown woman. She clearly reciprocated my interest. She said she's into older men, which makes me wonder if she had ever looked at me that way before, with even a fraction of the desire I feel for her.

She seemed to enjoy kissing me. Said she wanted me.

Ngh. My cock twitches as I replay those moments. I shift in my seat. Her lips were so sweet beneath mine. Her body all soft curves I'm still desperate to explore. I still crave her. If anything, I want her more. If I could, I'd pull her into my arms and kiss her again and again and again. I would make her feel good. Show her that she's the only woman in the world that I want.

But I *can't*.

What would my son say? About me, almost fifty, going after his best friend. A woman over twenty years my junior who's supposed to be in my care. Who Cliff *asked me* to look out for. It's possible he wouldn't mind. But am I willing to take that risk when Cliff and I have a rocky relationship to begin with?

And what if it doesn't work out? What if I break Quinn's heart, or she breaks mine? What if she feels like I've taken advantage of her? She might already be feeling just that.

God, why couldn't I stop myself from fucking everything up?

I've never lost control like that. I'm careful. Steady and reliable. I pride myself on it. When something goes haywire, I'm an expert at taking charge and righting the course. That's how I operated when I was a Green Beret, and I carried that professionalism into my career with Bennett Security. I do the same with Team Triumph when we respond to disaster areas.

I'm supposed to know how to pick up the pieces. But right now, I'm the guy who's caused a mess he can't find his way out of.

"Get yourself together," I growl. "Man the fuck up."

I have to fix this.

Starting with Quinn. I'll have a frank conversation with her, apologize again, and offer to let another Bennett Security bodyguard take over her detail. Not what I want to do. But what other solution is there? I can't be trusted around her.

I decide to grab some dinner for her as a peace offering. Besides, that woman has a bad habit of forgetting to eat. On my way out of the parking lot, I stop to chat with the guys on duty watching the building exit. They haven't seen anything odd all day. I let them know I'll be back in a few, then swing by a burger place I know Quinn likes. I throw in some of the sweet potato fries she loves because I'm not above groveling.

Back at the DA building, I park and use my temporary key card to swipe my way inside. The halls are eerily quiet, unlike Bennett Security, which always has something going on at all hours. Quinn seems to work harder than all her colleagues. Except maybe Lana, but even she's had to slow down with her pregnancy.

Does Quinn want kids?

That thought pops into my head out of nowhere. It just emphasizes the difference between us. I've got an adult son who's almost thirty. I've got more gray in my chest hair than black. But Quinn is just getting started. She should be with a man who can give her all the years she deserves.

And that's not me. I know that. But I can't help the sinking disappointment in my stomach.

"Shake it off," I say. "Worry about Quinn, not your own damn self."

There's a shout somewhere up ahead. Almost like a reply to my statement, but of course it's not.

Something's wrong.

I drop the bag of takeout burgers and sprint forward. When I turn the corner, I see a guy in a Halloween mask shove Quinn into a wall. She crumples to the ground.

No.

Shouting, I race to her. Her attacker is already running in the opposite direction, and I want to tackle that fucker and make him pay. But I have to see to Quinn. So I pull out my phone and radio to my men outside, reporting that our protectee is down.

"Attacker in a mask and hoodie fleeing to the south side of the building."

"*Roger*. We're on it."

"Get medical here. That's the priority." I lower the radio. They'll have an ambulance responding within minutes, but I kneel to check her over myself. My heart is beating like a fist against my ribs.

"Quinn," I say. "Can you hear me?" There's a lump forming on her head. She's not responsive.

My hands are fucking *shaking* like my first mission as a nineteen-year-old PFC. My memory flashes to the day that I found Lydia collapsed on the floor of our bedroom. She'd had a stroke. There hadn't even been time to call an ambulance for her.

My wife was gone within minutes.

I shouldn't be thinking about that. But I look at Quinn unconscious on the floor, and panic spreads like poison through my veins. This woman who cared for me and Cliff after Lydia died. Who's been my son's best friend. *My* friend. And...someone I wish could be more.

I can't sort out my feelings for her. Not right now.

I just know I can't lose her too.

~

THE FIRST EMTS TO ARRIVE ARE FROM WEST OAKS Fire. Danny Bradley rushes down the hallway with his medical bag and kneels over Quinn, nudging me out of the way. "We'll take it from here, Rex."

I don't want to leave her side. But I have to. A large hand rests on my shoulder as I watch Danny and another EMT working on Quinn. It's Matteo De Luca, another firefighter and someone I consider a good friend. I protected his now-wife, Detective Angela De Luca, when she was being targeted a year or two back.

"Heard on the radio West Oaks PD are on their way," Matteo says. "What happened?"

He knows what this is like. Watching helplessly when someone you care about is hurt. The look of concern on his face reflects everything that I'm feeling, but it doesn't make me feel one iota better.

"I can't talk now. I need to check in with my guys. We're supposed to be guarding Quinn, but some asshole got into this secure building and hurt her." I don't want to leave Quinn, but I have to do my job. Before I step away, though, I grab Matteo's arm. "Let me know if…if anything…"

He nods. "Go. We'll take care of her."

The next hour is a blur. Several patrol officers arrive. I find my teammates and am relieved to see they caught the piece of trash who attacked Quinn. He's kicking and screaming when I come upon them. The patrol officers take him into custody.

Meanwhile, an ambulance arrives, and the paramedics load Quinn inside. By the time I find that out, the ambulance is already on its way to the hospital. Just as well, because I'd probably insist on riding inside. And I shouldn't. Quinn doesn't need me agonizing over what happened and holding her hand right now. She needs me to be a professional. To find out how that guy got into her building right under our noses and make sure nothing like this happens again.

When I get to the hospital, Cliff and Quinn's friend Lark are already in the waiting room. I'm surprised they got here so soon. Cliff is in uniform, so I assume he heard from his colleagues at West Oaks PD. He might even have been on patrol himself. As for Lark, she's Danny Bradley's girlfriend. Yet I can't imagine that he took a break from EMT duties to call her.

Doesn't matter. What's important is that I've spoken to Devon and Tanner, the co-captains of the bodyguard team. They're calling in reinforcements to respond to the emergency. And to assess what the hell went wrong.

Cliff comes straight over to me. "Dad, I heard about Quinn getting hurt, but nobody knows anything more than that."

A fresh wave of guilt sickens my stomach as I look at my son. "I saw it happen. Some guy attacked her. Knocked her into a wall. She was unconscious last I saw her."

Lark is listening, and her eyes go wide, her hand flying to her mouth.

"But how?" Cliff asks. "How did this guy get close to her? I thought you were in charge of her security. Where were you?"

My throat feels like a fist is tightening around it, but I force the words out. "I left to pick us up some dinner." *Liar. That's not why you first left.* "My guys were supposed to have eyes on the building entrance. We are trying to figure it out."

"But this is about that trial, right?" Lark asks. "Amber Printz and all that ridiculousness."

"That's something else I'm trying to confirm."

Cliff takes out his phone, staring at the screen. Then he looks from Lark to me. "No, it's confirmed. No doubt. Look at what one of our friends just sent me. This was live streamed on Instagram about an hour ago."

He holds up his phone so we can see the video. It shows words being spray-painted in red on a door. *Lying slut.* Exactly what I saw outside Quinn's office. Fury makes me clench my fists, insides boiling with indignation.

And then, to my horror, the door opens and Quinn appears in the video. She yells at the guy. But her eyes are already red when she opens the door, and I know why.

Because of me.

The video cuts off almost immediately after. "It looks like this account is all about Amber Printz," Cliff says, studying his phone again and scrolling. "A fan. Anonymous, but not for long. We caught the guy, right? That's what I was hearing. I just got off duty right before it happened."

I nod. But at this point, I can barely keep myself standing upright. Knowing that this is likely my fault, that I could've protected Quinn if I'd been there beside her, is almost too much for me to take.

And Lark is peering at me like she can somehow sense it. Like she knows.

"I'll check in with Danny," she says softly. "See if he can find out anything more about Quinn's status. He knows a lot of the ED nurses. If Quinn's in surgery or anything like that, maybe he can find out."

I thank her, half in a daze. Quinn could be seriously injured. Head injuries are incredibly dangerous. I had teammates die from them in the Army. A TBI could change Quinn's life forever, alter the course of her career and her future…

She has to be all right. I can't live with anything else.

But I can't just wait around. I need to do absolutely everything I can for Quinn. I'm no doctor, so I can't be in there healing her right now. I have my own skills though. Contacts.

So I take out my phone, and I call Detective Angela De Luca.

~

FINALLY, WE GET AN UPDATE. QUINN IS CONSCIOUS and in stable condition. Since Cliff is apparently her emergency contact, the nurse lets him in first, and he agrees to let me come as well. If he knew what happened between Quinn and me earlier, what I did, he'd probably never let me speak to her again.

We walk inside, Cliff leading the way and me hanging back.

"Q! Never been so glad to see your face." He hugs her, taking a seat right beside her on the mattress. "How you feeling?"

"Not great." She's resting against the pillows, her golden skin too pale. It makes me want to go over there and just... hold her. Wrap her up so she's safe.

But I stand at the end of the bed. I'm not sure if she wants me any closer. She glances at me, and too many things bubble up within me. All that I need to say, but can't in front of my son.

"Did you know I'm your emergency contact?" Cliff asks. "That kinda blew my mind."

She laughs weakly. "Yeah. I didn't have anyone else to put down when I filled out those forms, so I went with you."

Shit. That admission strikes me in the chest. For a bunch of reasons.

"It was process of elimination?" Cliff rolls his eyes. "Just when I thought I was special to you."

She goes quiet.

I stick my hands into my pockets. I'm still wearing most of a suit, though I tossed my jacket in the back seat of my truck earlier. "What have the doctors told you?" I ask.

"They're running tests. They think I have a concussion. My head and my neck are killing me. My memory of the last few hours is pretty fuzzy."

I give her an update on what I've learned so far. That her attacker was a crazed fan of Amber Printz.

"The guy filmed himself tagging your door," Cliff says. "It's on Insta."

She pales even further. "Am I on the video?"

Cliff nods reluctantly. I wish he'd held back this development, because she's already dealing with a lot. I don't want Quinn stressing about how the entire internet could be talking about this. The very idea pisses me off enough to storm down to West Oaks PD and take off her attacker's head.

But Cliff is right. Quinn deserves to know.

"I saw some of it happen," I say. "I was bringing dinner when I heard you shout. I'm sorry I wasn't there in time to stop the guy from injuring you."

Her mouth twitches. I wish I could tell what that means. Whether she's thinking of all the other apologies I've issued today.

"Do you remember anything else about the attack?" I ask.

"I…" Her eyes narrow. "I'm not sure."

"That's all right," I assure her. "The memories will probably come back soon."

Quinn winces. "I hope so. I saw what amnesia was like for Lark, and it didn't seem fun. At least I remember my name." She points a thumb at Cliff. "And I remember this idiot."

"Hey!" he protests. "Do you remember the fact that you owe me fifty bucks?"

"Uh, nice try. You're the one who owes me."

My son grins. "Her long-term memory is working. Dang. Too bad."

Quinn punches his arm weakly.

"We need to get your statement for the police report," Cliff says, turning serious. "I can handle it. But it can wait if you're having trouble recalling the events of the attack. We want you to get better and not add to your stress."

"Detective Angela De Luca is going to handle your case personally," I add.

Cliff's brow creases. "De Luca? Are you sure? She's a senior homicide detective. This is trespassing and battery. Serious, but not her area."

"She's doing me a favor. I called her to put in the request."

Cliff whistles. "Okay. Glad to hear it. We would've had

good people on Quinn's case anyway, but having De Luca is as good as Chief Holt handling it himself."

"Unfortunately, we won't know much of anything until tomorrow," I say. "Detective De Luca won't interrogate the suspect until then. She's also going to work with our team at Bennett Security to find out how the guy got into the DA building. I spoke to Max, and he passed on a message from Lana. She's going to come see you as soon as possible. Is there anything else you need right now?"

Quinn avoids eye contact with me. "No. Thanks, Rex."

A ball of frustration and unease gathers in my throat. And I can't help wondering what else of the evening is fuzzy in her mind. Does she remember the kiss?

If she doesn't remember, do I tell her?

Cliff snaps his fingers. "Wait, Lark said something about bringing you ice cream? Also, she made me promise to get her in here to see you ASAP. I'll go get her from the waiting room." He jumps up, heading for the door. Then he returns and kisses Quinn gently on the cheek. "Really relieved you're okay, Q. We were worried."

He leaves, and Quinn and I are alone. Just the two of us and everything that's going unsaid.

13

Quinn

Cliff leaves, and the guilt on Rex's face speaks volumes. He looks like he'd rather be anywhere but here.

Yeah, me too.

Every part of me hurts, inside and out. I can't take much more today. I close my eyes and settle into the pillow. "You can go if you want."

"I don't want to go. Unless you'd rather I did?"

No, I think immediately. Because even now, I'd rather be near him. "I guess you can stay."

I hear his footsteps as he crosses the room. He picks up my hand like I'm fragile enough to break, cradling it between both of his. "What do you remember after we got back to your office this afternoon?" he asks.

"Not sure," I hedge.

The attack really is fuzzy, like I told them. I wish I could say I don't remember what happened before that in my office. But I do. Every mortifying moment of it, including when Rex apologized profusely for kissing me. For *wanting* me.

Would it be better if I pretend not to remember? Will he

be relieved? We can both go forward from this and try to act like it never happened.

For a while, we watch one another. Maybe to see who will crack first.

"You need to know," he says. "I kissed you in your office."

Of course he decided to tell me. Because he's just that upstanding and honorable. At least, when he's not making out with me against my desk. I'm not sure if his confession makes me feel better or worse.

"Pretty sure I kissed you first."

"So you do remember."

"Yep."

"You know I'm the one who escalated things."

"Maybe we got carried away, but it was nothing I didn't want. You decided it was a mistake."

"In the moment, I thought it was."

In the moment? I repeat in my head. Does that mean he feels differently? I don't want to hope. It hurts too much. But I can't stop myself from asking.

"What about now? Do you regret it?"

"I've been beating myself up over it, that's for sure." Rex sits on the bed beside me. His eyes search mine. He runs his thumb below my lip like he's recalling the same thing I am. How it felt when our mouths were entwined, sharing the same air. "But the truth is that I don't want to regret it. Unless it hurt you."

"It hurt when you took off the way you did."

Anguish flashes in his eyes. "I left because I knew if I stayed, I'd end up kissing you again. I was afraid of what Cliff would think if he found out. And that's never a good sign. I'm not the kind of man who does things in secret, behind closed doors."

"You think we're *wrong* together."

He tips his head back to glare at the ceiling, running his

fingers through his hair. "We're complicated. I'm still worried about how Cliff would react to…us. But Quinn, when I saw you collapse on the ground… It made me think of when Lydia died. *That* is true fear."

"Because you're not over Lydia's death."

"I am, though. It's been eleven years. I've witnessed plenty of traumas since then. It was seeing *you* hurt. The thought of losing you like I lost her." He rubs his eyes. "Dammit, I'm not good at this. Explaining my feelings. I'm out of practice."

"Keep trying," I deadpan. "You're a capable guy. You'll get the hang of it."

A smile sneaks onto his lips.

Then he lifts my hand and presses a kiss to my palm, his gaze locked on mine. And despite how much I'm aching right now, in so many ways, desire flares low in my belly. The hitch in his breath says he feels it too.

"I didn't always see you this way," he says. "Not at all. But I've cared about you for a very long time. And now that I *do* see you, all of you, you're the only woman I want."

"Oh." That's all I can manage. I can barely breathe, much less come up with an adequate response to that.

Voices come from the hallway, getting louder. Rex lets go of my hand and stands up just as the door bursts open. Cliff barrels inside, followed by Lark.

Worst. Timing. Ever.

Lark takes one look at me and scowls. "Sorry, I just have to say this. I really want to punch that Amber Printz bitch in the face."

I have to stop myself from laughing because it hurts to move that much. But between Rex's declaration, Cliff's golden retriever energy, and Lark's fierce attitude, I feel light-years better than I did half an hour ago. I do love my friends.

If I could just go back to that moment with Rex. We were kinda in the middle of something.

Lark comes over and gives me a gentle hug. “I brought ice cream. The nurses let me put it in their break room freezer. How are you doing? With…everything.” She subtly nods her head toward Rex and Cliff, who are chatting by the door. I know what she means, and it’s not just a reference to my injury. I’m sure Cliff already updated her on that.

“I’m better. A lot better. Actually.”

What happened? Lark mouths silently, her expression morphing into a huge grin.

“Be cool,” I mutter. “They’ll hear.”

“But I have to know everything,” she whispers back.

Where to even begin? I can barely process it myself. “We’re still trying to figure it out.”

“Oh crap, did I interrupt the declarations of undying love? Or at least lust?”

I clench my teeth, checking over her shoulder. No sign the guys are listening. “Maybe?” Way too soon to think a word like love. It’s so big I can’t get my head around it.

But it seems like it’s more than lust. Isn’t that the point of what Rex was trying to tell me? That even if we’re complicated, this could be worth the risk?

I’d really like to find out if he’s thinking the same thing.

Lark nods, as if she was eavesdropping inside my brain. “I’ve got you.” Swiftly, she straightens and raises her voice. “What am I thinking? You should be resting. Cliff, we should leave Quinn alone for a while. Don’t you think?”

“Huh? But you just got here.”

Lark grabs his arm and drags him to the door. “Come on. We’ll come back after Quinn has a chance to relax. We can dig into the ice cream stash.” She winks at me as they leave.

“I assume she knows about us,” Rex says with a smirk.

"She does. I called her earlier after you left my office. I needed someone to talk to."

He nods, but he studies the floor.

"She's not going to tell anyone," I assure him. "I'm not even sure what there is to tell."

He comes over to me and reaches for my hand. "That depends on what you want."

What *I* want? That's never been a question. I want Rex.

But I've never imagined saying that to him. I don't blink at speaking in front of a courtroom full of people. Yet the thought of telling him about my years of desperate yearning makes me want to hide under the covers.

But if there's ever going to be a right time to tell him, this has to be it.

"I want to be with you. I know it's complicated because of Cliff and because you're my bodyguard. But I know how I feel. I've known for a while. I just never believed it was possible."

Please don't think I'm pathetic, a tiny voice says in my head. This is bad enough, and I haven't even confessed the most embarrassing parts.

"Quinn," he murmurs. Rex sits on the bed and brushes his nose against mine. "You don't know what it does to me to hear you say that."

I put my hands on his strong shoulders. Then move them down to his chest and feel his heart beating rapidly under my palm. He comes even closer. Bracing on either side of the bed, he brings his lips to mine. He's being careful with me, which is what I need. But dang it, I want a real kiss like earlier. Full of passion and heat. It's almost worth the pain so much motion would cause in my head.

He sits back and affectionately adjusts the collar on my hospital gown. "I want to give this a chance. See if we can be more. What do you say?"

"Are you kidding? Yes."

He smiles. "There's also the issue of your security. I can't be objective when it comes to you. The wisest thing would be to step aside as your bodyguard. Assign someone else to protect you."

"Uh, I disagree. That sounds like the worst idea ever."

"But my feelings for you distracted me earlier today. If I hadn't left you in your office, it's likely I could've prevented you from being hurt."

"You can't blame yourself for that. Today wasn't the first time I stayed at the office working late after you went off duty. That's why you have a team. We all believed my building was secure. Those precautions failed today, but it was never your assignment to be with me twenty-four-seven."

"Then maybe it should be." He strokes my chin. "I would put another bodyguard in charge of you if I had to, but honestly, I'd fucking hate it. I'd much prefer to keep you with me. "

"There is no one in the world I trust more than you."

He exhales. Whether relieved or resigned, I'm not sure. "I'm going to do everything I can to keep you safe. That includes not letting you out of my sight." He kisses me again and lightly sucks my lower lip. "I don't want to be apart from you," he whispers into my ear.

I tremble with the weight and wonder of that sentence. A few simple words, nowhere near poetry. Yet it's the most beautiful thing I've ever heard.

If this is a dream, please don't let me wake up.

I don't want to spoil this. But my lawyer-brain raises her hand with a question. "What about Cliff? Do we tell him?"

This has to be Rex's decision. He's probably right that Cliff won't be okay with us together. I would never want to come between Rex and his son. Of course, I don't want to lose my best friend either. But Cliff and his father have their own issues, and I'm worried that Cliff will blame his dad rather than me.

Rex is quiet for a bit, thinking. "If you want me to tell him, I will. I don't intend for you to be my dirty secret."

"I'm okay with waiting. We can keep this just between us for now. When we're ready and it makes sense, we can tell Cliff about it."

"All right."

"I have one more condition, though."

"Anything," he says automatically, and that makes me all gooey inside. As if I wasn't already.

"You delete that dating app. I don't want Denise messaging you anymore."

He chuckles, tugging out his phone then and there. He deletes the app icon, showing me. "I wasn't interested in her anyway. I only downloaded the app in a futile effort to get my mind off of you. You have no competition."

"I kind of lost it when I saw that message from her."

He leans in. "I nearly lost it when Christian Hayworth asked you to dinner. And when you said you might accept."

"Only to further the investigation into the secret witness!" I cringe when my headache pulses a warning. I'm getting too riled up.

"Let's just agree we don't want anyone else. There's only you and me. And we'll go from there."

"I suppose I can live with that. What about finishing what we started in my office? The part where I was on my desk, and..."

His nose trails along my jaw as a rumbly, possessive sound rolls from his chest. "As soon as you're better, I'm planning to do just that. But not a moment before. Now get some rest." He kisses my head. "I'll be right here. I'm not going anywhere."

14

Quinn

I stay overnight for observation, and Rex stays right there by my side.

I wish I could say it's non-stop sexy touches and smoldering tension. But I feel way too crappy for that. This headache won't quit, and every time I get up, the room spins. My balance wavers, and at one point, I lose my battle not to throw up. It should be mortifying. But Rex has seen me sick before. He's seen me crying with mascara streaks down my face. I saw him racked with sobs in the days after Lydia died. We're already comfortable around each other. So having him here with me in the hospital is like bringing a cozy blanket from home. I wish I could curl up in his lap and not worry about who'll see.

Mid-morning the next day, Rex leaves for a couple of hours to get cleaned up and changed. Another Bennett Security bodyguard stands outside my hospital room, someone I don't know well. Lark stops by for a bit, but I'm all pouty and listless.

I have no idea how I managed to stay away from Rex for

those six months before the infamous gala night, because now it's torture not to have him around.

I only perk up when there's a knock on my open door.

"Can we come in?" Angela De Luca asks.

Rex is right behind the detective, and we share a smile as they walk into the hospital room. It's like sparklers are going off in my veins. I want to reach for him, but of course Rex is being all professional. He stands with his hands in his jeans pockets while Angela approaches the bed. She's wearing a colorful dress with a blazer over it. Her small piercing is in place above her upper lip, and braids cascade over her shoulder.

"I'd better run," Lark says, kissing my forehead. She greets Angela and Rex on her way out, shutting the door.

"How're you feeling?" Angela asks.

"My head's a little better, thanks."

The hospital finished up the tests. I have a concussion, a lump on my head, and a big bruise on my shoulder. They warned me it'll take some time to heal. I'm lucky it wasn't worse.

"How's little Brent?" I ask.

She smiles warmly. "Adorable. And getting into everything."

Angela used to be Detective Murphy before falling in love with firefighter Matteo De Luca. I never would've expected fun-loving Matteo to end up with tough-as-nails Angela. But she's been showing her softer side, especially after the birth of their son, Brent. Then they surprised us again by getting hitched in a spontaneous ceremony at the county clerk's office. They have a beautiful family, so full of joy and love whenever I see them together.

"I heard your memories of the attack are fuzzy," Angela says, directing us back to the matter at hand.

"Last night they were, yeah. But it's coming back. I

remember opening my office door and finding the guy outside. I tried to chase him down. Probably not my smartest moment. But I was pissed."

"Can't blame you."

"I should've been there," Rex mutters.

"I keep telling him it wasn't his fault, but he doesn't want to listen."

"Hard of hearing in his old age?" Angela smirks at him. "Rex is one of the good ones. He and Bennett Security took care of me when I needed help. He told me you're someone special, so I have no problem returning the favor."

"Thank you." I can't keep my eyes off Rex, and he's got his head tilted, watching me intensely. Angela glances between us, a small smile forming on her beautiful face.

I have a feeling the detective is picking up on some clues. Or maybe I'm just that obvious.

"I'm planning to personally supervise the investigation into the harassment campaign against you," she says. "I'll clear it with Chief Holt first, and if needed, I'll do it on my own personal time. I don't want any accusations of preferential treatment. But given the media frenzy around the Printz case, Holt might agree we need to keep a tight rein on this one."

"We've got Sylvie Trousseau on it as well," Rex says. "She can share whatever her team digs up. Have you spoken to the suspect in last night's attack?"

"I did this morning. The guy confessed to everything. Between the video he posted on social media live-streaming the incident, and the cameras in the DA building, we had him dead to rights anyway. But he swears up and down that he was working alone. He claims nobody put him up to it. And that Amber had nothing to do with it."

I huff. "Of course. Same as the others." Like the guy with the perfume bottle at the gala and the one who threw the milkshake. But the asshole last night went so much further.

What will someone try next? Will they escalate even more as the trial nears?

"I'm guessing you haven't checked social media this morning?" Angela asks. "There was another development. Courtesy of Amber Printz's Insta account."

"No. I haven't seen anything about it."

Rex says he hasn't seen it either. Angela brings her phone over to the bed. It's hard for me to look at it because focusing makes my headache worse, but I get the gist.

It's a video of Amber. She's sitting tucked into a comfy chair, hair back in a ponytail, face washed clean of makeup. *"I just heard what happened at the West Oaks District Attorney's Office last night, one of their lawyers being confronted by an overzealous protester, and I just want to say I don't condone it. Violence is never the answer. Even in the face of injustice."*

Angela switches off her screen. "As you can see, Amber's once again fanning the flames while pretending to play innocent. It's no wonder there are reporters outside the hospital."

"What?"

Rex steps closer to me and rests his hand on my shoulder. "I'm aware of the situation with the reporters. You don't need to worry about it. I won't let them anywhere near you."

"We did learn how the suspect got inside your building," Angela says. "He works for the cleaning company, and he got hold of a keycard that way. No doubt he'll be fired, and we intend to recommend his case to the DA for prosecution on every possible charge."

"I guess I'm glad to hear that," I say. Even though it doesn't take away my concussion or the damage to my peace of mind. "But who knows when the next crazed Amber fan comes after me or Lana or one of our colleagues."

Rex crosses his arms. "Exactly why we have to keep you protected. The next threat could come from anywhere."

"What about transferring Quinn to a safe house?" Angela asks. "I know Max Bennett has several. It's not fun to be cooped up, but you should probably step up your security until this dies down."

Rex nods. "That's my thought as well. If Quinn is willing."

I shrug. "Whatever you think."

His eyebrow arches. "Not going to overrule my advice this time?"

"Not when your advice is reasonable instead of annoying."

I'm not so sure about this safe house idea, actually, if it'll keep me away from the office. No matter what, that trial is coming up, and I have to be ready.

But would I object to cozying up in an isolated location with Rex to guard me, day and night?

No, I would not.

Maybe I should be more frightened than I am. So far, Amber has never told anyone outright to harass our trial team. Not that we can prove. But she implies plenty in her posts. With her social media campaigning, Amber can create chaos while never being implicated directly herself. It's so frustrating. She killed her husband, and she's trying to use the media to get away with it. Celebrities have done it before, I suppose, but it's no less disheartening.

Meanwhile, that secret witness who contacted me is nowhere to be found. I need that irrefutable evidence against Amber Printz even more. Yet on the very day we found leads to the witness's identity, I'm attacked.

Makes me wonder if the timing is a coincidence. Or if Amber—or someone else entirely—is pulling the strings.

~

The doctor has just given me clearance to discharge when Lana arrives. My boss sweeps into my hospital room, her presence equal parts nurturing and commanding. She knows how to mother-hen like nobody else. The pregnant belly only adds to the effect.

"Sorry I couldn't make it here sooner," she says breathlessly. "I've been so worried about you, not to mention furious, and I've been making calls nonstop. I just finished with an emergency phone conference with the judge and defense counsel for the Printz case. Plus my back is *killing* me."

Rex pulls up a chair beside my bed so she can sit down. "Is Max here?" Rex asks.

"You think he's letting me go anywhere by myself after what happened to Quinn? He's in the waiting room." She turns back to me. "Has Rex been taking good care of you?"

"Um, yep." *Don't look at him,* I tell myself. Lana is too smart, and I already gave myself away to Angela.

"Derek Keller was adamant that his client had nothing to do with last night's 'unfortunate incident,' as he kept calling it. Derek vigorously opposed my request to continue the trial. But the judge agreed to push our start date by two weeks."

"Two *weeks*? That's not necessary. I can get back on my feet and do my job. I'll be fine by tomorrow. Maybe the day after."

Lana eyes me skeptically, and Rex looks ready to jump in and start issuing orders. I keep arguing.

"A two-week continuance means we'll be that much closer to your due date. That's more stress on you."

"I appreciate you thinking of me, but I'm sure this baby will hold out. I'm far more concerned about you. If by the time the trial starts, you're not feeling up to it—"

"Please don't say you'll pull me from the trial team." It

would be giving Amber exactly what she wants. "I can handle this."

"Hey, let's not jump to conclusions." Lana scoots her chair closer to place her hand over mine. "You're a key part of our team, and I'm not letting you go so easily. But your health is important. Concussions are no joke. We need that brain of yours functioning at full capacity. Your job is to rest. I mean complete downtime. Even though I know that's hard for a workaholic like you."

"Okay," I say reluctantly. "I'll try."

"Do better than that. This is an order from your superior, soldier," Lana jokes. "Take this time to heal. No work for at least several days. Preferably a week."

"But what about the investigation into the secret witness? The new evidence we're trying to find against Amber?"

"The evidence that may not exist? Bennett Security can keep working on that. But not you. You, my dear, are out of commission for the moment." She glances at Rex. "What about Quinn's security?"

"I'm arranging a safe house," he says. "I assume Max is setting you up somewhere as well?"

"Oh, yes. We're moving back into his old apartment at Bennett headquarters. There's no place that's more secure. Quinn, I'd ask you to stay with us, but it'll be crowded and noisy with Joy running around."

Joy is the little girl Lana and Max adopted. While I'd love to spend time with her, because she's adorable, I'm counting on lots of privacy. I won't get that at Bennett headquarters. "It's all right. I trust Rex to handle my arrangements."

"Then I'm sure you're in good hands."

That's what I'm hoping for. Rex's *good hands* all over me. As soon as the headache and dizziness go away, at least.

Finally, Lana says goodbye. All I need is the paperwork for my hospital discharge. The doctor said I need rest, just as

Lana advised, and I'll need to come back if my headache worsens. I'll also have to be careful in the future to avoid another concussion, which could be even more serious.

As soon as the coast is clear, Rex stands by my bedside and brushes a few strands of hair from my face.

"You're tired," he says. Not a question.

"Exhausted." I appreciate the concern and love that my visitors have shown, but I'm ready for quiet time. "Are we going to the safe house after this?"

"That's my plan. We have a few options. Max has several safe houses in the region, as Angela said. A few the police are aware of, and more that they have no idea about. But my preference is to take you to my beach house. It's outside of town. Secluded. Just as secure as Max's places, but I think it'll be more comfortable for you."

"Absolutely." I remember Rex bought a cabin by the water a few years back. I've never seen it. "I just want to be alone with you. I want to be able to touch you."

He glances left and right. "We're alone right now."

My breath hitches. I reach up and stroke his stubbled jaw. It's such a simple gesture, but so intimate.

Wow. This feeling is indescribable. I keep wondering if it's really happening, but here he is. Flesh and blood and smiling like he's as swept up as I am.

Rex leans into my touch. "You're beautiful, you know that?" he says.

"On the inside, right? Because I know for a fact my outside is a mess. I have hospital hair."

"Always with the arguing. You're an incredibly sexy woman, Quinn. That clear enough for you?" He comes closer and presses a soft kiss to my mouth. "Is it bad if I use the safe house as an excuse to get you all to myself?"

"I won't tell."

"You don't have to worry about anything. Leave the

details to me." He touches my chin. "I'm going to take *very* good care of you."

"Is this real?" I whisper.

He chuckles softly. "I keep wondering that too. If it's not, it's the best kind of dream."

Could this really work out? Could he really be mine?

If I lose him, my heart won't just break. It'll shatter. There won't be anything left. But I have to take the risk.

If it means finally having Rex, I'm all in.

15

Quinn

Getting me to Rex's beach house turns out to be a clandestine operation.

After the hospital gives me the all-clear, Rex sneaks me out through a delivery exit and takes me to Bennett Security headquarters. I hang out in the infirmary, and that's where Cliff, Lark and Danny meet me. They stopped by my apartment to pack a suitcase for me. Rex already packed a bag for himself earlier this morning. Right now he's upstairs, doing whatever bodyguards do at Bennett headquarters.

"There were reporters outside your apartment building," Lark says. "Cliff and Danny stood by the entrance looking all gruff and scary while I went inside."

Danny grins. "It was kinda fun, actually."

I groan. "Not to me. This is awful." I'd much rather go back to obscurity. I'm mostly internet famous, and I'm sure it'll die down as soon as the next viral video or controversy hits. But this is too much attention for me.

I'm sitting in a comfy upholstered chair, and Lark perches on the arm. "I tried to cover all the bases when I was packing. You said this house is by the beach, so I grabbed your swimsuit. Just in case. And, ya know, *other stuff*," she mutters with a wink.

I'm guessing that means my sexy underwear. I really hope I'll feel well enough to wear it.

And I can't believe Rex will see me in it. That thought makes sweat prick all over my skin.

Soon, Rex comes in with his duffle over his shoulder. "Ready?" he asks.

There's an SUV with tinted windows waiting for us in the underground parking garage. Rex insists on wheeling me out in a wheelchair, just like the hospital did.

"Dad," Cliff says, "are you sure the beach house is the best idea? What if the media figures out Quinn is with you and tracks you both there?"

Rex loads our bags into the trunk. "I thought about that. It's not an issue. Technically, an LLC owns title to the beach house. It would take a lot of steps for anyone to connect the dots."

"Really? I didn't know about the LLC."

"Guess I never mentioned it," Rex says.

I doubt he keeps much from Cliff. Of course, there are plenty of recent things my best friend doesn't know.

"The beach house has a Bennett Security alarm system," Rex explains. "And we'll have a team on-call in case anything happens. But it should be nice and quiet and isolated."

"Perfect for Quinn to recuperate," Cliff says. He claps his father on the shoulder. "Thanks for looking out for her, Dad."

There's a flicker of guilt on Rex's face. The same discomfort I'm feeling. We haven't outright lied to Cliff. But this is a pretty big omission.

By the way, Cliff, your dad and I are hot for each other. If the safe house is rocking, don't come knocking.

Lord, no. I need to come up with some better word choices for when we eventually break the news.

Lark and Danny give me hugs, and Cliff adds a kiss on my cheek. Rex helps me into the SUV and buckles me in. I put on sunglasses to shield my eyes from the sun. "So what's this LLC that owns the beach house? Do you have some spy identity I don't know about?" He did look like 007 in that tux at the gala.

He laughs. "Nope. I'll tell you all about it. But I want you to rest on the drive up. It'll be about an hour." His hand gently slides over my knee, below the view of my friends standing in the parking garage. "I'll wake you when we get there."

"With a kiss?"

"If that's what you want, I'm happy to oblige you."

Christian Hayworth joked that Rex was treating me like a princess. But shockingly, I don't mind it. I don't like the reasons this escape is necessary, but I'm going to make the most of it.

I drift off quickly. Before I know it, Rex's large hand is cradling my cheek, and soft kisses are raining over my face. "Wake up, gorgeous girl. We're here."

"Mmmm." I blink my eyes open. Even with the sunglasses, it's bright. We're in a driveway in front of an angular modern house made of white stucco and glass. I yawn, sitting up straighter.

Rex gets out and rounds the SUV to open my door. He leans across me to unbuckle my seatbelt, then lifts me up into his arms. "Carrying me inside too?" I ask. "This is five-star service."

"I aim to please. I also don't want you falling over walking into the house. You sway around like a drunken sailor every time you get up for the bathroom."

"Rude. But true."

He grins. I rest my head on his chest as he carries me inside. The house looked impressive on the outside, but inside, it's breath-taking. Soaring ceilings, polished concrete floors. The entire back wall is glass doors and windows. The panoramic view overlooks a stretch of sand leading to white-capped waves and endless blue sky.

He sets me down on the couch, then sits next to me. Our sides are pressed together, and he wraps an arm around me. "What do you think?"

"This place is amazing." I was expecting a small cottage or cabin. Not this.

It's not massive in size, but it still looks like a page from an architectural design magazine. Yet the space isn't cold. Far from it. Plush rugs in bright colors make it cozy and inviting. The furniture in the dining and living rooms is especially striking, made of weathered wood.

"How the heck can you afford this?" I blurt out.

Whoops, that came out harsher than I meant it.

But Rex is laughing. "I had some money saved up from my Army days. Lydia and I were supposed to travel more after I retired and took my pension." His smile turns wistful. "There was some life insurance money as well."

My heart hurts for him. "I'm sorry."

He smooths my hair back. "It's all right. Does it make you uncomfortable when I mention her?"

"No. Not at all. But I don't want to say something that makes you sad."

"God, you're sweet." He pulls me closer and kisses me, feather-light, at my hairline. "So good to me."

"You're the one who's been taking care of me. Doing a pretty great job of it, too."

"I hope so. You're very precious to me, Quinn. I want you to know that."

I'm seriously swooning, which unfortunately adds to my

dizziness. It's all a little too much. I put my head on his shoulder. "You were telling me about buying the house."

"Sure. For several years after Lydia died, I pondered what to do with the money. I used some for Cliff's college. But after he was off living his own life, I stumbled across a listing for this place. There'd been a fire here, including water damage from the mitigation. The owners wanted to take their insurance money and move on. They'd loved this house and had spent happy years here, but it was too hard to rebuild after seeing it destroyed. The price was a steal. It was going to get snapped up fast. In my purchase offer, I told them my plans to rebuild it instead of tearing it down." He rests his head against mine. "I said I really needed this project. Something totally different from the life I'd shared with Lydia. I was just like the house, in a way. Almost destroyed after the loss I'd been through. But still standing."

I bury my face against his neck. He holds me tighter. I didn't expect this story to get so personal for him, and I'm honored he's sharing it with me.

"I created an LLC to buy the house because I assumed I'd sell it after I was done. Maybe a new business, you know? Even though I hate numbers, it seemed like a viable idea. Something different. A fresh start."

That shocks me. I'd had no idea. "Did you think about quitting Bennett Security?"

"Considered it. Max let me cut back on my hours. I still volunteered for Team Triumph, but I spent a lot of time here on the renovation. I did a lot of the work on my own."

"I remember hearing you'd bought a beachside cabin, but I didn't realize you were here so much."

"This was when you and Cliff were in college. And then you had law school, and Cliff was starting out on patrol. You were both plenty busy with lives of your own."

"That's true." But still, I feel like I should've noticed Rex being gone all the time. I guess I was focused on myself then. Discovering who I was and expanding my horizons. Growing up.

"It took me a long time to finish. I decided I wanted to keep this place, but I gave up the idea of renovating houses for a living. I was ready to get back to Bennett Security and using the skills I'd developed in the Army. It was good for me, though. Taking that break. Restoring this house helped me finally heal as well."

"Thank you for bringing me. And telling me all that." I'm overwhelmed at the story he just shared.

"I've never invited anyone else here except Cliff, and I'm glad you're the first person aside from him to see it. I hope being here will help you heal, too."

I blink away tears. One escapes, and he catches the drop with his thumb.

This incredible man. What can I do but kiss him?

I go up on my knees and wrap my arms around his neck. The kiss is tender. Deep. Lazy swipes of tongue, both of us in no hurry. I swear his kisses have healing power. My headache lessens and the dizziness fades whenever our lips are connected. I wind up straddling his lap and rocking myself against his swelling cock.

He pulls back and kisses my forehead instead. "We can't. You need to get better, and I'm not going to risk being rough with you."

I whimper. "But I really, really want you to be rough with me. Pretty please?"

He kisses the tip of my nose. "Be good, and I will. When you're ready. I'll show you to your room."

Rex helps me to the main suite. It's another stunning space, with patio doors overlooking the ocean and a dramatic king-size bed constructed of more weathered wood, like his other furniture. "I get to stay here with you?" I ask.

"No, I'll be sleeping in the guest room." He must see my disappointment, because he slides his arms around my waist. "We're just getting started. We're not going to rush. I want you to focus on healing."

"You're being annoyingly reasonable."

His grin goes lopsided. Devious. "When we share a bed the first time, I plan to spend a lot of time exploring you. I don't want any concerns about hurting you."

"I'm sorry I'm not well enough for more."

"Don't you dare be sorry. Just having you here is wonderful. And it's not about me, anyway. I'm taking care of you, not the other way around."

"For now."

Rex brings my suitcase into the room. He agrees to lie down on the bed with me to cuddle, after I make a convincing argument that it's not the same as sharing the bed overnight.

I'm starting to wear down and get tired again. Yet I force my eyes open, not ready for this moment to end. "Kiss me some more?"

He shakes his head. "See? This is why we can't share a room. You're too tempting." But then he's dipping toward me, his tongue swiping across my lower lip to gain entrance again.

Finally, we have to come up for breath. I'm not ready to confess the true extent of my feelings for him. But I could show him. I want to be as close to Rex as possible, sharing every part of my body with him, as if the act of joining could seal our hearts and souls together too. That's how gone I am for this man.

I sneak my hand between us and cup the bulge in his jeans. "I want you inside me. So badly."

He groans. "Soon. I promise."

ON MY FOURTH MORNING AT THE BEACH HOUSE, I wake in Rex's bed feeling more clear-headed than ever. I stretch out on his soft sheets. When I sit up, there's a faint trace of fog in my brain. The doctor said the fuzziness might take a while to go away. But otherwise, I feel great. Like my old self. My headache has faded, and the dizziness and nausea are nearly gone.

Jumping out of bed, I catch a glimpse of myself in the mirror and find myself grinning. My hair is wild and I'm in pajamas, but I stopped being self-conscious around Rex after that vomiting bout in the hospital. By comparison, I look glamorous right now. After brushing my teeth and washing my face, I head into the main part of the house. It's quiet. The door to the guest room is open and the bed is empty, so he's clearly up.

"Rex?" I ask. "Where are you?"

But he isn't in the living room or kitchen. I find coffee in the pot and pour a cup, sighing as I take a sip. There's a blueberry muffin on a plate, so I take a few bites.

I can't remember the last time I went so long without logging in to my work email or doing research for upcoming cases. I've always been ambitious. The kind of person who can't sit still without some kind of goal or project. Rex and I are alike that way. I've rested my brain the last few days, just as Lana ordered.

But my heart? That's been getting a workout, because Rex has been in top form. So freaking charming and wonderful it's hard to believe he's real.

I check the alarm panel, which shows the system is activated. While it feels like we're on vacation here, Rex is still treating this as a safe house, and he talked me through all the security protocols I'm supposed to follow. *No leaving the house without him. No answering the door.* There's a panic button and a gun safe where Rex keeps his weapons. He changed the settings so my fingerprint as well as his will open the lock.

He mentioned there are cameras aimed at the road and the beach to monitor anyone coming and going. But he keeps the cameras around the house itself off whenever it's occupied.

Rex must be around here somewhere because I can't imagine he left me alone. He's still my bodyguard.

Of course, we're so much more than that now.

Rex has been cooking for me. Cuddling and napping with me on the couch. We can sit quietly on his patio for hours together until the sun sets over the ocean. I'm still avoiding screens because they don't make me feel well, so we listen to music instead. He's introduced me to some of the jazz greats. Miles Davis, John Coltrane, Thelonious Monk. I've played my favorite indie singer-songwriters for him, and now he's into Phoebe Bridgers.

Don't get me wrong. There's been plenty of kissing and touching. Full-body snuggles that almost turn to more. But it's a slow build of tension and anticipation. Longing looks, when I feel like I'll get lost in the consuming desire I see in his eyes. He's as eager for me as I am for him, while also making clear that he wants more with me than some hot, forbidden hookup.

He wants me. I'm still marveling at that fact. Maybe at some point, it'll really sink in.

I wander through the house that's already becoming familiar to me. Rex's family photos decorate the feature wall in the living room. There are a few pictures of Rex and Lydia from when they were younger. Snapshots of Rex with Cliff at varying ages. Even some photos of Cliff and me, like at our high school graduation ceremony. There's a shot of Cliff, Rex, and me together on the day I graduated from law school.

I've looked at these pictures several times in the last few days. But today, I spot one I didn't notice before. It's of Lydia, Rex, Cliff and me at a school track meet. Probably the only photo ever taken of all four of us. I remember that day, not long after the Eastons moved to West Oaks. Right after my eighteenth birthday. My own parents were gone so much, and I was thrilled that Cliff's family didn't mind me hanging around all the time.

I used to hate the quiet when I was home alone.

When Cliff's mom died, it wasn't a big sacrifice for me to stay with him and Rex to help out. I genuinely cared for the Eastons and felt terrible about their loss. But now, I wonder how Cliff might view it. Would he think I was trying, even back then, to take the place of his mom?

Ugh, that makes me feel gross to even think it.

For the vast majority of the time Rex has known me, he didn't see me as anything other than Cliff's best friend. Now, we're about to become lovers. What I've wanted for so long. Dreamed of. Ached for.

If we don't work out, could we ever go back to the way we were before? What about Cliff and me? Cliff and his dad?

And what would Lydia Easton say if she knew?

When Rex is right next to me, our connection feels natural. Effortless. Like this is exactly where I'm supposed to end up. I need to find him and stop second-guessing the best thing that's ever happened to me.

Then I hear something coming from the garage, which is off the kitchen. Rex gave me a tour when we first arrived, but I only glanced into the unfinished space. He mentioned that he turned the garage into a workshop of some kind.

Now, I crack open the door and peer inside. Rex is bent over a work table, sanding a piece of wood. His salt-and-pepper hair is messier than usual. He's dressed in sweats and a Team Triumph T-shirt with the sleeves cut off, leaving his flexing muscles on display. So sexy.

"Looking good," I say, loud enough that he'll hear me over the Air Pods he's wearing.

He looks up and grins, tugging the Air Pods free. "Hey. How are you feeling this morning?"

"So much better." Just being in his presence makes those upsetting thoughts about Cliff evaporate. "What are you up to?"

"Come here and I'll show you."

I pretend to be undecided. "If I come over there, will you make it worth my while?"

"Only one way to find out."

I saunter over, and he hooks me around the waist, drawing me closer. He brings his mouth to mine. His beard is growing in, and his whiskers are slightly prickly against my skin. I trail my fingers over the bristles. His beard is almost entirely gray, a recent change in the last few years. It makes him look handsomer than ever.

"What are you working on?" I ask.

Without letting go of me, he turns us both to face the worktable. "A hobby. After I finished renovating this house, I needed something else to fill my free time. What little there was. I started working with reclaimed wood."

I think of all that furniture inside the house made from weathered slats of wood. "Wait, did you make the pieces you've got in the house? Like the dining table and your bed?"

He nods. "Do you like them?"

"I love them. I can't believe you made those. I mean, I *can*, but I'm impressed."

His eyes light up. As if it means a lot to hear me say that. "I've done smaller things too, but as far as bigger pieces, only those that you saw. The table, the bed, a few chairs. It's been a learning process. But I love taking something worn out and making it beautiful again."

It's such a Rex thing to do. I point at the board he was sanding. "What's this going to be?"

He runs his fingers over the surface. "I'm not sure yet. But with you here, I was inspired to start something new." He nuzzles my cheek. "You do seem better today. What do you feel like doing?"

"I would say *you,* but that's way too cheesy a line."

He laughs, but his gaze has taken on a darker gleam. "I did make you certain promises about what would happen when you got better."

A thrill of excitement runs through me, like I'm a live wire. "Yeah. You did." I wiggle in his arms.

"Are you nervous?" he asks, his voice deep and melodic.

Part of me wants to sprawl out on his workbench and let him do whatever he wants. But the other part of me? "A little nervous," I say. Because once we cross that line, we can't ever go back.

"We don't have to do anything you don't want to do."

"That's not it. I've just wanted this for so long."

"How long?"

I bite my lip. Am I really going to tell him this? "About ten years. Off and on."

He inhales slowly, nostrils flaring. "Quinn…you've had boyfriends though, right? I thought you did."

"Of course. Mainly this one guy in college. But aside from him, there hasn't really been anyone. I know. It's ridiculous."

He holds my chin so I'll look at him. "Not ridiculous. I'm flattered. I didn't know. And even if I had…"

"You couldn't see me that way back then. I get that. I'm glad you didn't. I'm glad it's happening the way it is. Even with all this drama."

"I'm not happy you're in danger. Certainly not happy you

were hurt. But I think it's happening when it's meant to. When we're both ready." He stares at me for a long time, eyes searching mine. "I have my work cut out for me. I'd better make it worth all that wait. Let's spend the day together."

"We've been spending every day together."

"I mean a date. I'd take you out, but we're safer here. So I'll have to make it special." He lifts an eyebrow. "You brought a swimsuit, right?"

"Lark packed one for me."

"Good. Put it on and meet me by the door in twenty minutes. I have big plans for you."

"I can't wait," I say.

I'm itching to check my email. But I know the rest of my colleagues are covering for me right now. Lana had a point that I haven't taken time off in a while.

I have no idea how much longer I can spend with Rex without the rest of the world interfering. The Printz trial is still looming, and we haven't made any progress on finding the anonymous source or new evidence. Who knows what crap is being said about me online.

But for now, I want to enjoy being with him and shut out everyone else for as long as I can. Including all my fears and doubts. After ten years, I'm finally about to have the man of my dreams.

16

Rex

Ten years. Quinn has had a thing for me for almost ten *years*?

As I strip off my clothes and grab my spare swim trunks from the guest room dresser, I repeat her confession in my head. I have so many questions. Did she just mean that she was attracted to me back then? That she'd actually wanted to *sleep* with me when she was a teenager?

Even the thought of that makes me uncomfortable. I never looked at her that way until recently, and if she'd made any sort of advance, I would've kindly but emphatically turned her down.

I'm flattered, of course. But the scary thought is that some men *wouldn't* have turned her down. I certainly hope Quinn didn't mess around with any such creeps. Yeah, she was eighteen and a legal adult then, but honor and morality have to mean something too. If I find out some asshole took advantage of her, no matter how long ago, I'll hunt him down. I don't care who he is or where he is.

Then my anger falters as I remember how Quinn was

avoiding me earlier this year. She stopped coming to weekend dinners with me and Cliff. Moved out of the Pink House, where I chatted with her whenever I saw her.

Was that because it hurt her to see *me*?

Shit, I hate that. Had she felt unwanted or sad because my thick skull failed to notice what an incredible woman she'd become?

But I notice her now. The past led us to this point, where we are now, and we're getting our chance.

Then a new source of anxiety occurs to me. She's been waiting to be with me for ten years. What if she's disappointed? What if we really try this, and Quinn decides *Nah, didn't live up to expectations. One star.*

I can show her a good time in the bedroom. Not so much worried about *that*. But my relationship skills are beyond rusty. I've been alone for so long. Gotten set in my ways. And I want so much more than a good time with Quinn. I want a future. Yet we haven't discussed what that would look like.

I tug on my swim trunks and banish all that self-doubt from my head. I'm not usually the type to get neurotic about my every decision. True leaders assess a situation, make a choice, and follow through. In my thirty years as a soldier, Special Forces operator, bodyguard and volunteer, I've seen so much shit. So many people suffering. The only way to keep going is to believe there's a silver lining. Some way to turn all the bad to good.

After I lost Lydia, I lost that faith for a while too, and it took me a long time to get it back again. Working on this house made a difference. Same with building my furniture. It's symbolic. When I take something that others see as ruined and transform it into something useful, even beautiful, it's like I'm restoring part of the world to where it should be.

But in all this time, I've never fully put *myself* back together. I've found peace. I'm no longer grieving. But that's not the same.

I've been in the position where I've held the person I love in my arms and had to watch her slip away. I *never* want to go through that again. Being able to actually aid in Quinn's recovery has meant everything to me. I see the potential that we could have. I can't focus on the obstacles. I've overcome plenty before.

This is my shot to be happy, truly happy, in a way I haven't been since Lydia died. And to make Quinn happy too. I have to take it.

I don't see Quinn in the kitchen or living room. She must still be getting changed. I head into the garage and pull out a couple of wetsuits in our sizes, plus two surfboards. Once I've transferred everything we need to the back patio, I go looking for her.

And nearly forget my name when I see her emerge from the bedroom.

She's wearing a yellow string bikini. Between her golden hair, tanned skin, and those tiny triangles of fabric, she's pure sunshine. Or perhaps lemon meringue pie. My mouth waters and my eyes rake over her. We each cross the distance until we're standing close enough to touch.

I hum appreciatively. "You look good enough to eat."

"So do you." She openly admires my bare torso, running her hand from my Adam's apple down the swell of my pecs.

"Not too much gray for you?"

"*No*. Are you kidding? It's hot." She presses a kiss above my heart, and my cock gives an eager twitch.

"Right. Because you like older guys." I should rein in this jealousy, but it's out in full force. "Any other older guys in your history I need to know about?" The thought of her with another man, especially one my age, makes my blood boil again. Even if she wasn't a teenager at the time, I'm still not okay with it. *She's not for you,* I tell this imaginary guy, right before my imaginary fist connects with his imaginary face.

Quinn is smiling and shaking her head. "I told you about my college boyfriend. He was a classmate. My few hookups have been my generation too. The only older guy I've ever wanted is you."

I'm relieved to hear that, but then I make a face. "Please don't say the word *generation*. Makes me feel ancient."

She laughs. "It's true, though. You're Gen X, right? I'm a millennial. I like how we're different. Even though we have plenty in common too. I like everything about you." She drags her nails across my chest hair. Then she turns her attention to the tattoo on my right bicep. "I've never been able to see your ink close up before. What is this?"

"The coat of arms for the Easton family."

"Very hot." Quinn pushes her bikini-covered breasts against me. "You're so sexy it makes me crazy."

I almost throw her over my shoulder and carry her to my bed. My *real* bed, the one she's been sleeping in without me. But I squeeze the curve of her butt cheek instead and step back.

Worth the wait, I remind myself.

"Ever been surfing?" I ask.

"A couple of times. I wasn't great at it. Will you teach me?" She says this seductively, and I have the feeling that Quinn could figure it out for herself. She can do anything she sets her mind to.

But this is foreplay, and we both know it.

"Of course I will." I smooth my fingers over her bikini straps, adjusting them. Her nipples bead. *Ngh*. It's all I can do not to slide my thumbs over them. Tweak them and tease them. "I'll show you just what to do."

"*Will* you?" She's laying it on thick. "You'll show this poor, innocent California girl how to surf?"

I laugh. "I know you're not so innocent. Come on. Let's go."

On the patio, we each tug on our wetsuits, and then I grab both boards. I'm glad she's feeling better, but I don't plan on her lifting a finger today. It goes way beyond my title as bodyguard.

I love taking care of her. In fact, it turns me all the way on.

The water's always cold here, but it's a warm, sunny day. The waves are decent. Not too big that I'd worry about Quinn's recent concussion. There are a couple of surfers about a half mile down the beach, but otherwise it's quiet. This is something I love about this spot. It doesn't get much foot traffic. And my nearest neighbors are off in the distance, those houses often empty while their owners are away, so we've got some privacy.

There is a camera on the beachside of the house, since an intruder could approach from the water. But that feed, like the others, is encrypted and only goes to myself and Bennett Security.

I set our surfboards on the sand. "I brought you a wider board since your balance might still be off. We're going to take it slow."

"So, no getting barreled today?"

"I think you underestimated your skills to me."

She laughs. "Cliff and I used to go surfing sometimes after track practice. We picked up a few terms. It's been a while though."

Soon we're out in the water. It's been a while since I've been out here myself, and it feels great. Being out in the sun and waves. It's a chance to turn off my analytical, strategizing brain and just be.

The fact that I get to be here with Quinn makes it even more perfect.

She gets up on her board easily, and I watch her ride a few waves in. She tires quickly since she's still recovering. I leave my board on the sand and we both sit astride hers, paddling lazily when we need to so we don't drift too far in the current.

"It's so beautiful here," she says. "I can't believe Cliff didn't tell me. If it were me, I'd be here every weekend."

"He's only been out a handful of times. I've invited him, but he's busy."

She snorts. "Yeah, playing video games and bumming around with our roommates." Then she looks guilty. "Sorry, I shouldn't say that. I must be breaking some kind of best friend code right now. "

"It's okay. I know my kid. I love him and I am proud of him. But I'm not sure that always gets through."

"Do you say that to him?"

I'm sure I must have told him countless times. But now, I can't think of a single one. "I think so. Probably not as much as I should."

She stretches out her legs so her knees are hooked over mine. "I don't want to mess things up with you and Cliff. I know it hasn't always been smooth between the two of you."

"Maybe. But that's my fault, not yours. We're much closer than we used to be, but I still need to do better with him. I feel like I'm always saying the wrong thing. Offending him without meaning to. He doesn't get outright mad at me. Not like when he was a teenager. But I can tell he gets annoyed, and sometimes I don't even know what I did." I'm trying to be careful about this conversation. I don't want to make Quinn feel uncomfortable or stuck in the middle. As much as I'd like to ask her for some insights into my son, it's not right of me. Cliff has probably told her things in confidence as his best friend. I can't violate that trust.

"But I am grateful that you've been there for him all these years," I add. "And there for me too after Lydia died."

She reaches out to squeeze my hand. I link our fingers together. I might be out of the habit of sharing my innermost thoughts with a partner, but I'm trying. Bringing Quinn here was a big part of that. Letting her see who I am in a way that I never share with anyone, not even Cliff.

"What about your parents?" I ask. "Do you want me to try texting them again? They might like hearing from you."

"Not necessary. They know I'm safe. But they're not the types to fuss over me. You know that."

The first day we arrived, Quinn asked me to text her mom and dad to let them know about her concussion and that she would be out of touch for a few days. I've been monitoring her phone, but they only acknowledged the message. Didn't ask for details or for a phone call. If it had been Cliff, I would've dropped everything to be there. Even though Cliff might not want me to.

"I know how your parents are," I say. "They haven't changed much. But I don't like it any more now than I did when you were younger."

She glances at the horizon. "It's fine. I have you." She's speaking lightly, but I feel what she's asking underneath.

"You do have me, Quinn. Always. No matter what happens."

When we're ready to head in, I jump off the board to push us back to shore, while Quinn sits on top of it. I help her up, then grab both boards and head back toward the house.

"I have an outdoor shower around the side," I say, pointing. We need to wash off all the sand before we go back inside. I drop off the boards on the patio, and we strip the wetsuits.

I follow Quinn around the side of the house. There's a partial enclosure constructed of teak wood, sheltering the shower from the view of the road, but leaving it open to the beach.

Quinn turns on the water. She waits a moment for it to heat, since I've got the hot water feeding out here. She steps under the spray. Streams cascade over her body. All her curves are on shameless display.

She turns to face me. I'm still standing in the opening to the enclosure. A wicked grin spreads on her face.

Her fingers hook the tiny straps on her bikini top, and she tugs them down.

I groan. Her breasts are full, with rosy, pink nipples jutting out. Just begging to be sucked. My cock starts to fill in my board shorts.

"See something you like?" she asks.

I walk toward her. "I do. I see a sexy woman who wants my attention."

"Is it that obvious?"

I bend to close my lips around her nipple. She moans, fingers threading into my wet hair. Her skin is slightly salty. Warm and smooth. My hands go to her hips, squeezing gently. I lick and suck until she's writhing against me. Then switch to the other side to lavish her other nipple with attention.

I'm fully hard now, my dick throbbing. "Wash off," I command. "I can't do everything I want to do to you here." Quinn goes to pull her bikini straps up again, but I untie the back so it falls to the ground. "That stays off."

Smiling, she steps back under the spray. I crowd in with her, quickly rinsing the sand from my body. Quinn bends her arms over her head like she's a pinup model.

Growling, I grab hold of her and hoist her up, my arms

cinching around her hips. Her breasts jiggle right in front of my face. I give the right nipple another lick as she laughs, but I need to get her inside the house before I burst. I'm not so much worried about public indecency as the fact that I want my mouth on other parts of her. I need more room.

I manage to slide open the patio door, not bothering to shut it. We're safe here. A salt-scented breeze follows us inside. We make it as far as the sectional couch before I set her down. I'm trying not to jostle her too much given her concussion. But Quinn flops backward, lying with her arms stretched up, knees bent, breasts on display. The tent in my board shorts is downright obscene. I keep my cock in his place, though.

I have to stop and admire her as I stand over her. Quinn, my beautiful blond-next-door, is sprawled on my couch wearing nothing but string-bikini bottoms.

Life is good.

"Here I am," she says. "What should I do now?"

"Untie your bikini bottoms." My voice is raspy, drenched with lust.

"Yes, Rex." She slides one hand along her side until she reaches the left tie. Pulls the bow until the strings open. Slowly, she undoes the other tie. "What now?" she asks.

I'm salivating. "Take them off."

She shifts around and tosses the yellow fabric onto the carpet. But her knees are knocked together, hiding the view.

"Open your legs. Let me see you."

She sucks in a breath. Quinn's pulse jumps at her throat. My own chest is tight with anticipation, my heart rate speeding.

Her legs spread, revealing the pink center of her, the rosy folds glistening with wetness. Fuck.

I drop to my knees.

"You want my mouth on you?" My voice is ragged. I'm already strung out with desire. But I remember her nervousness earlier. No matter how teasing and sexy she's being, I need to make sure she's excited about every single thing we do.

"Please," she whispers. "Please, please, please, Rex. Put your tongue inside me."

Doesn't get any clearer than that.

I place a hand on the underside of each of her thighs, supporting her legs and spreading them wide. Then I bow forward. Ready to worship her. But still, I pause. Drawing out the moment and building the anticipation.

The flat of my tongue slides over her pussy, and Quinn cries out. It's a needy, desperate sound. "Finally. *Yes.*"

And I lose control.

I feast on her. Licking, sucking, and nipping at her sensitive folds. My tongue flicks over her clit before I thrust it into her opening as deep as I can go. She tastes faintly of ocean water, but mostly her own sweet liquor. I drink her in and she goes straight to my head.

She's chanting my name, and that just urges me on. I swirl and pulse my tongue at her clit. Her thighs are shaking under my hands. I hike one of her legs even higher, my other hand moving to push a finger into her opening. And she cries out. "*Rex*. Right there. Don't stop."

I keep up the rapid ministrations of my tongue while my finger pumps in and out. She convulses and shudders, her channel tightening on my digit. More of her sweetness coats my fingers. She continues to shake, and I pump another finger inside her to draw out her orgasm.

After she's done, Quinn goes limp. "That was…that was…"

"I know." I climb onto the sectional, shoving my swim trunks down and off along the way. My cock is so swollen it pops free and slaps my abs. I straddle her, one knee to either side of her waist. She closes her slender fingers around my shaft and strokes me up and down.

I tip my head back, eyes closing briefly. "So good."

I add my own hand over hers to tighten her grip, quickening her pace as she jacks me. Precome leaks from my tip and spills onto our overlapping fists.

"Need to kiss you," I say.

I lower my upper body over her, bracing a hand by her head while my other keeps up that fast pace on my cock. Our lips and tongues tangle. It's messy and unpolished and perfect.

"Wait," she says breathlessly. "Come in my mouth? Please?"

My cock bucks in our joined grips. "Fuck, yes."

She lets go of me. I lay to one side of her on the wide sectional couch, propped on an elbow. My fist holds on to the base of my cock, keeping it upright. Quinn bends over. Her soft, wet mouth closes around the tip.

I make a strangled sound. It's mind-blowing how incredible this feels. I stroke my shaft, and she sucks the head, her tongue swirling over my slit.

The tingle in my balls becomes an explosion of pleasure.

"*Ungh,* Quinn. That's perfect. You're making me come. Yes."

I keep saying dirty things, barely aware of the words. She hums as I shoot into her mouth. Her throat works as she swallows. I'm carried away by the waves of good feeling.

I don't want it to end.

It does, of course, and Quinn stretches out beside me. I grasp her chin. Crash my mouth onto hers. We taste one another, our flavors mixing. I have no idea how long we kiss. Eventually, I'm aware of her breathing. The caress of a warm breeze coming through the open patio door, and the faraway screech of a seagull.

I give her another soft kiss. Another. "My gorgeous girl," I murmur against her lips. "Where did you come from?"

"I've been here waiting for you."

17

Rex

At some point, we'll have to get up. I'd stay naked on the couch with her all day, but my stomach is growling. If only I could get my brain to work. Somebody sucked it right out of me.

"We need lunch," Quinn says. "You're hungry."

"Hmmm?"

"You need to move. You're half on top of me, and you're heavy." She pushes at my shoulder and laughs. "Aren't you supposed to be my hyper-vigilant bodyguard? You're useless right now."

"That's mean." Summoning all my energy, I get into a pushup position over her. I drop a kiss on her nose and then launch myself up to standing.

"Now you're just showing off."

"You insulted my abilities. My ego got involved." I hold out a hand to help her up. She's deliciously naked, breasts swaying as she stands. So tempting. I want a repeat of what we just did. But I'm not twenty anymore. I need my recovery time.

Also, food. For myself, sure, but I also need to feed my girl. I'm supposed to be taking care of her.

I scoop up my board shorts and tug them back on. "What would you like for lunch?"

"I don't care. Anything. I can make it if you want."

I give her a side-eye. *"I'm* taking care of *you,* remember?"

"Yeah, I know. It's very sweet of you. But I think you like controlling how everything goes, too." She leans into me and whispers, "I think you get off on it."

I swat her bare butt. She giggles and disappears into the main bedroom. I hear the shower running a moment later.

While I'd love to join her in there, I should get the food going. We've got all day and all night to enjoy each other. If I'm lucky, all of tomorrow too.

By the time she emerges, I've got sandwiches and fresh-cut veggies arranged on plates. Her hair is damp and wavy. She's wearing my Team Triumph shirt, the one with the sleeves cut off. It hangs low on her thighs, and when I pull her close and slide my hands beneath, I find she's wearing a skimpy pair of lace panties. In fact, I can peek in the cut-off sides of the shirt and get a nice show.

After we both eat, I go to clean myself up. I suggest strongly to Quinn that she lie down for a nap. She agrees to rest on the couch, and I find some blankets to keep her cozy while I'm gone.

I quickly shower and dress in my gray sweats, not bothering with a shirt. But when I get out to the living room, staying quiet so I don't wake her, I find Quinn sitting up at the kitchen table.

And she's got her phone, thumb scrolling rapidly across the screen.

"Hey, I thought you were resting."

"I couldn't rest while I thought about all the emails that

had probably built up in my inbox. And I was right. This is a horror show."

I go over to the table and lean a hand against it. "The screen isn't making your headache act up?"

She shrugs. "It's bothering me a little. But this email from Derek Keller? Ugh, that's a freaking pain."

"Keller? He's the defense lawyer for Amber Printz?" I remember seeing him in the DA building the other day. The same eventful day, in fact, that we took the trip to LA, and afterward Quinn was attacked. "Why does he keep bothering you?"

"It's kind of his job. But I'm sure it's a passion too." She smirks. "Derek wrote to express his sincere concern for my health and welfare, and he wants me to call him to discuss the Printz case. Whatever. I'm not writing him back until I'm good and ready." She turns off the screen and sighs. "The rest of these emails can wait. But I was hoping for an update from Sylvie and her team. Have you heard anything from them?"

"Sure, I have. I've been checking in with her every day. I know how important the Printz trial is to you, so I wanted to make sure I knew the latest."

"And?"

I shake my head. "Nothing to report. But we could try Sylvie again now if you want."

"You wouldn't mind?" she asks guiltily. "I'm sorry. I know today is supposed to be a date, and I should be thinking about you and me, but this is nagging at me."

I bend to kiss the top of her head. "Don't be sorry. I love how dedicated you are. I respect the hell out of that. Come on, let's sit in the living room and use my phone. If you're up for it, we can call Detective De Luca and see if she has anything for us as well." I hold out my hand, and she takes it, getting up from the chair and following me into the living room.

"Thank you for understanding."

"I'm the last guy to complain about work being a priority. You don't have to worry about that with me." I know some guys who gripe about their women working or having hobbies, as if they can't bear not to be number one at all times. But Quinn wouldn't be who she is without her career. I wouldn't change anything about her.

"Good," she says. "Same here. Sounds like we're a pretty good match."

"Seems like we are." We pause for a few kisses, but before things can get heated, I sit on the couch and tug her onto my lap. Just because we're taking a break for work doesn't mean we can't cuddle up at the same time.

But I'm going to keep these calls audio only. No need to give Sylvie or Angela an eyeful.

First up, I call Sylvie's work number. "Hey, Foxy," she drawls. Quinn covers her mouth, but her laughter must carry. Because Sylvie asks, "Is that Quinn?"

"Yes. You're on speaker."

"How's Foxy's beach house? Beachy?"

I roll my eyes, though of course Sylvie can't see me. "It is quite beachy, yes."

"We're having a great time," Quinn adds. "Thanks to Rex, I'm feeling much better."

That's probably giving a lot away to a woman like Sylvie, who's one of the shrewdest people I've ever met. Sylvie's going to give me a hard time later. But I don't mind. Not really. Not when Quinn looks so happy.

"I bet you are," Sylvie says.

There will inevitably be questions and comments when word spreads that I'm dating a woman over twenty years younger. That's an issue for another day, though.

"But I assume you called to find out what's up with the

search for your secret witness? Not just to share the good vibes?"

"You guessed it," Quinn replies. "Please tell me you've got news."

"As a matter of fact, I just met with my team. They've been trying to track down Pete Diamond."

Quinn sits up excitedly. "Did they find him?"

Pete Diamond was the former chauffeur for Thompson and Amber Hayworth. Quinn thinks he could be the secret witness who contacted her and promised new evidence against Amber. The same witness who seemed to vanish into thin air.

"Yep. Christian Hayworth did send Pete to a set in Nevada a little over two weeks ago, but from there, Pete went AWOL. Apparently, nobody has seen him since. From what we've learned, he got a phone call and walked off the set without a word to anyone."

Quinn taps her lip. "It's been a little over two weeks since we texted with the secret witness at Bennett Security headquarters."

"Exactly. I tried to track the burner phone the witness was using, and I was able to confirm he or she was in West Los Angeles during that initial conversation. But since then, that cell hasn't pinged a single tower. The witness hasn't turned it on."

"Damn," I say. "This would be easier if it had turned up in Nevada."

Sylvie chuckles. "If only our targets would be more cooperative. But no, they rarely are. My team will keep trying to track Pete down. If we do, Quinn, what's your preference? Do you want me to make contact, or would you rather I pass on his info to you?"

"Give it to me. If he's the witness, then he spoke to me before. We have no idea why he decided not to follow through. Maybe it's whatever danger he was talking about. The reasons he was staying anonymous in the first place. He might have gotten spooked. But if I could talk to him directly, I could convince him to turn over the evidence. In a way, this concussion bought us some more time before the trial. But it's still coming up fast."

"Got it," Sylvie says. "Foxy, we'll catch up later. See ya." She ends the call.

Quinn turns in my lap to face me. "So it's still possible Pete Diamond is my witness. And that Christian Hayworth knows Pete has something to hide. Maybe Christian sent him off to Nevada to keep him quiet. But I keep wondering *why*?"

"Maybe this evidence doesn't just incriminate Amber. It could be damaging or embarrassing to Christian. Or to the reputation of Thompson Hayworth or Hayworth Productions. His son would care about that."

"Except Kendall Simms, Thompson's assistant, told me that Christian doesn't seem to care about his father's legacy at all."

"Give Sylvie a little more time. She's just about as relentless as you are. She'll use her hacker skills to sniff out Pete Diamond wherever he's hiding. Then we can find out from him what's going on."

Quinn sighs." I just hope we can make that happen before the trial. Lana's counting on me. I'm getting more and more worried that our case won't stand up in front of the jury without that missing piece. I just hope it really exists."

And I hope that Quinn doesn't put all the pressure to win this case on herself.

18

Quinn

I'm disappointed by how little Sylvie's team has found so far. I don't blame her, of course. She's working hard on this, and my problems aren't the only ones Bennett Security has to deal with. I just feel like I'm not doing enough. I want to make some kind of progress toward finding the witness.

Maybe Angela De Luca has had more luck with ending the harassment campaign against me and the trial team.

Unfortunately, my call with her isn't any more satisfying.

The suspect who attacked me at my office building continues to insist he was working alone. But he was able to make bail, and Angela is trying to find out who put up the money. The suspect earns minimum wage making pizza deliveries, so it's doubtful he's flush with extra cash. But that's barely a lead. For all we know, the guy's parents bailed him out, not some nefarious puppet master. Angela and West Oaks PD are no closer to finding out if Amber Printz or someone else is really behind these threats.

I'm left feeling tired out and frustrated. So much so that I don't argue when Rex orders me to take a nap. For real this time. "Okay," I say, "I'll rest. But I don't want to sleep through our day together. Wake me up after a few hours?"

"I can handle that." He surprises me by lying down on the couch and patting the space beside him on the wide sectional cushion. "Snuggle up."

I lie next to him, and Rex covers us with a throw blanket. His chest makes a great pillow. If a little on the firm side.

My mind drifts away from thoughts of work to our surfing date earlier.

I've rarely spent time alone with Rex until recently. I've had a crush on the man for a decade, yet I only knew parts of him. Now, I'm getting the opportunity to know Rex as a complete person. Not just a father and a hero, but a man. Someone with insecurities and dreams and raw desires.

We enjoyed hanging out the night of the gala. But my time with Rex in this house has proven what great chemistry we have together. Not just romantically but as friends.

And the sexual chemistry? Off the freaking charts.

I've always admired Rex's upstanding, heroic qualities. It's hard not to. He's so honorable. The kind of man who stands up for justice, which matters to me. But when it comes to sex, I had no clue he could be so down and dirty.

And I love it.

Rex seems to enjoy ordering me around, and I've got to admit, I'm into it too. I might prefer taking command in my real life, especially in my job. But in bed? Rex's dominance takes over, and my submissive side comes to the forefront. We're perfectly matched. At least, I think we are. The hot-as-fire things we did together on this couch, just a few hours ago, suggest that's true.

I'm excited to put my theory to the test later in the bedroom. I want a lot more than trading orgasms. I'm ready for him to *wreck* me.

I squirm against him just thinking about it.

But just as wonderful are moments like this. When there's a sense of calm between us, and Rex is affectionate and protective. Can it always be like this? I don't know. Reality will inevitably intrude, dragging us back to our regular lives. The Printz trial will end, and Rex will have his own work and responsibilities aside from guarding me.

I just hope that we can find this same connection when we're back in West Oaks. Because I can't imagine feeling this way with any other man.

Maybe he's already wrecked me, I realize. After having just a taste of Rex, I know for sure I'll never want anyone else.

"WAKE UP, GORGEOUS." KISSES LAND ON MY forehead and cheek. "Time to get up."

I stretch and yawn, not yet opening my eyes. "This is a great way to wake up, you know. Whoever invents the kissing alarm clock will make a fortune."

He chuckles and then pokes my side.

I yelp. "Hey!" My eyes pop open. "What happened to the gentle kissing?"

"Wasn't working. You told me not to let you sleep too long. I have plans for you." He's sitting on the couch. He must've sneaked away at some point during my nap. He's added a T-shirt instead of just rocking those sexy gray sweats.

"Why did you put a shirt on?"

"I was doing prep work in the kitchen. Some people consider chest hair in their food to be unappetizing."

I snort. "I've never been that picky," I joke.

He pinches my chin playfully. "Yet another new thing I'm learning about you. Gotta say, I'm concerned."

I jump up and pounce on him, straddling his lap. "You're

into me. Admit it. You like my weirdness." He gives me a deep, sexy kiss, lots of tongue. I probably don't taste great after my nap, but he doesn't seem to mind.

"I do like it," he murmurs. "I like every moment with you."

After a few more kisses, Rex makes us get up and go to the kitchen. So bossy, this one.

He's got a bunch of bowls already set out, some with chopped vegetables and other ingredients. "We're making a stir fry. I called in an order for supplies, and one of my guys dropped it off while you were asleep."

"Yum. But do I have to put on more clothes for this?" I point at the T-shirt with cut-off sides I'm still wearing. It's not actually covering that much of me.

"Definitely not." He winks. "You're the dessert."

"And your lines are terrible. But I like it." I wrap my arms around his neck. "'Cause I'm into you, too."

We're both smiling like idiots, and it's the best thing ever.

Rex asks me to make jasmine rice in the rice cooker, while he slices up steak and assembles the other veggies. It's not a complicated meal, yet it takes us far longer to finish because we keep taking breaks to kiss, or joke around, or cop feels.

Finally we get our dinner on the table. Rex lights a tea candle in the middle, and we sit side-by-side, our seats close enough that we're pressed together. He pours a couple of glasses of wine too. Half a glass for me, since I'm trying to avoid alcohol as my concussion heals.

"I don't think I've ever enjoyed making dinner that much," I say. I nudge his knee with mine. "You're a lot of fun, Easton."

He lifts an eyebrow and takes a bite of rice. "Am I? A lot of people would be surprised to hear you say that. Especially Cliff. I have a reputation for being the most boring guy in the room."

"What? You can be quiet at times, but quiet doesn't equal boring. You're the strong, silent type. But you can loosen up, too. I always have fun with you. I don't just mean now that we're...more."

"I guess you bring out that side of me. Having fun with you is easy." He brushes his thumb over my cheekbone, smiling fondly. "What you and I have is different from anything else I've had before. But it feels...big. That's something I recognize."

I can't say anything for a few minutes. There's just too much inside me.

"I know it's happening fast," he says.

"Fast?" I sputter. "For me, it feels like ten years."

He grins and laughs. "Okay, fair enough. What I mean is that this new dynamic between us is developing quickly. But I'm in this with you. I want to follow wherever it goes. For as long as you want it."

Forever, I want to blurt out. But that seems like too much, even with the romantic, wonderful things he's saying. "Me too," I say instead.

We finish up dinner. "I've got strawberry shortcake for dessert," he says. "You always ordered it at that restaurant we used to go to with Cliff."

"Sounds delicious. But I thought *I* was the dessert."

His eyes do that molten-fire thing they do as his gaze travels down my body. "If you want to be. You're certainly sweet enough. But we don't have to rush."

I lean closer, placing my hand on his thigh. "Ten years, Rex. *Ten. Years.*"

He cracks up. "All right. I'm getting the picture."

"You said you'd fulfill all my needs."

"But I didn't realize you'd be so demanding about it," he teases. He pecks my lips, then gets up. "I'll wash the dishes, and then I have a few things to do in the bedroom."

"Watching you do the dishes sounds surprisingly erotic, but I can pull my own weight. Division of labor. That will be much faster." He clearly has more planned for tonight, and I'm impatient to find out.

Rex disappears into the main bedroom, and I handle the dishes and the mess in the kitchen. I'm about to knock on the door to hurry him up when he steps into the main room. Soft music is playing from inside.

He tilts his head in a silent, beckoning gesture. It's so quietly commanding. So *him*. Desire tingles up and down my body as I walk toward him. Rex steps aside in the doorway, giving me just enough room to pass by.

The overhead lights are dimmed in the main bedroom, and candles flicker on the tables and dresser. Sultry jazz music plays from his phone. Rex links our fingers together, drawing me closer to the bed, where there's a vase with long-stemmed white and yellow roses on the nightstand.

"You did all this for me?"

"Sure. You deserve it. I requested the flowers in today's delivery." He says this like it's no big deal. And maybe it didn't take him that long to set this up, but it means a lot to me. I don't think anyone has ever bought me flowers. Even my corsage on prom night, I bought myself. Tears prick my eyes.

"No one has ever done anything like this for me."

Rex pulls me so I'm in front of him, my back to his chest, and he wraps his arms around my waist. "You've brought beauty and joy into my life again. It's like I've been asleep for all these years, and I finally woke up and saw what was right in front of me." He kisses my neck. "I'm thankful you waited for me." His voice is thick with emotion now.

My heart is so full. "I thought it was hopeless. I tried to stop feeling the way I do for you, but it didn't work. I'm glad it didn't."

"I hate to think you were hurting because of me."

I turn around and pull him down for a kiss. "It was worth it. So worth it. I get to have you."

"We have each other." He kisses me again, even slower than before. His lips skim the surface of mine. "But Quinn, you can still say no to me. Whatever we do together tonight, it's your choice. I'd be satisfied just being near you. I'm yours already."

"Thank you for saying that. But I want all of you. Including all the naughty bits."

He laughs. "You sure about that?"

"Very." I nip his bearded chin with my teeth. "I've seen glimpses of your darker side, but I want to know just how bad you can be, Rex Easton."

His nostrils flare. "I hope that's not a challenge."

I shrug one shoulder. "You can say no."

"Such a tease. What will I do with you?" His fingers grip the back of my neck, and his teeth catch my lower lip. Then his tongue smooths over the sting. "Get naked and get on the bed. Face down. Legs spread."

Oh, wow. I shiver at the commanding tone in his voice. "Yes, Rex."

I back away from him toward the bed, unable to tear myself from his gaze. He's never looked more like a predator. But this is a safe kind of thrill. I trust Rex more than anyone in the entire world. No one has ever shown me such care. We're guaranteed to have fun together, but despite his warnings, I know he would never come close to going too far with me.

He's one of the best men I've ever known. His goodness is clear to anyone who meets him.

But this sexy, sinful side? It's all for me.

First, I slide my panties off and kick them aside. I kneel

on the mattress to pull the shirt over my head. After tossing it to the rug, I turn around on all fours.

He makes a low, rumbly sound as I stretch out on my stomach.

Rex gets onto the bed beside me. He takes my hands and moves them until they're up near my head, elbows bent so it's not a strain. "Keep your arms like this," he says. "Don't move unless you get uncomfortable."

"Okay."

"If your head hurts at all, tell me. Or if you feel dizzy and need to stop or need a different position."

"I will."

Next he grabs a pillow and tucks it beneath my hips to prop them up. He pushes on my inner thighs to spread them a little wider. For a long minute, he kneels at the end of the bed and doesn't do anything else.

I turn my head to the side. "Getting a good look?"

"Hell yeah, I am. This is a great view. I don't want to miss out."

I snicker. "Not fair. I want to see you."

"Soon." Rex gets up to grab a tube of lotion from the nightstand beside the roses. "I'm going to give you a massage," he says. "If anything doesn't feel good, tell me."

After warming the lotion in his hands, he spreads it over my shoulders, somehow zeroing in on the very spots where I hold the most tension. I sigh contentedly as his thumbs work at the knots in my muscles. The lotion is rosewater scented. Subtle and delicate. His rough, strong hands knead my lower back, then my arms and legs. And as he does, he drops kisses onto my bare skin.

He leans toward the nightstand again. And then something impossibly soft brushes my skin. "Mmmm. What is that?" I ask.

"Guess."

He brings whatever it is up along my spine, then across each shoulder. The scent of rose gets stronger, and I realize it's one of the flowers. He touches it to my nose, confirming my suspicion. "That's nice," I say.

"That's the idea."

It feels amazing. Smoother than velvet, warmer and softer than leather. I've never been into the idea of rose petals on a bed. But this is *heaven*. Goosebumps and tingles dance across my skin wherever the rosebud touches. Then Rex's lips and rougher whiskers as he kisses the same spots. I get lost in a relaxing sort of trance.

But when he sets the rose aside and his fingers trail closer to the cleft between my legs, my awareness zeroes in. My heartbeat quickens. My clit throbs, and I feel arousal dripping from me in anticipation.

His fingers sweep closer. Closer. "This okay?" he asks.

"Don't you dare stop."

He finally slides his fingertip into my opening. It's still a tease, but I whimper at the relief of friction. "I have lube, but you don't need it," he rasps. "You're soaking. You're desperate for me to touch you, aren't you?"

"*Yes.*"

He spreads my wetness over my labia. My clit. I moan shamelessly as he massages my most sensitive places. But I still want more. I wiggle my hips, and he presses his body against me to keep me in place. His erection is long and hard against my thigh through the fabric of his sweatpants.

Just when I get close, the pressure of his fingers turns feather-light and ultra-slow. "No," I whine. "Not enough."

He huffs a small, smug laugh. "You've waited ten years. You can wait a little longer. It'll be worth it."

"You're evil." I finally see his sadistic plan. He's torturing me with slow, drawn-out pleasure.

Rex gets me close again. And stops. *Again*. But before I

can complain, he tugs my hips up a bit more, my back arching.

And then I feel his hot, wet tongue.

I cry out, grasping the sheets in my fists. He's tonguing my clit from behind. Somehow my body is even more responsive from this angle, because the sensations are driving me wild. He licks my opening before pushing his tongue inside. I can't control the desperate sounds I'm making. It's too good.

Rex holds my hips in his rough grip and fucks me with his tongue. Sucks on my clit. And I fall apart. Moaning and shaking. The orgasm is almost violent, it's so overwhelming.

When I can think again, Rex is lying beside me, cradling me in his arms. He kisses my forehead. "Was that too much? You okay?"

"I'm…yes."

He grins. "Yes, that was too much?"

"No, it was perfect. We should do that every day after breakfast."

"Might be difficult with our schedules when we're back to work, but I'll see what I can do."

We're joking around, but I like that idea. Waking up with him. Having our routine. Our life together. Is that too much to hope for yet? Can Rex possibly be feeling as much as I am right now? I don't mean the orgasm. I mean this connection. The way my heart jumps when I look at him.

I want more. I want to make him feel as incredible as he did me.

My hand presses against the hard cock in his sweatpants. "Tell me what to do next. Let me make you feel good." I lick my lower lip. "Please?"

"I want you to ride my cock."

I nod vigorously. "Yes. Definitely that."

He reaches behind his head to fist his shirt, pulling it off. Lying down again, he orders, "Take off my sweats."

Smiling coyly, I hook his waistband with my fingers and inch them down over his hips, while Rex lifts up to help me. His swollen cock pops out. He wasn't wearing underwear. Very nice. I discard the sweats over the side of the bed. He leans over to open the nightstand drawer and fishes out a condom.

Rex holds out the foil packet. "Put this on me."

Oh, I like this. I climb over him, straddling his thighs. I make a show of tearing open the wrapper and rolling the condom down his shaft. It's possible I stroke him a little more than necessary to make sure it's in place. "What next?"

He bends his elbows and puts his hands behind his head, relaxing. "Put me inside you. Nice and slow. Show me how much you've been dying for this cock."

"I *have* been dying for it."

And I have never had this much fun in bed. He's giving me that devious grin I'm really starting to appreciate. Who knew Rex was so dirty?

I do as he said. I hold his cock, position my opening at his tip, and start working him inside of me. I gasp at the first pressure of him breaching me. His hands fly to my hips.

"That's it," he coos. "Just like that."

Once I'm fully seated, he runs his hands over my legs and stomach. I bend forward to kiss him. My hair falls across his shoulder, and he cups the back of my neck, holding me there.

Rex is inside me. Finally.

"How're you feeling?" he asks.

"Incredible." I move my hips, loving the way he's filling me.

"Is it as good as you hoped it would be?"

"So much better."

"For me too. I had dreams about this. You riding me."

I suck in a breath, sitting up slightly, and we both moan at the movement of our bodies against each other. I'm ultra-sensitive. "When did you dream about me?"

Rex pulls me close again. His chest hair tickles my breasts. "Started a few weeks ago." He nips at my mouth. "Wanted you so much. And now you're mine."

"You didn't have to wait as long as I did," I point out wryly.

"Didn't I?" He brushes my hair back from my forehead to see me better. "For years, I didn't want to admit how lonely I was. I was…treading water. Told myself I wasn't ready to find someone new, but I think maybe I *was* waiting. I just didn't know I was waiting for *you*."

When I rock against him, the movement is deep and steady. Rex's fingers press into the flesh of my hips. Our eyes stay locked. I want to remember everything about this. Every word he said.

After a while, he rolls us over so he's on top of me, but we don't break our rhythm. I wrap my legs around his waist. His thick cock strokes inside my channel again and again, so much pleasure I can't think straight. He takes my hand and presses my palm flat to his chest. As if he wants me to feel how hard his heart is beating for me.

He rolls us again. I'm back on top, but he's fully in charge this time. Moving my body against him. Building up the perfect amount of friction I need. "*Rex*, I'm…*oh*…"

"I'm close too. Let me hear you come. That'll push me over the edge."

I gasp and moan as I climax, and his fingers tighten on my hips, digging in. He shouts, and his cock pulses inside me. We keep rocking against each other, trading open-mouthed kisses as the most intense pleasure I've ever experienced courses through me.

Is it possible to be this happy and make it last? I have to

believe it. Because I don't want to lose this exact, perfect feeling.

I'm in love.

I'm in love with Rex. The realization takes my breath. At times over the past ten years, I thought I might love him, but I didn't truly know him. Not the way I do now. I know how devoted he is. How funny and sweet and sexy too. I know his doubts and his secret loneliness. How he makes love.

Now, I know exactly what's at stake if I lose him.

19

Rex

When I wake up, I feel Quinn snuggled against my side. Her breathing is deep and regular. I open my eyes, and there she is. Golden hair spread over my pillow. Long eyelashes and pouty lips. Vibrant even in sleep.

She's the first woman I've ever had in this bed.

We've started something real. I just wish I could see where it's going.

Moving carefully so I don't jostle her, I reach for my phone and check my messages. It's later than I realized. Quinn and I slept in. But then again, we were up late. My morning wood stiffens as I think about what we did.

After that first round of lovemaking, we got up and made strawberry shortcake. We fed each other, kissing between bites. And then I fucked her against the kitchen counter.

I want her again. I can't get enough.

But I'm going to let her sleep. I tried not to be too rough with her last night, and she's still recovering.

I don't have any new messages from Bennett or West Oaks PD. There's a missed call and text from Cliff. Looks like he was up early this morning. The preview of his text says, *Hey Dad, how's Quinn? I just wanted to…*

Clearly it's not urgent. So I don't open the message or listen to his voicemail. Immediately, I feel like an asshole. Before this thing with Quinn, I would've been eager to hear anything from Cliff. It's rare enough that he contacts me instead of me having to hound him.

But I'm naked in bed with his friend, and my conscience is nagging at me. I just want to set that aside for now. I'll figure out how to handle Cliff later. Soon. Just not yet. Not when Quinn and I are so new. It's perfect now, what we have. What we're starting to build. I look over at her and warmth fills my chest.

I've felt tenderness toward Quinn for years. This extra element to our relationship is a shift. A seismic one. Yet that deep affection is still there at the core of my feelings for her. It would be easy to keep on falling. Let this take me over completely. It should be scary to risk my heart like that again, knowing how it feels to lose everything. But stopping this would be even worse. I can't go back to being half-alive. Quinn makes me whole again.

There's no way this can stay a secret for long, nor do I want it to. Lark knows, and I'm pretty sure Sylvie and Angela do too. The rumors are likely spreading through my bodyguard team after that delivery of roses I requested yesterday. Luckily none of them are close to my son.

But I have this thread of worry that telling Cliff too soon will break the bubble of happiness we're in. As if he'll point out all the reasons that Quinn shouldn't want me. The ways I'm not enough.

And then she'll come to her senses and call this off.

"Are you staring at me?" she asks sleepily, her eyes still closed. "It feels like you're staring at me."

I turn onto my side and drape my arm over her. I press a

kiss to her forehead. Then one to her nose. "Just your kissing wake-up service. As requested."

The dazzling smile she gives me when she opens her eyes steals my breath. "Morning."

"How's your head?"

"I wish you would stop asking me that. Answer's the same as yesterday."

Which means she feels pretty good, but not one hundred percent yet. Would she tell me if she felt worse after last night? "I can't help it. It's my job to take care of you."

"I like the other ways you take care of me." Quinn shifts so her bare ass is up against my crotch, and she wiggles closer. A clear invitation.

"Are you sure you feel up to that?" I ask. "I had you up late."

"If you're up to it, then I am. Come on, old man. I think you're making excuses."

With a growl, I pounce on her. Gently, of course. I thrust my erection against her cheeks. Quinn turns her head to kiss me, both of us too aroused to worry about morning breath. Soon, I've got a condom on and I'm sliding into her tight, wet heat from behind as we lie on our sides. Quinn's eyelids are heavy with lust as she looks over her shoulder at me. Her whimpers, our heavy breathing, and the slick sound of our bodies meeting heighten the experience.

"Touch me," she begs.

I trail my hand down her stomach and between her legs to play with her clit. My fingers feel the pressure of my cock pumping inside her. I'm not trying to draw this out. I'm too worked up. She comes undone quickly, her cries muffled by my tongue in her mouth, and a few hard and fast thrusts later, I follow her. Pleasure shoots like lightning as my balls empty into the condom.

We lie there, catching our breaths.

"Before the last couple of days," she says, "I thought sex wasn't as amazing as people talk it up to be. Now I see what they're always going on about."

Chuckling, I drop kisses all over the side of her face. "I thought I could live without it, too. I *was* living without it. But with you, I just want more every time."

"Let's stay in bed all day."

"I would love that."

I don't know how many more times I can come today. But my body has been rising to the challenge so far. Pun intended. It's like Quinn is infusing me with her energy and vibrance. I've got to keep up with her. My ego won't allow anything else.

An unexpected sound reaches my ears, and I sit up rapidly.

I think that was the front door opening.

And then the quiet beeps of someone pushing buttons on the Bennett Security alarm panel. There's only one person who knows my code to disarm the system. Only one person with a key to this house.

Quinn's eyes are wide. She's realized something is up too. But we don't have a chance to do anything. Footsteps cross the small main room. Then Cliff's voice rings out.

"Dad? Are you here? Quinn's room is empty. Where is she?"

Quinn vaults out of my bed. "What do we do?" she hisses.

I'm cursing myself inside my head, but now is not the time to panic. I get up and grab my sweats from the floor, trying to think.

My son raps loudly on the door a few feet away.

Fine, I might be panicking a little.

"Dad?"

"I'm here," I choke out. "Just a second. Everything's fine."

"But Quinn..." Cliff's voice trails off, turning strange at the end. Like he might be having a realization.

I glance at the state of my bedroom. Sheets in a tangled mess, condom wrappers on the floor, roses and candles everywhere. The moment I open that door, it's going to be obvious what happened in here. Wouldn't take a cop to put together these clues.

And my son *is* a cop.

Fuck.

Quinn pulls me into the en suite bathroom. "Here's what we'll do," she says. "I'll pretend I was feeling really awful, and you were taking care of me. You had to sleep in here to keep an eye on me. Hide the trash and the flowers under the bed."

I'm shaking my head. "Quinn, I don't—"

"It'll work. Just go with it. I'll fix this." She goes to grab some clothes out of her suitcase. I put a shirt on. Once we're dressed, I turn her to face me, resting my hands on either side of her waist.

"I am not going to lie. Cliff deserves better than that, and so do you. I'll tell him the truth."

"But I don't want him to be mad at you," she whispers.

I can't stand the look of guilt on her face. This is my fault. I never should've let something like this happen, and it was all too foreseeable. I've been an idiot. Cliff probably called and texted this morning to let me know he was on his way. Why didn't I just read the damn message?

Because I was avoiding him. Like a man with something to hide.

"I'm not going to treat you like a shameful secret," I say. "I made my choices. It's time to accept the consequences."

She frowns, but nods resignedly. "I'm coming with you. It was my choice too."

We go to the door. I hold my breath and open it while Quinn stands just behind me, looking past my shoulder.

Cliff is leaning against the wall opposite, arms crossed, a cautious expression on his face. He looks from Quinn to me. From our disheveled state, it's clear we just got out of bed.

Before I can say anything, Quinn asks, "What are you doing here?"

"I wanted to come see how you're doing. I called when I was on my way. What's up? Q, why are you in my dad's room?"

Her nose scrunches. "So, um, the thing is—"

I can't let her take responsibility for this. I look at her sternly. "I need to do this. Okay?"

She nods, glancing at the floor.

"What is going on?" Cliff demands.

"Quinn and I are together."

"What?"

He still seems confused. Maybe he just doesn't want to believe the evidence in front of him. Guess I'll have to spell this out, even though it feels like peeling back my skin.

I step out of the doorway, keeping her behind me. "We're involved. She spent the night with me."

"But you…she's…"

"We're having sex," Quinn blurts out. "Get it now?"

My son goes from confusion to shock to rage in a moment. "The *fuck*?"

I grip his shoulder and march him toward the patio doors. "Let's discuss this outside." If Cliff needs to vent, I don't want Quinn to hear it.

She starts to follow. "I'm coming too."

"No, you're not," I say firmly. "We'll be back."

I slide open the patio door, push my son through, and close it behind me. It's a gorgeous morning. Or midday, really. The sun is high. Bright enough I have to squint.

Cliff is glaring at me with disgust. "Please tell me she was kidding."

"No. It's true."

He explodes. "You had *sex with Quinn*? What the fuck, Dad? What fucking universe is this?"

I flinch, resting my hands on my hips. I figured this could be bad, but no. It's worse.

Cliff is digging his fingers into his hair, pacing the patio. "I don't get this. Why? What possessed you? She's young enough to be your daughter!"

I'm ready to accept his ire, but he's going a little far. "She's twenty-eight. We're both adults. We have feelings for each other."

"Since *when*? How long has this been going on?"

"Not long at all. I've had romantic feelings for Quinn for close to a month, I guess. We got together only recently."

"So it's about you being her bodyguard? You thought that's what I meant when I asked you to look out for her? Or was it just convenient?"

Ouch. I suppose I deserved that. But Quinn doesn't. "This is serious for us. Protecting her brought us closer, made me see what I'd been too dense to realize before. That I care for her very deeply. Quinn means so much to me."

He scoffs. "Only you could make sleeping with your client sound heroic."

"What does that mean?"

Cliff shakes his head. "Forget it. So you're her boyfriend now? Do you have any idea how ridiculous that sounds? What do you have to offer her? She wants to have a family. You're suddenly going to start over? Try to get it right the second time around?"

It's nothing I haven't thought before myself. But hearing Cliff say it is pretty brutal. "All of that is between Quinn and me. I understand that you're angry, and you have a right to be. I should have warned you. But you're reacting emotionally and—"

"Of course you would say that. I'm the fuck-up, and you're the stoic warrior. The chivalrous hero. Even now, after what you've done, *I'm* the problem."

"I didn't say that."

"Do you know how obnoxious it is to have Rex Easton as my father? I'm constantly compared to you, and I always come up lacking."

"What are you talking about?" I have no idea where this is coming from. "I don't see you that way."

"Never mind. It's nothing." He starts to walk toward the beach.

I follow him onto the sand. "Cliff, if you need to say something to me, do it. I want to know what you meant. Please. I want to understand."

He whirls around. Cliff's jaw clenches a few times.

And then, the floodgates open.

"Do you have any idea what it was like when I was a kid? You were deployed somewhere on the other side of the world, and I was supposed to get on the phone with you and act like everything was fine. Like Mom and I were doing great without you. You expected me to be as strong and perfect as you were, and I was constantly failing. It sucked when you were gone. Okay? I know how selfish that sounds, but I hated it."

"Son, that's okay. I didn't expect perfection of you. You were a little kid."

"But I felt like I was supposed to be better. I was supposed to be more like you. And after mom died, I was supposed to get it together and stuff down my emotions."

"You think that's what *I* did? I was a mess."

"Were you?" Cliff asks. "Because you never showed that to me."

God, didn't I? Was I trying so hard to be strong for my son that I hid my grief from him? Made him feel guilty for his?

Quinn saw me at some of my weakest moments when she was helping us get through those awful days. But did Cliff?

"Even at the police academy," he says, "I got questions about my Green Beret dad who now worked with Max Bennett guarding celebrities. And let's not forget, rebuilding disaster areas on the side. My instructors got this look on their faces when they saw my scores, like they couldn't figure out how the son of Rex Easton was so damn mediocre."

"I can't imagine that's true. You did well. You should be proud of yourself. I'm proud of you."

Cliff goes on like he didn't hear me. "I figured out how to be satisfied with what I could do, even if I could never measure up. Maybe I wasn't superhero material, wasn't going to be a SWAT sergeant or chief of police, but at least I had my friends. I had a life that was mine. I had Quinn, standing by me no matter what. But now, once again, I'm coming in second place to you."

My stomach churns. "Are you saying you have romantic feelings for her? What about Lia?"

"No, it's not like that with Quinn. I think of her like she's my sister, which makes this even creepier. But that's not even the point! It's the fact that you decided, out of all the women in the world, to fuck *my best friend*!"

Cliff's chest heaves.

I'm reeling. Sick to my stomach. What can I say to all of that? Did I really fail him that badly?

At least I can explain what happened with Quinn.

"I didn't fall for her intentionally. When I realized how I felt about Quinn, I tried to deny it and ignore it. I didn't want to risk hurting you."

Cliff snorts. "Sure. But you still did it. Would you have told me at all if I hadn't shown up today?"

"I was planning to, yes. I was waiting for the right time. But I see that was a mistake. I've made a lot of them. It seems like you had a lot you needed to say to me that has nothing to do with Quinn, and I should've made it easier for you to talk to me."

Cliff scoffs and looks away. I don't know what caused this fresh offense. But I keep going. Trying to say what I need to say, even if I'm messing this up.

"I tried to put a lid on what I was feeling for Quinn, but I couldn't stop it. Then I found out Quinn feels the same way about me. Neither of us wanted to upset you, but we had a chance at being happy together. I know firsthand how rare that is."

"I guess," he mutters.

"Can we talk about the rest of what you said? How you feel…less than me? Because I have never, ever, felt that way about you."

"I can't right now, Dad. I need some time to process this. I didn't even mean to say all that. It just came out."

"I'm glad it did. I want you to know how much I love you. You and I are different, but that's okay. I'm sorry that I haven't been more clear about my feelings, but I'm so fucking proud of who you are."

Cliff doesn't acknowledge what I've said.

He walks back to the patio, slides open the door, and goes inside instead.

"Damn it," I mutter, dropping my head into my hands.

I've screwed up with him. Not just lately, but for years.

And now, maybe my words are too little, too late.

20

Quinn

Cliff is yelling at his father on the patio, and it takes everything in me to stay inside and not defend him. This is my fault as much as Rex's.

I busy myself with making breakfast and coffee instead. I find a canvas tote on the ground, which I assume Cliff brought with him. It holds a box of my favorite apple fritters from Westside Donuts.

Then I sit at the dining table, sipping a cup of coffee and catching up on email until Cliff comes inside. He glances at me, then quickly away.

"What happened out there?" I ask.

"I said some really shitty things to my dad. And I already feel bad about it." He stuffs his hands in his jeans pockets.

I glance at the patio. Rex is sitting out there, staring at the ocean. I have the feeling he'll stay there for a while. "Are you going to go apologize?"

"Not right now."

I roll my eyes.

"I can't even talk to you about this, can I?" Cliff asks. "You're going to take his side."

"I'm not on anyone's side. But you're still my best friend. I'm not giving up that title." I point at the box on the counter. "Want a fritter?"

He pulls up a chair and starts pulling one of the pastries apart. "I can't believe you and my dad…"

"I know. Me neither. I should have broken the news with more subtlety." I grimace, remembering what I said. "You just weren't getting the picture."

"It did, but it shocked me. I didn't mean to yell. Especially around you."

"You don't hate me for seducing your dad?"

"*Ew*. I will hate you if you keep saying things like that."

We look at each other. I smile first, then Cliff cracks. We both start giggling.

"This isn't funny," he says. "I don't know why I'm laughing."

"Better than the alternative." I take another bite of fritter, and then I blurt out, "I kissed Rex first."

"I don't want details."

"I get that. But I need you to know that he didn't push me into anything." It's hard to get this out, because it's been my secret for so long, but I have to. "I've had feelings for Rex for a long time. Years."

"What? How many years?"

"Since senior year of high school."

He gapes at me. "And you didn't say anything to me?"

"You wanted me to tell you I had the hots for your dad?"

"On second thought, gross. All right, I see why you didn't say anything. I may have overreacted today. It's just so weird."

"It isn't weird to me. It feels right. Like I'm finally where I belong. For what it's worth, Rex has been amazing to me. He's been protecting me and taking care of me. I couldn't ask for a better bodyguard."

Cliff's eyes lift to the ceiling. "I get it. He's the perfect hero. I'm the asshole."

"Your words, not mine."

"No, you know how it is. Everybody admires my dad. It's always been that way. I barely scrape by, while he's running laps around me. I don't blame you for being into him. Do you know how many teachers used to ask if my dad was single?"

I make a face. We both laugh, more genuinely this time.

"The thing is, he is a hero. When I was a kid, he was *my* hero. Why else do you think I became a cop? I wanted to help people like he does. I just suck at it."

"You're a great cop and an amazing best friend. Do you remember the time you went and bought me tampons because I was home alone with terrible cramps and had nobody else to ask? Or the time I had the flu, and you made homemade chicken soup? You forgot the salt, but it was the thought that counted."

"Had to mention that part."

I squeeze his hand. "You've taken care of me plenty of times. And the rest of our friends too. You're the guy we can always count on if we need someone. You're more like your dad than you give yourself credit for."

"I need to tell you something." He blinks a few times. "I'm thinking about quitting West Oaks PD."

"Yeah?" This isn't a complete shock to me. Cliff gets along great with the other patrol officers, and I know his superiors love him for his dedication. But he's told me before that he doesn't feel passionate about it. Doesn't really feel like he fits there.

"I think what I really want to do is go back to school. I'm interested in social work." He exhales. "You're only the second person I've told that after Lia. Feels good to say it. I know going back for a new degree will be hard. I wasn't that great in school the first time around." His eyes light up. "But

I work with social workers all the time. I see how they help people solve problems in a more direct way. Especially with kids. I think I'd be good at that."

"I think so too." Cliff is a people person. Easy to talk to. That's been a great quality for him on patrol because he gets along well with people in the community. But I can also see how that would translate into social work, and he'll be able to put that skill to use in a different way. One that he feels more in tune with.

"But I'm terrified to tell my dad. I don't want him to be disappointed in me."

"Why would he be?"

"Because I'm quitting. I'm choosing to sit at a desk instead of carrying a gun."

"Lots of cops work a desk."

"You know what I mean. He was a Green Beret. His whole career has been about kicking ass."

I snort a laugh. "And looking hot while doing it?"

"You're not my best friend anymore."

I playfully punch his shoulder. "I'm pretty sure I understand what you're saying. But you should give Rex a chance. That's all I'm going to say, because I don't want to dictate your relationship with him. That's not my place. But I promise, he wants you to be happy."

"I want that for you too. My dad makes you happy?"

"Happier than I've ever been in my life."

He sighs. "My dad seemed like he wanted to listen. I give him credit for that. I *will* talk to him. I just can't handle it yet. I don't want to say anything else to him that I can't take back. This has been a lot."

"Want a hug?"

"That's still okay?"

"Don't be a dumbass." I open my arms, and he gives me a bear hug. Same one I've been getting from Cliff since high school. It ends in a noogie on the top of my head, because he's matured *so much.*

"I love you," I say.

"I love you too. We've been through a ton together. I've thought of you as family for a long time. Stepmom is family, right?" He cringes. "Nah, I'm not ready for that yet. But I'll get there, okay? Just give me some time."

The thought of being Cliff's stepmom is *a lot.* I'm not ready for that either. But…I could definitely get there. If Rex wants that.

I give Cliff another hug goodbye. I ask if he'll stay for a while longer to hang out, hoping that he'll get another chance to talk with Rex, but Cliff insists that should be another day. He takes off. But I'm left feeling lighter. He and Rex still have a bunch of issues to figure out, which is up to them. I can't micromanage their father-son communications. But I'm hopeful they'll talk and be better for it.

Then I see the dejected look on Rex's face outside, and my heart squeezes. I need to give him a sense of what Cliff said. Not betraying my best friend's confidence, but I have no doubt I can share some of it.

I'm about to head outside when my phone makes a noise on the table. I go to check it. It's a new text from Sylvie.

> We found the chauffeur. I've got Pete Diamond's contact info for you. And get this. He's in West Oaks.

21

Rex

I sit and watch wave after wave crash into shore. At the same time, the things my son said keep repeating in my brain.

What do you have to offer her?

And the rest of it. All the ways I failed as a father. I've known that I could do better, that I wasn't the best at communicating with him. But I had no clue he felt like I wanted him to hide his emotions. To project some fake, idealized image.

I have no idea how long I sit there. But finally, the door slides open, and Quinn steps out. My chest tightens with nerves. But she's got a small, hesitant smile. Which can't be all bad.

"Is Cliff still here?" I ask.

"He decided he should go for now. But we talked. It's going to be okay."

I'm sitting in an oversized patio chair, and Quinn comes over to lower herself down into my lap. She wraps her arms around my neck and kisses me. It's sweet and tender. The kind of kiss that's not intended to lead to more. But it's a balm to my soul.

"Cliff is sorry about what he said."

I should be happy to hear that, but my stomach drops even further. "Did he tell you what he thinks of me?"

"Not exactly. He admits he overreacted, though."

"He made some decent points. Quinn, I'm not perfect. I would never claim to be. I messed up with Cliff. It's entirely possible I'll mess up with you."

She pushes her forehead against mine. "I don't want perfect. Perfect is boring, and you're the furthest thing from that. To me, anyway. But you're devoted. I've always known that about you. Even before I really knew you, like I do now. That's how I know everything will be okay with Cliff eventually. I know you'll never stop trying because that's the kind of man you are. The kind of father. Cliff is lucky to have you."

"And I am damn lucky to have you."

After a couple more kisses, Quinn sits back. "I wish we could go back to bed and spend all day there. But I have news." She shows me the message from Sylvie and the contact info for Pete Diamond. "Do you still have the burner phone from Sylvie that we used to initially contact the secret witness?"

"Sure. I was holding onto it. It's in my bag."

We go inside. After some food and coffee, which I was desperately needing, we set up at the dining table. Quinn holds the burner in her hands, contemplating what she'll write to the chauffeur.

"Are you going to let Lana know you're contacting him?" I ask.

"I will. But I don't want to waste any time getting in touch. Nobody knew where this guy was, and who knows if he'll stay in West Oaks or go somewhere else. If he's the witness, I have to try to get him to talk to me. And find out why he cut off contact and disappeared."

I rest my arm on the back of Quinn's chair as she types out her opening message to Diamond.

Mr. Diamond, my name is Quinn Ainsley. We met before. I'm one of the district attorneys on the Amber Printz case. I was hoping we could chat.

How did you get this number?

"He's skittish," I say.

"Figures."

From a reliable source who will be discreet. As can I. Do you have time to meet today? I've been trying to reach you for a while.

There's a long wait. Quinn drums her fingers impatiently on the table. I massage her shoulder.

Finally, Diamond writes back.

I can meet you at the Sunset Cafe. 3 PM.

I'll see you then.

Quinn looks over at me, smiling triumphantly. "One step closer. Either he's the witness I've been looking for, or he has something else we can use. I'm going to hope for the best."

That's something I like about her. But when it comes to Quinn's safety, I can't operate based on hope. I have to plan for the worst-case scenario.

I might be the man she shares her bed with. Maybe even her significant other, if I get to use that title. But this afternoon, I'm back to being her full-time bodyguard.

Anyone who intends to harm Quinn will have to do it over my dead body.

~

Pete Diamond looks like shit.

When we walk into the diner, there's only one guy who matches his description. His eyes are bloodshot, his hair is disheveled, and his clothes look like he hasn't changed them in a few days. The guy is glancing back and forth and startles when he sees us.

He's the very definition of squirrelly, and I don't like it.

But this isn't my call. Quinn is determined to find out what this guy knows. Still, I outright refused to let her go in here alone. She gave up that argument pretty easily, probably guessing that this was one of those times that I wouldn't back down.

Quinn slides into the booth across from Pete. I sit down beside her. The guy stiffens, eyeing me. "Who is he? Doesn't look like a lawyer."

"He's my bodyguard. Amber has been encouraging her fans to go after the DAs prosecuting her case. Especially me."

He looks at his hands. "Yeah, no kidding. I've heard. When Amber Printz wants to get rid of you, that's not a good place to be."

"Speaking from experience?" Quinn asks.

He shifts around in his seat. "Look, why did you contact me?"

A server comes over, and Quinn orders a milkshake and fries. Pete is hesitant, but then he orders the same. Quinn smiles at him and folds her hands on the table in that disarming manner she has.

"I've been following up on some things in preparation for the trial." She nods at me. "Rex and I went to Los Angeles to speak with Christian Hayworth, and I found out he'd sent you to Nevada. Why is that?"

Pete hunches over in his seat. His eyes dart around the diner. "If I talk to you, I need to know I can trust you."

She leans in, mirroring his posture. "You can trust us both. If you need protection, I can arrange that. And I can talk to DA Marchetti about immunity, depending on what you tell me. But you have to talk to me, Pete. It's clear you're going through something, and I want to help. But I can't help unless I know what it is."

His hands shake. "I wanted to come forward before. But they were watching me. Even meeting you like this is dangerous. They put you in the hospital, right? You already know."

I tense, my hand reaching protectively for Quinn. But she's entirely focused on the man across from her. "Pete, did you leave that note for me several weeks back? Are you the anonymous witness I texted with?"

Eyes down, he nods.

I've got my hand on Quinn's leg beneath the table, and I can feel her vibrating with excitement. The server chooses that moment to bring the food over, and Pete jumps in his seat at the interruption.

It takes a few minutes for him to settle down again. He picks at his fries, and Quinn sips her vanilla milkshake. But I can almost hear her brain working. Strategizing how to get him to open up. She should probably be recording his statement. Preferably down at her office or West Oaks PD headquarters. But I know she would veto that idea. Pete looks ready to bolt as it is. Any mention of police stations or cameras could scare him off.

So I sit quietly and wait for the guy to speak up.

"I didn't always want to be a driver," Pete says. For the first time since we got here, the guy almost smiles. "Not exactly my dream career as a kid. I wanted to be an actor.

That's why I moved to LA. Me and half the other people in the service industry around here, right? It didn't work out. But I still liked being near all the action. The big Hollywood deals and Oscar-nominated flicks. I've had my name in the credits of six different movies." He lifts his chin proudly. "I loved driving for Thompson Hayworth. He was as A-list as you could get. And I was right there with him, every day. Then Amber came along. He was infatuated with her, and I couldn't blame the guy. Supermodel looks, but she was real sweet to him. In the beginning. They were crazy about each other."

Pete takes a gulp of water. "Things changed when Thompson made Amber the star of his last movie. The other producers couldn't stand her, and they pressured him to fire her. She cried all the time. I felt so bad for her. She and Thompson started arguing more. Spending time apart. Their marriage was on the rocks. But I thought they were giving it one more chance. That's why they were in their house in West Oaks that weekend. To get away from everyone else and reconnect."

Quinn nods along. "I remember what you said in your original interview. But you know more, don't you? You drove Amber the day of the murder."

She's taking a slight risk by pushing him, but I understand. She's trying to keep him focused. I have the feeling this guy could wax poetic about Thompson and Amber all day long.

He runs a hand over the stubble at his jaw. "Yeah, I drove her to the spa on Ocean Lane that day. Thompson planned to stay home as usual. I waited for Amber to finish up, but it was taking a while. So I walked down the street to get a sandwich. On the way back, I cut through an alley. And I saw her."

Quinn reaches for my hand under the table and squeezes.

"She was wearing a floppy hat and sunglasses. She came out of the side exit of the building. Walked off in the opposite direction and got in a sedan that was parked there."

"Was anyone waiting for her?" Quinn asks.

"No. She was alone. She took off in the sedan. I checked my phone, thinking that something had come up, and she couldn't find me, so she arranged another car, strange as that would be. But she hadn't said a word. I had no idea what was going on. So I just went back to my car and waited."

"You didn't go to the Hayworth residence?" I ask.

Pete's eyes widen at my voice, as if he forgot I was sitting there. "No way. I had no idea what Amber was doing, and if she wasn't back at the house, I couldn't just show up without her. Thompson might be mad. I waited, and after a few hours, she walked out of the front of the spa. Like she'd been there the whole time. I was confused, but I figured maybe she'd snuck off to meet some guy." His Adam's apple bobs as he swallows. "Wouldn't have been the first time."

There, I think. A tell. The man's jealous. Pissed at the thought that Amber might've been having an affair. Makes me wonder what else the man is leaving out.

Quinn is mesmerized. "Then you drove her back to the house."

"Yeah." He pushes his plate of fries away. "We walked in and found the house a wreck and Thompson dead."

"Yet you didn't tell the police about seeing Amber leave the spa?" I say.

"They said it was a burglar! I didn't think she'd killed him. Not then."

"Did she know you'd seen her in that alley?" Quinn asks.

"Well…I let it slip. I was trying to be there for her after Thompson's death, offer whatever help I could, and she got all uptight."

I read between the lines. He came onto her, and she

rejected him harshly. As she had every right to do. Murderess or not.

"I might have gotten offended and said too much in the heat of the moment," Pete goes on. "Dropped some hints that I knew she had a secret. That she hadn't been where she claimed on the day of the murder. She started crying and begged me not to spread rumors about her. It was weeks before the detectives actually suspected Amber of the murder, and by then..." He suppresses a shudder. "By then I'd already gotten a glimpse of the real Amber Printz. Some goons in masks showed up at my door and threatened me. Said they'd mess me up if I said anything against her."

"She'd already recruited some new fans," Quinn says. "The murder was a sensation even before Amber was suspected, and she was milking that sympathy on social media for all it was worth. She must've spread the word that you had damaging information."

"I kept my mouth shut," Pete finishes.

"Then why leave that note for Quinn?" I ask. "Why come forward at all?"

"Because it's not right. Thompson was a good man. And the closer the trial gets, the more she's milking it for fame. Do you know how much money she's making through her YouTube channel? Amber's using his murder to become a star. Who needs an Oscar-bait movie when you've got millions of followers hanging on your every word?"

"Sounds like you're envious," I say. "You came to Hollywood to make it, and Amber succeeded where you failed."

Pete glares, and Quinn gives me a small shake of her head.

"What about Christian Hayworth?" Quinn asks. "How does he fit into this? Why did he send you off to Nevada right after you contacted me a few weeks ago?"

"I think Amber's blackmailing him. With what, I don't

know. Christian hates her, so he wouldn't lift a finger to help her otherwise. All I know is, Christian tried to get me out of the way. I got spooked. I was afraid some thugs were going to come after me in the night and shut me up for good. So I took off and came back to West Oaks to keep my head down until the trial. I have no idea how you really got my new number, but I'm glad you did. I just want to make this right. See justice done for Thompson."

Quinn studies him. "Are you willing to repeat what you've told me? Without you speaking the truth, Amber might get away with it."

"Yeah. I'll testify. If you can guarantee my safety. I don't want Amber's psycho fanboys to track me down."

"I know how you feel. I'll make some calls. In the meantime, keep the low profile." Quinn holds out her hand, and Pete shakes it. "I'll be in touch tomorrow."

22

Rex

"What did you think of his story?" Quinn asks. "Do you think he's telling the truth?"

We just got into my truck after leaving the diner. On the nearby boulevard, evening traffic streams by.

"You're the one who has to decide that," I answer. "This is your case."

"But I trust your opinion."

Quinn seemed confident and self-assured with Pete, but now that we're alone, she's not afraid to show me the lack of surety underneath. I'm glad she can be herself with me. The same way I can be myself with her. I reach across the console and tangle our fingers together.

"His story has some holes in it. The defense will point out every one. They'll make him seem like a rejected suitor who wants revenge for Amber turning him down."

"There's something else that bothers me," Quinn says. "It's odd that he actively contacted me before, slipping that note into my purse the night of the gala, then went silent for so long. He didn't fully explain why. He could've found some way to contact me from Nevada. Or after returning to West Oaks."

"I agree."

"But the substance of what he told us matches. The anonymous source promised eyewitness evidence that Amber wasn't where she claimed to be on the day of the murder. And that's exactly what Pete is providing. He promised to testify." She purses her lips. "But the part about Christian Hayworth bugs me too. He claims he wants Amber to go to prison, yet he tried to hide the one eyewitness against her? Is she really blackmailing him, and why? What does Amber have on Christian?"

"What are you going to do?" I ask. "The trial is in two weeks."

She bites her lip. "Lana's the DA. It's her decision, ultimately. We'll see if Pete will repeat his statement on video and in writing. And then go from there."

"Sounds like a plan."

"This could be *huge* for our case." Her excitement is returning. A spark of hope shining in her eyes.

"And you're the one who made it happen."

"With the help of Bennett Security. And you."

I run my fingers through her hair, then turn to buckle my seatbelt. "Where to? It's a drive back to the beach. Or I could take you to your apartment or my place here."

Her eyes widen. "Your house?"

"If you're comfortable with that, sure."

I'd like to take her back to my West Oaks home. But there's no denying the significance.

I've been in communication with my team. They've been on standby, and as soon as I know where we're going, I'll have a car tag along after us for extra security. Since we're back in West Oaks for the first time since the attack on

Quinn that left her in the hospital, I'm not taking any chances.

If Quinn wants to head back to the beach house, I'm fine with that, despite the drive. I'm confident in her safety either way.

But I'd like to take her to the home I've lived in for over a decade now. She's been there countless times as Cliff's friend. As the girl who lived next door. Taking her to my bed there, having her spend the night as my lover, is a very different thing.

"I'd like that," she says breathlessly. "If you're sure it's okay."

"I want you in every part of my life. Nothing is off limits." I touch her chin, then lean over to peck her on the lips. "Come home with me?"

She nods, and I put the truck in gear.

WE PULL INTO MY DRIVEWAY. MY WINDOWS ARE dark, but the ranch-style house next door is lit up. There's a TV playing some kind of action movie inside, visible through the front window. Quinn stares at it. Her parents haven't lived there for years. Yet I have no doubt she's remembering what it was like to grow up there.

I was holding her hand on the drive, so I lift it to my lips and kiss it. "Let's go inside."

After another glance at her childhood home, she follows me into my two-story brick bungalow. I switch on lights as I go from room to room. Except for the home where I grew up in Michigan, this is the house I've lived in the longest. It's as familiar to me as my own name at this point. I could probably navigate it in pitch dark.

Yet somehow, it looks different to me now. Probably

because I'm not the same guy that I was when I left here about a week ago. I had realized my attraction to Quinn by then, but I had no idea how deep those feelings already ran within me.

The last night I spent here, I was still achingly lonely. But now I have Quinn. I'm happy. I feel that sensation bubbling up and pushing on my lungs. I am truly happy for the first time in ages, and it's all because of her.

Things are a mess with Cliff, and that's a constant thorn in the back of my mind. I texted him before we left for West Oaks earlier, just to tell him again that I love him no matter what. He hasn't written back yet. But I have to trust Quinn when she says that Cliff and I will be okay.

"I have a frozen pizza on standby," I say. "If you're hungry."

"Maybe later." She's looking at a wall of family photos that's just past the kitchen. I go over and stand behind her, resting my hands on her waist. There are photos of me and my Army buddies, brothers who I still keep in close contact with. Max Bennett is in a couple of them. But most of the photos are of me, Lydia, and Cliff. I took a few with me up to the beach house, but this is my treasure trove. All our best memories together.

There are none of Quinn because I took those to the beach house. My sanctuary when I was healing. Maybe that should've been a clue.

"I can't wait to add photos of you and me," I say. I rest my chin on her shoulder. I have to hunch over to do it, but she nuzzles into me affectionately. "Lots more memories to come."

Quinn is silent for a couple of moments. Then she says, "Do you think Lydia would be okay with this? You and me together?"

I turn her around so I can look at her. "She'd probably be surprised. But she loved you. She thought you were a great influence on Cliff." We both laugh softly. "More importantly, she thought you were an intelligent, thoughtful young woman. I don't know why things happen the way they do. That's way above my pay grade. But I'm sure, down to my bones, that if Lydia can see us now, she's happy for us." I rest my forehead against Quinn's. "She'd want us to take care of each other."

"Thank you," she whispers, lips trembling.

Neither one of us feels like eating right now. So I take her hand and lead her upstairs to my bedroom instead. We pass Cliff's old room, where Quinn spent the night so often. When she and I were completely different people to each other.

My room is neat, the bed made, just like I left it. Quinn hesitates in the doorway. I can guess what she's thinking.

"I got new furniture and a new mattress in here years ago," I say. "I've, um…had other women here. Not many. But a few."

I want her to know, without me spelling it out, that I don't view this as the same room I shared with my wife. While I have no problem discussing Lydia, that's part of my past.

Quinn is my present. My future.

She makes an annoyed face, but she comes into the room. "Just lie to me and say they were awful in bed and you kicked them out immediately."

I laugh. "I didn't do that. I was a gentleman. But they didn't mean anything to me, and the experiences were lackluster." I draw her against me, mouthing at the side of her neck. "Nothing like the fireworks I have with you. I am *wild* for you, Quinn Ainsley."

I keep the lights off. Outside, the sun is going down. We

undress each other, down to my boxer briefs and her panties, and I lead her to my bed.

We touch and kiss each other all over in the shadowed room. Rolling back and forth over my king-size bed. I moan when she tugs down my boxer briefs and kisses the tip of my cock before smoothing her tongue over my sensitive slit.

"After my prom night, I used to fantasize about being here with you," she murmurs. "I imagined sneaking into this room and into your bed. I would kiss you to wake you up, and you'd be mad at me at first. You'd tell me we couldn't. But you'd finally give in because you wanted me too much. I didn't *actually* want all that to happen, but I wore tracks in my brain with how many times I imagined it."

There's a stark difference between fantasy and reality. Even so, I never had such thoughts about Quinn. There were lines my mind wouldn't have crossed. But *now*? Hearing her say these words in that breathy, needy voice?

"I wanted you to take my virginity," she says.

"Fuck, Quinn. You're killing me." I gently nudge her onto her back. My boxers come off, and I tug her panties down her legs. I need to be inside her. Claiming the woman she is, here and now.

Kneeling, I grab a condom from my nightstand, give my cock a few strokes with my fist in anticipation, and roll the rubber down my length. Soon I'll want to go bare with her. Take her completely and mark her as mine, inside and out. But this works for now. We'll get there.

I slide into her tight warmth. Coming home.

She puts her arms around my neck, clinging to me as we make love. We don't say anything because our bodies are saying it all. Neither of us thought this was possible. I certainly never imagined I could be this happy again after losing so much. Much less with her.

But it's happened.

When I fell in love for the first time at sixteen years old, I was naive. I had no idea what challenges lay ahead of me. For the longest time after I lost Lydia, I would've given anything to go back and change her fate. But it's impossible to change the past. That kind of decision is out of my hands. It's not up to me, and I've never been grateful for that fact before.

I'm a different man now. Older, more experienced. Hopefully wiser. What Quinn and I have is unique and special in its own way. It's incredible to think I'm getting a second chance at love.

That's where I'm headed. I'm falling hard and fast.

We both had dreams of each other, different ones at different times, but they're coming true. No more secrets. No more fears about what others will think, because I know we'll make it through.

Now that we're together, I'll do everything in my power to ensure we'll never be apart.

23

Quinn

Two weeks until the trial.

The morning after my meeting with Pete Diamond, I call Lana and tell her everything. We get on the phone with Diamond, and he confirms what he said the night before. Upon his request, we arrange for protection with the local US Marshals' office.

We also have to make a supplemental report to the defense, letting them know about Pete's new testimony. I expect Derek to explode, and yet he's quiet. That surprises me. But I have plenty of other things to focus on than his trial strategy.

Another week goes by while I work remotely from Rex's home in West Oaks. Every day, the last of my concussion symptoms are fading. And spending all this time with Rex is bliss. He's still protecting me, but given how the lines have blurred, he's decided to take a short leave from Bennett Security until the Printz trial is over. Rex says he doesn't want to be paid for guarding me when he's really acting as my boyfriend, which makes me all warm and gooey inside.

But he still coordinates with the other bodyguards who

keep an eye on his house. Thankfully, we don't have any other random creeps coming near. I stay off social media and never, ever google my name online.

Lark pesters me for info on my relationship with Rex, and I can finally gush about how wonderful he is and how happy I am. I'm less effusive with Cliff, who still hasn't had a real conversation with his dad. But Cliff and I are good, and I know that he and Rex have at least exchanged a few texts.

As the trial approaches, I'm nervous but confident. We've got a powerful case against Amber. I'm ready.

The night before jury selection begins, Rex makes salmon and roasted potatoes for dinner. We sit on the couch later, cuddling and listening to jazz. I hold up my phone and take a selfie of us with our heads together.

Rex smiles when I show it to him. "Send it to me. I'll get it framed. First new addition to the photo wall."

He's the sweetest. I kiss him to show my appreciation, which leads to me straddling his lap as we make out. And then a trail of clothing leading upstairs to his bedroom.

I was a little unsure the first time he brought me here. In that moment, all the complications of our history were impossible to ignore. But I've finally put my guilt over wanting my friend's father to rest. Rex isn't my best friend's dad anymore. I mean, he is, but his place in my life is so much more than that now. We're equals. He's my boyfriend. My lover.

As soon as this trial is over and I can focus fully on Rex, I'm going to tell him that I love him. I don't want any distractions when I say those words. It'll be worth the wait.

~

AND NOW, IT'S HERE. THE START OF THE TRIAL.

We begin with jury selection, which takes a while given

all the media attention this case has received. Every eye is on Amber at the defense table. Her hair is pinned half up, and she's wearing a skirt suit and heels. She looks like she stepped out of a 1940s movie. Old school glamour, but conservative too.

After a couple of days of questioning potential jurors, the judge impanels the jury, and it's time for the opening statement.

Lana gets up to speak. "This is a case about greed. The evidence will show you a young woman who simply couldn't get enough. Enough money, enough fame. When Amber Printz married Thompson Hayworth, she gained a life of luxury and privilege. But when her husband failed to give her every advantage she craved, when she feared she'd lose it all, she chose to get rid of him instead."

Lana places a hand on her belly, her other hand bracing against our counsel table. "You'll hear testimony that Amber created an elaborate scheme to hide her tracks on the day of Thompson Hayworth's murder. She set a scene worthy of a movie. She went to a day spa, created her alibi, and sneaked back home to do away with her husband. She trashed her own house to make it look like the work of an intruder. But the evidence will show that Amber wasn't where she claimed to be that day. She's an actress. But ladies and gentlemen of the jury, do not be fooled."

When she's finished, Lana returns to her seat. But as soon as she's turned away from the jury, her face twists with discomfort. Her hand presses to her belly.

"Lana, are you all right?" I whisper.

"Just Braxton Hicks. I'm fine." She takes a few gulps from her glass of water.

Derek Keller makes his opening statement for the defense next, railing against the incompetence of West Oaks PD and touting his client's innocence. "The People's case is entirely circumstantial. Based on speculation and unfair assumptions about a beautiful young woman falling for an older man. The prosecution just implied Amber is a gold digger. But she's a grieving widow who loved her husband and was devastated to lose him."

I somehow keep a straight face, my eyes on the table in front of me. But inside, I'm triumphant. Derek Keller claims our case is circumstantial, but Pete Diamond will provide eyewitness testimony that Amber lied about her whereabouts. Keller will try to say Pete is lying, of course, but I'm confident the jury won't buy it.

When it comes to putting on a murder prosecution, there are a few different ways to go. One is to start with testimony, usually from police witnesses, about the victim and the crime scene. Walk the jury through the procedure, step-by-step, as the DA slowly builds a powerful case pointing to the defendant. But a far more dramatic strategy is to begin with the single most damning piece of evidence. Create a first impression that the jury won't be able to forget throughout the rest of the trial.

Our trial team has already discussed our strategy. And we're going with the drama.

After the opening statements and the judge's comments to the jury, Lana stands once again. "Your honor, the People call Pete Diamond." She takes a step.

Suddenly, Lana stumbles, crying out in pain.

There are gasps all over the courtroom. I jump up, rounding the table to hold Lana up before she falls. I send a panicked glance at Rex, who's in the audience with Max. Lana's husband looks ready to vault over the barrier to get to her.

"Get paramedics here," the judge tells the bailiff before excusing the jury from the room. A few minutes later, the judge has called a recess until this afternoon and paramedics are checking Lana's vitals.

"Your contractions are coming pretty fast," one says. "More than just Braxton Hicks. You may be going into premature labor, Ms. Marchetti. Let's get you to the hospital."

Max is next to her, holding her hand. Rex has his arm around my shoulder as I look on, barely able to breathe. Lana is only seven months along now. This isn't supposed to be happening.

I just want her and the baby to be all right.

And then I remember—we're in the middle of a trial right now.

Max and Lana head to the hospital, but I stay at the courthouse. Every moment is tense as we wait for news. Finally, Rex looks up from his phone. "Max just texted. Lana wants you to go ahead with the trial."

I'm stressed and worried. Not just about Lana and the baby, but about going on with the trial without her. I won't be alone up there because I have the two other members of our team. But I was Lana's second chair. With her gone, that makes me first. I'm suddenly in charge.

Rex walks over to me and rests his hands on my shoulders. "You can do this. Lana believes in you. So do I."

I breathe out slowly. Having Rex here settles me. He said exactly what I needed to hear. I need to talk to my colleagues about our plan going forward. But Rex is right. I know this case. I know the evidence. Lana was going to question Diamond, but I'm the one who secured his testimony.

"Okay," I say. "I'm ready."

"THE PEOPLE CALL PETE DIAMOND."

I stand in front of the courtroom as Diamond approaches the witness box. The bailiff swears him in. I ask my preliminary questions. His name, occupation.

"I was the driver for Thompson and Amber Hayworth."

"Did you work on the day of Thompson's murder?"

"Yes, I did."

I guide him through the events of that morning. How he took Amber to the spa on Ocean Lane. "What did you do while Amber was having her appointment?"

"I stayed parked nearby. Then I got hungry and walked a block away for a sandwich."

"What route did you use to return to the spa?"

"I cut through an alley."

I nod. We're on track. He's giving all the answers I expect. "What did you see in the alley?"

"Nothing. I just went back to my car to wait. Listened to a couple of podcasts."

I halt in my tracks when my brain echoes what he just said. It doesn't make sense. "I'm sorry, could you repeat that?"

"I saw nothing."

There are murmurs among the jury and the audience. Chills sheet my skin. *What the hell is he doing?*

"Did you see anything *unusual* in the alley?" I prompt. "Any*one?*"

"Objection," Derek barks. "Leading the witness."

"Sustained," the judge says, squinting at me with concern.

But Pete answers my question anyway. "I didn't see anything unusual. Like I said, I went back to the car. I waited. And after her appointments were all done, Amber came out the front of the spa. Just like she said she would. She was there the whole time."

This can't be happening.

Now, sweat is pouring down my sides in my suit. I go to the counsel table, where my colleague is staring at me with wide, panicked eyes, and I grab the transcript of Pete's prior statement.

"Mr. Diamond, didn't you tell the district attorney that you saw Amber sneak out a side entrance into the alley, get into a sedan, and leave during the time period she claimed to be inside the spa?"

A few people in the audience gasp. "Objection!" Derek cries. "Lack of foundation. Improper impeachment."

"Bailiff, please escort the jury from the room," the judge says. "Counsel, approach the bench. *Now.*"

The jury files out so they won't overhear the conference. Defense counsel and I crowd in front of the judge, who crosses her arms over her robes. "Ms. Ainsley, explain yourself. What is going on?"

"Mr. Diamond changed his testimony," I sputter. I point to the statement of what he told us before, which I'm holding in my hand.

Derek cuts me off. "I'd say that's no surprise at all. Diamond has no credibility whatsoever. It's not my client's fault the prosecution decided to make a known liar its star witness. Not only *that*, Miss Ainsley needs to review the rules of evidence and how to properly question a witness."

Another wave of nausea rocks me. But it's not Derek's smug little digs that are getting under my skin. I can't understand what happened. Did Amber or one of her thugs get to Pete?

But he didn't look frightened on the stand. He seemed shockingly calm. *Satisfied*, even.

"Mr. Diamond made a proffer of his new testimony last week. If I could have a few moments to get in touch with the district attorney—"

"We strenuously object to any delays," Derek says. "If the

DA wants to suborn perjury, she needs to do it in a timely manner."

"That's quite enough, Mr. Keller. You've made your point." The judge heaves a sigh. "Since Mr. Diamond now contradicts his prior statements, the People may impeach him *if* they set the proper foundation. No more leading questions without moving to declare him as hostile. And of course, Mr. Keller may cross-examine the witness about his flip-flopping testimony as well, if he wishes. I urge you both to be careful. I won't have any more outbursts in my courtroom."

Before he can return to his table, I grab Derek's arm. "Did you know about this?" I hiss. "Did you convince Pete to hide what he saw the day of the murder?"

Derek scowls and yanks his arm away. "I don't have a clue what you're talking about."

The judge orders quiet, and the jury returns to their box. I try to get myself back on track. But I'm shaking. I clasp my hands in front of me to hide it.

Get it together, I tell myself. *You can't fall apart. Not in front of everyone.*

The judge didn't allow cameras, but there are sketch artists and reporters here. I briefly glance over at Rex. He's sitting in the front row of the audience, his expression both hard and brittle. I know he's worried for me. But he nods, and that gives me just enough reassurance to catch my breath.

"Mr. Diamond, would you read the statement that you gave to the district attorney just days ago?" I ask, handing him the paper.

He does. But when I ask why he's changing his testimony, he says, "You and the district attorney pressured me into saying this. I was coerced. If anyone was threatening me, it was *you.*"

My insides drop through the floor.

It all goes downhill from there. My colleagues and I call our other witnesses, but I can feel the jury's skepticism. They don't trust me, and that's fatal to our case. I succeeded in creating an indelible first impression. Unfortunately, it was the exact wrong one. All our other evidence is circumstantial, and Derek pokes holes in each witness during cross-examination.

It takes four days for us to put on our entire case, and at the end of it, I'm exhausted down to my soul. The only bright side is that Lana has stabilized, and the doctors were able to stop her premature labor. She's on bed rest for the foreseeable future, but that's far better than her baby being born too soon.

After we rest our case, I barely sleep that night. I can hardly even speak to Rex. There's nothing in my mind except evidence and trial strategy. I'm still searching for some way to turn this around.

The next day, the defense barely puts on any case at all. Amber is their sole witness, testifying on her own behalf. She might not have range as an actress, but she's got the innocent act down pat.

I manage to get myself together enough to cross-examine her. My voice is stronger today. My hands are steady. I question her about her internet searches on forensics and on methods to kill someone. I drill her about her motive to do away with Thompson and all she stood to gain. I'm relentless.

"You sneaked out of the spa through the alley, didn't you?"

"No."

"You drove home and found Thompson napping on the couch, didn't you?"

"I didn't."

"You picked up the heaviest object you could find, and you hit him over the head until he died." My voice rings out in the silent courtroom.

Amber stares at me, her innocence morphing into murderous rage. There's a shift in the air. The jury is sitting forward. Listening. A spark of hope feeds me.

Maybe I can win them over. Make them *see*.

"Then you staged the house to look like a burglary," I say. "Just like the burglary scenes you'd researched online."

"Good luck with that theory," she spits out. "Because you have no fucking proof."

She's finally dropped her facade. *Please let it be enough.*

We make our closing arguments, and I reconstruct the day of the murder piece by piece. I do my best to explain what happened with Pete and his changing testimony. Of course, I can't outright accuse Amber of tampering with a witness because I *don't* have proof of that. Still, I can draw inferences and hope the jury connects the dots.

The judge instructs the jury, and they retire to deliberate. They return a verdict after only three hours, which could be good for us. A quick deliberation often means a guilty verdict.

The judge calls everyone back into the courtroom.

Please, I think. *Please*.

When the foreman announces the verdict, the sound is muffled. Like I'm hearing it underwater. But it echoes all the way down inside me.

Not. Guilty.

24

Rex

Quinn is shell-shocked.

After the verdict, she leaves the courtroom with her head held high. But when I reach her in the hallway, she slumps against me. I lead her out of the courthouse and across the street to her building. A few people try to speak to her along the way, but she ignores them, and I frown at them until they step back.

When we reach her office, we go inside and I shut the door. She sits in her desk chair and stares blankly at her dark laptop screen.

"Not guilty," she says in a monotone. "I lost the case."

"It wasn't just you. You were part of a team. If anything, you held everyone together after Lana had to leave."

"No, Rex. I insisted on investigating the anonymous source. I brought in Pete Diamond as our star witness. *Me*." She wipes her hands over her face. "Was it all a trap from the beginning? I just…I don't understand."

I kneel in front of her, taking her hands in mine. "Maybe you should take the rest of today off and debrief with your team tomorrow."

She pulls away from my touch. "I have things I need to do. Calls to make. Could you wait in the hall, please? I'd like some space."

I stand. "Of course. I'll be there if you need me." I'm trying not to let her dismissal bother me. In fact, I'm proud of her for soldiering on. Exactly what she's been doing this whole time. I just wish I could take this burden from her. Shield her from the disappointment and scrutiny.

But she doesn't want that from me, nor should she. I'm not her mentor, and I'm certainly nothing like a father to her. I'm the man who loves her.

This isn't easy for me, though. Standing in the hallway as if I'm nothing more than a bodyguard.

She leaves her door partway open, and I hear her speaking quietly on the phone. The click of her keyboard. Then voices come from the front of the building. Some kind of commotion.

I radio to the guys I have stationed in the front of the building. "What's going on?"

"Reporters. The assistant DA came out and made a statement about the Printz verdict, but they're not satisfied. They want to talk to Quinn since she's the one who tried the case. There are news trucks all over the street."

I curse. The media presence during the trial has been obvious, but we've been avoiding them as best we can. The reporters were satisfied with shouting a few questions at her on her way in and out of the courthouse before, but I guess now that the verdict has been read, they smell blood in the water.

Quinn steps into the doorway. "The media?"

I guess she heard what my teammate radioed. I nod, and her eyes go round. "Rex, please get me out of here."

Resolve settles into my bones. Man, it feels good to have a mission.

It takes me a few minutes to come up with a plan. Then I put it in motion. I find an admin who has golden hair and Quinn's build. Quinn hands over her blazer, plus a pair of sunglasses.

"Thanks for doing this," Quinn says.

The admin smiles, adjusting her disguise. "Hey, most exciting part of my week. You did great with the closing, by the way. A bunch of us watched it. And the cross you did on Amber? Powerful. You did the best you could with the hand you were dealt."

Quinn's expression doesn't change. "Thanks," she mutters.

I feel her dejection in the pit of my stomach.

Next, Leon comes inside to meet us. He's on duty today, and he's all business. Which I appreciate. The kid does come through when it really counts.

"Leon, when you get the signal from me, escort our decoy outside through the front. You can drop her off when you reach the end of the block. You're okay walking back?" I ask the admin, and she nods. Then I turn to Quinn. "You know what to do?"

She nods. "Head to the conference room. I've got it."

I leave the building. The throng of reporters gets excited when they see me approach, but they deflate when they realize I'm just security. I breeze past them. Then into the parking lot, where I start up my truck and drive around to the rear of the building, where a first-floor conference room window overlooks a quiet side street.

The window in Quinn's private office is painted shut, but this one works well enough as an escape route. As soon as I pull up, Quinn climbs out and dashes to the truck. The moment she's inside, I take off.

But then I see heads turning and fingers pointing. One of

the camera crews has spotted us. They must've realized the decoy was just that. Shit.

"Buckle up."

I floor it.

A couple of news trucks try to follow, but I make a quick left turn, then cut through an alley. We come out on a different street.

"Pretty sure we lost them," I say.

She sighs and closes her eyes. "Never imagined I'd be running from paparazzi."

"Have you spoken to Lana?" I've been texting with Max over the last few days about her condition, though we avoided talking about the trial. I wasn't going to commentate because that felt too much like talking behind Quinn's back. I have no doubt Quinn wanted to break the news to her boss herself.

"I did. I'm so relieved the baby is stable, but telling her about the verdict… It was awful. The absolute worst."

"I've been there. Reporting back to the brass after a mission goes tits up is never fun."

"But I doubt you ever screwed up as thoroughly as I did."

I would disagree. I've got plenty of stories from my twenty years in the service that don't reflect me at my best. But this isn't about me.

I reach for her hand and squeeze it instead. "Do you want to get dinner somewhere? Get your mind off things? Or—"

I pause, studying a low-slung hatchback in my rearview. I realize it's been a couple of car lengths behind us for a while. It's got an oversized spoiler and racing stripes.

"What is it?" Quinn turns around to look behind us, probably noticing the way my eyes keep flicking to the mirror. She gasps as the hatchback revs its engine and accelerates, passing another vehicle so that it's now directly behind us.

The driver is wearing a mask. That creepy face from the Halloween movies. Just like the rabid Amber fan who attacked Quinn in her office about a month ago.

"What is with these creeps?" Quinn shouts. "They already won. Why won't they leave me alone?"

It's revenge, I think. For Quinn's cross-examination of Amber today. But the reasons don't matter.

"Hold on."

I brake suddenly and steer hard to the left, cutting across the opposing traffic and leaving horns honking in our wake. Then I radio Leon, who was hanging back until I let him know our destination.

"I've got a shadow." I describe the hatchback. "Where are you?"

"Ocean and Fifth."

I glance in the mirror. Our masked assailant managed to keep on our tail. He accelerates again and taps our bumper.

"Dammit!" My truck swerves before I regain control of the steering. That probably did more damage to the little car than my huge truck, but Quinn yelps in fear, grabbing for anything she can hold on to.

"Rex?" Leon asks on the radio.

"This guy is really starting to piss me off." I press the gas.

What's the man trying to do? Just terrify her? Or actually make us lose control and crash? This is a crowded area. Who knows how many others could be hurt.

"Any vacant lots near you?" I ask Leon. "Open space?"

"I see a lot up ahead. It's blocked off by some cones for the farmer's market tomorrow. Ocean and Seventh."

"And you passed the tactical driving course earlier this year, right?"

"Sure did, Foxy. Flying colors."

I grit my teeth, already knowing this will end up on the

evening news. But I don't have a lot of options. "I'm bringing him to you."

"Copy. I gotchu."

Quinn is breathing hard beside me. I lay on the horn to warn people ahead of us. A light turns red. I blow through it and steer left. Yet I can't gain any distance from him. His car is faster and more maneuverable than mine.

I'm on Seventh now, on a straightaway. Almost there. I see Leon's vehicle idling on one side of the empty lot. He's got a tricked-out Acura, just as I remembered.

Orange caution cones are scattered over the lot. I assume Leon plowed into them to get them out of the way.

I steer into the lot's entrance, my tires bumping over uneven concrete and crushing a caution cone. The hatchback follows in my rearview mirror.

Leon's vehicle is already moving. He knows what to do. As the hatchback flies past him, Leon knocks the hatchback's rear bumper at an angle, sending it spinning. It skids, coming to a rough stop against a dumpster.

I brake hard and bring my truck to a halt at the other end of the lot.

In seconds, Leon and his partner are out of their vehicle and aiming their weapons at the hatchback. Sirens wail. Probably approaching West Oaks PD units responding to bystander 911 calls. But miraculously, no pedestrians were hit that I'm aware of. No damage except to the hatchback itself.

I tip my head back, exhaling. At the same time, I reach for Quinn.

"You okay?" I ask.

She doesn't say anything. Instead, my girl starts *laughing*.

"Quinn?"

"Sorry, it's just..." She covers her mouth, giggling.

"It's the adrenaline rush. C'mere." I unbuckle my seatbelt, then hers, and pull her as close as I can across the center console. She's shivering. I tighten the grip of my arms, and she rests her head against my shoulder.

"It's just so surreal," she says. "After everything."

"I know."

She takes a few deep breaths, calming down.

Squad cars arrive, lights flashing. Quinn and I get out of the truck, our hands clearly visible so everyone can see we're not a threat. The patrol officers recognize me. My son's not among them, but they know Cliff, and I've met several of them before.

We stand off to the side while they get our masked assailant out of the hatchback and place him under arrest. He seems dizzy at most, but otherwise unharmed. "Recognize him?" I ask her when they pull his mask off.

"Nope. A rando. Just like the others."

Once again, we're playing whack-a-mole. When are these psychos going to stop coming out of the woodwork?

We give our statements, and finally, we're back in my truck. But instead of driving off, I put my arms around her again, holding her tight. "I'll take you to the beach house. We'll get away from all this for a while. I'll drive straight there."

"I would like that. Curl up, let you take care of me. You're really good at it." Then she lifts her head, separating from me. "But I can't."

I look down at her in confusion. "It would be the safest choice. Until—"

"*No,*" she says sharply.

I shut my mouth, looking down at her and waiting for her to go on.

"I tried to quit the DA's office today. I offered Lana my resignation."

I cup her cheek. "Quinn, no."

"She refused to accept it. She said we all have failures, and it hurts in the moment. I didn't quit, but I still felt like giving up. I can't change the fact that I lost the case. I have no possible way to make that right. I let the victim and anyone who loves him down, and it hurts *so bad*."

She takes a breath, and I smooth back her hair.

"But not that long ago," she goes on, "I was ready to give up on the hope of ever being with *you*. I thought that was smarter. Safer. But if I had, if I hadn't taken a risk of kissing you, I would've missed this. So I appreciate you wanting to protect me, but I'm going to stay here. I have to find out what's really going on, and find some way to fight back. Maybe that's dumb and I'm just making life harder on myself, but I have to try."

This astonishing woman. How did I ever fail to see her for who she is?

"Can I say something?" I ask.

"Yes." Her mouth flattens. Like she's bracing for me to argue with her.

"I love you."

"You—what?"

I brush my lips over hers. "I love you. I'm lucky to call you mine."

She takes a stuttering breath. "I love you too. I've loved you for so long, and I never thought I'd ever hear that back."

There was a time I didn't think I'd hear those words again, either. It's a lovely thing, sometimes, to be proven wrong. "Then I'll have to say it over and over. I'm in love with you, Quinn."

Who says I can't talk about my feelings?

I keep repeating the words, kissing her in between. There are tears in her eyes, but I know it's not despair. It's this too-big sensation of knowing you've found the right puzzle piece and slotted perfectly into place.

"You'll go to war with me?" she asks. "Because that's what I want. That asshole who just tried to run us off the road was getting his orders from somewhere. I don't have evidence of that yet, but I know it in my gut. There's a reason Pete Diamond lied. An explanation for *all* of this. I'm going to find out what it is."

The idiot driving the hatchback in that creepy mask made a crucial mistake. And so did whoever's been pulling the strings behind the scenes. They could've chosen to take that not-guilty verdict and let their vendetta against Quinn go. But instead, they've solidified her resolve. Given her the fire she needs to gather herself up and go on.

I like to think I've played a role in that, too. By being here for her.

But that adrenaline rush cleared away any trace of destructive self pity. My lady is ready to fight.

Where else would I be except right next to her?

"I would be honored to go to war with you. No need to keep advocating. You won me over at least ten minutes ago, counselor. I'm reporting for duty."

"At ease." She pats my cheek. "Take me home, Foxy."

We both laugh softly. I know which home she means. My house here in West Oaks, where we've been staying the last couple of weeks since returning from the beach house. The house that's starting to feel like *ours*.

~

I HAVE TO ADMIT, WHEN QUINN TALKED ABOUT going to war, I had certain expectations. I imagined I would be the five-star general to Quinn's commander-in-chief.

Instead, I'm baking frozen pizzas in my kitchen while she conference-calls with Lana and her fellow attorneys.

But that's all right. I'm currently on doting-boyfriend

duty, and my secret is that I don't mind it one bit. Though I'm not going to admit that to the other guys the next time we're shooting the shit at headquarters after a sparring session.

There's a knock at the back door, which then cracks open slightly. "Can I come in?" Cliff asks.

"Yep," I say. "All clear." That's the closest I can get to making a joke about what happened at the beach house. Judging by my son's bright red face, he's not ready to make light of it.

"Uh, hey Dad," Cliff says, barely looking at me.

His girlfriend Lia is right behind him, followed by Lark and Danny. I called Cliff about the disastrous trial verdict, and he organized more of Quinn's friends to come here and cheer her up.

I greet the others, asking what they'd like to drink, while Lark and Lia unload the snacks and desserts they've brought. "Quinn's on the phone in the living room with DA Marchetti at the moment," I say. "She'll finish up soon."

Danny grabs the beer I hold out. "We heard about what happened after the trial ended. The car chase down Ocean Lane? I saw the news footage. How your Bennett Security teammate stopped the perp with a PIT maneuver. A lot of shit's gone down in West Oaks over the years, but dang." He whistles.

"It was memorable." It turns out a news chopper was in the air and caught the ending of the chase. Leon is milking it for all it's worth. He's going to be crowing about that perfectly executed PIT maneuver for months.

Once again, we caught the suspect in the attack, but he claims to have acted alone. Just another devotee of Amber Printz who was incensed at her unfair persecution. Where are all these wackos coming from? When is this going to end? I want to see Quinn safe and smiling. I want to know she can go for a run without fearing who'll come after her.

I'm ready to start our life together. But we can't. Not until this is finished.

"Not so fun for me and Quinn though," I add.

Danny grimaces. "No, I hear you. That's why we're here. To help in any way we can. I, uh, hear congratulations are in order? You and Quinn?"

Cliff glances up, then away, conspicuously silent considering my son's usual talkative nature.

"Yeah," I say cautiously. "We're both very happy. Not about the drama around the Printz trial, obviously, but about falling in love."

On the other side of the kitchen counter, Cliff goes completely still.

I'm not sure if Danny will have an issue with our age difference. He was one of Quinn and Cliff's roommates at the Pink House. He saw me around plenty, but mainly as Cliff's dad or a representative of Bennett Security.

Now, I'm dating his friend.

But Danny grins. "I'm thrilled for you. Makes all the difference, doesn't it? Finding the right person. Lark is it for me. And Quinn is one of the best people in the world, a great friend, so I'm really glad to see she's found you." He clinks his beer bottle against mine, then heads into the living room, where the women have gone to join Quinn.

Now, it's just me and my son in the kitchen.

"You're in love?" Cliff asks quietly.

I turn to him. "Yes. We are."

"Isn't that kind of fast?"

"I can't speak for Quinn. For me, I've known her a long time. So much of what I admire about her hasn't changed. I see her differently now, but it's more like I've seen her for who she really is. In one sense, yes, it's fast. But loving her is the easiest thing in the world. It feels right to me. And I won't apologize for it."

"I wouldn't want you to. I didn't mean to sound judgmental." He comes around from the other side of the counter. "Dad, I need to apologize to *you* for what I said before. A lot of it was...pretty awful."

"You were upset."

"But that's not an excuse. You were right that I was reacting without thinking about why. I've talked about it a lot with Lia. I hope that's okay."

I tuck my hands into my jeans pockets. Quinn and I both changed out of our court clothes when we got home. "Of course. That's what's so great about having a partner. They'll act as a sounding board." Something else I was missing the last decade I spent alone.

"There's something I need to tell you."

My brows tense. "Oh?"

"I'm going to leave West Oaks PD. I'm going back to school."

For several seconds, I have no idea how to respond. And I have a hunch I'm about to say the wrong thing. So I try a different approach. "Tell me more."

His mouth curves as he explains the social work program he's interested in. To be honest, I'm concerned. He's giving up a career he's spent years building. Cliff is a good cop. The kind who cares about people.

But he can help people through social work too, I reason with myself. And he's seen the work they do firsthand. He knows what he's getting into. He's clearly done a lot of research into the program, tuition, and job opportunities too.

Most importantly? Cliff's entire expression lights up as he talks about it. In a way I've never seen him get passionate about police work.

So no, I don't get it. But my son is a grown man. This isn't my decision. Or my life.

"I can't wait to see where this goes for you. If I can help or give advice, let me know." I open my arms. "Proud of you."

We hug. I still want to talk more about the other things he said at the beach house. About his childhood. About improving communication between us. But we don't have to do all that in one night. The door is open now, and we'll get there. Like Quinn said, we'll be okay.

"Thanks, Dad. I'm happy for you and Quinn. You deserve someone as amazing as her. Just be good to her, okay?"

"I will, son. I promise."

25

Quinn

"How's it going in here?"

I look up to see Lark crossing the living room toward me. Lia is right behind her. "Not so bad, actually," I say. "Who knew a dangerous car chase would boost my mood?"

I hug each of them. "Uh oh," Lia says, "sounds like we have a daredevil on our hands."

I laugh. "Hardly. It's funny, I used to be the cautious type."

"But love makes us daring," Lark says.

I think of everything Rex and I have been through. "If you want to hold on to it, yeah."

Lia folds her arms over her chest. Her lustrous brown hair is pulled up in a high ponytail, and she's wearing a West Oaks SWAT T-shirt. "We heard you're planning some kind of op?"

I wave them over, and we all sit down on the couch. "I'm not that far yet. I just got off a conference call with the district attorney and our team from the trial. I assume you know what happened? The not-guilty verdict?"

They both nod. "The trial has been hard to avoid on my newsfeeds these days," Leah says. "Plus everybody at the station has been talking about it nonstop. Your witness changed his testimony? Are you going after him for perjury?"

"That's something that I discussed with Lana. It's her call as DA. She's considering it, but it would be nearly impossible to get a conviction. Not after Amber was acquitted."

Lark's face scrunches up. As usual, her long black hair is spilling over her shoulders, and her elaborate botanical tattoos are visible beneath her black tank top. "But there must be some way to challenge that not-guilty verdict, right? Can't you show that Amber influenced Diamond somehow? That has to be what happened."

I shake my head. "That's what we think too, but proving it is another matter. Double jeopardy prevents us from ever trying her on the murder charges again. But we can still try to figure out what really happened. And if there are any other charges we could bring against Amber or anyone else who's been exerting undue influence."

Danny walks in and goes to stand behind Lark, rubbing her shoulders. "Don't mind me," he says. "Just listening in."

Lark glances up at him and smiles. "I was about to say, it would be nice for the world to know the truth about Amber, even if she manages to avoid prison."

"Exactly my feeling. And then there's the fact that her crazed fans continue to come after me. If we can uncover the truth and show everyone who Amber really is, it could stop the harassment."

Lia nods, ponytail bobbing. "So you're putting together an investigation team. I know Detective De Luca has been supervising the investigation into the attacks on you."

"Right," I say. "She's been trying to find out if someone is coordinating the threats and attacks. They've seemed random, inspired by Amber's social media posts but not coordinated. But I'm convinced there's organization behind it. I just don't believe random actors can keep getting this close. And I think what happened at the trial, with Pete Diamond changing his testimony, could be connected to the harassment campaign as well. We know Amber Printz is the link, but we've been looking at things piecemeal. I want to go back to the beginning and look at the whole picture again. Find new leads."

Cliff and Rex join us in the living room. I share a glance with my man, feeling the contentment and affection radiating from him. And I notice that he and Cliff are standing close to one another. Cliff looks happy too.

Rex gives me a small nod. I take that to mean he and Cliff have made up and talked through some things. I knew it would happen, but I'm relieved for Rex. I know that was weighing on him.

"Can we eat now?" Cliff asks. "The pizza's ready, and I'm starving."

"When are you not starving?" I say with an eye roll.

The doorbell rings, and Cliff perks up. "That must be Shelby. I forgot to mention I invited her and Nash. I figured you would appreciate all the brainpower you could get."

"Absolutely." Madison and Nash Jennings know plenty about investigating tough cases on a less-than-official basis. Besides, it's been too long since I saw them.

Cliff and I go to meet them at the door. "Look at you!" I say when Madison walks in.

Madison's older brother Aiden used to be my roommate at the Pink House. But since Aiden moved to Colorado, I haven't had as many excuses to run into Madison or her family, which includes Nash's daughter Emma. Career success and a happy home life look very good on her.

She used to be Madison Shelborne, hence the nickname "Shelby." Even though her last name is Jennings now. She's a hostage negotiator for West Oaks PD, while Nash is a SWAT sergeant. She's also tall and blond with model looks, and she's got the cutest baby belly.

Maybe that'll be me someday.

Then I have a brief moment of shock at the mental image. Not so much the career part as the *pregnant* part. Rex and I haven't talked about if he'd want more kids. But the idea of us having a baby together sets off waves of longing in my chest. Somehow, Lana's pregnancy didn't trigger that same desire in me. Probably because I've known Madison since she was single and watched her life change. She's my age, married to an older guy who already had a kid...

Shaking off those thoughts for later, I give Madison a hug. "You look amazing. And you have excellent timing. Pizza just came out of the oven."

"Good, I'm starved." Madison pats her stomach.

"Quinn gave me crap when I said that," Cliff complained.

Nash steps over the threshold, broad and intimidating as usual. "That's because Madison is eating for two," he says gruffly. "You just love food someone else paid for."

"Yes, Sergeant," Cliff squeaks.

Madison and I crack up. "Come on," I say. "I think the others went into the kitchen."

We all grab food and eat, gathering around the kitchen counters, laughing and joking. It's exactly what I need. Time with friends and family. I'm not related to any of these people, but they've shown me what a family truly should be. People who stick together no matter what happens. Even through fights and uncomfortable truths. People who forgive each other.

My classmates used to think I was lucky that my parents were so hands off. I don't think I've ever had a fight with my mom or dad. Not even when I was a teenager. I'm glad I had stability, of course. They were never cruel to me. I could've had it so much worse.

But they didn't try very hard with me, either. They didn't work to show they cared. When you really love someone, you're willing to push through the hard parts. You step up when your loved one needs you. Exactly what everyone in this room is doing for me right now.

Especially Rex. The man I love with my entire heart. Whether he wants more kids or not, I'm his. There's no other option for me.

And when he puts his arm around my waist and gives me a peck on the lips, in front of everyone, I'm beyond grateful that we get to show those we care about what we mean to each other.

After dinner, we gather in the living room. I sit on the couch with Rex snuggled against me. Madison takes one of the easy chairs, Nash perching on the arm beside her. Danny and Lark hold hands on the other end of the couch.

"Why don't you start at the beginning?" Madison asks. "I'm guessing we all have a different level of familiarity with the case."

"That's what I was planning on," I say. "Maybe you all can help brainstorm. We need a fresh look at what's been going on, because I've hit a dead end."

I start with the murder of Thompson Hayworth. Everyone in the room has been keeping track, at least vaguely, of the Printz case. It's impossible not to, given the level of media scrutiny. Plus the fact that nearly all of us are involved in law enforcement in some way.

I tell them about our initial preparation for the trial. Amber's social media campaign to gain sympathy, and her legion of young male fans convinced she was innocent and in need of saving.

"She went the damsel in distress route," Nash says. "No

wonder she had so many admirers willing to believe whatever she said. Way too many guys are ready to do anything as long as the ask comes from a pretty face."

"Just like too many women will believe anything a charming man tells them," Madison adds wryly.

"Good thing nobody in this room would ever fall for such manipulation," Lia says, planting an affectionate kiss on Cliff's head.

His brow wrinkles. "Hey, wait a minute."

"It's not just you, Cliff," Danny says. "Let's face it. All the guys in this room are suckers for our women."

Everyone laughs. Rex's thumb brushes my neck, and he winks when I look over.

Then I continue. "After the West Oaks Bar Association gala, the threats against Lana and me turned into real-life harassment. But that same night, someone left a note in my purse. They claimed to have information on the Printz case. I contacted the source, who said they had to remain anonymous because it was too dangerous to come forward yet. But they promised eyewitness testimony that Amber left the spa during the key time period."

"Which is exactly what Pete Diamond provided," Lark says.

I nod. "I was out of commission for a while after I got the concussion, thanks to another attack by one of Amber's fanboys. During that time, I didn't hear another word from the anonymous source. Then Sylvie Trousseau at Bennett Security tracked down Pete Diamond's information."

Rex touches my thigh. "But he's not the only person you suspected of being the witness."

"Right." I tell them about our trip into Los Angeles to speak with Christian Hayworth, Thompson's son, as well as Thompson's assistant, Kendall Simms. "But I didn't think either of them fit the profile of the witness. Pete Diamond seemed to be the most likely person. He was Thompson's chauffeur, and he drove Amber to the spa that day. So when I finally spoke to him, I was more than ready to believe he was telling the truth about being the secret witness who had contacted me. That's why I called him as our star witness." Guilt sours my stomach. "I did have some reservations, but I needed his testimony so badly."

"And Lana signed off on it," Rex reminds me. "I couldn't tell he was lying either. Assuming he was lying at all. Someone could've threatened him after that. Or persuaded him some other way not to tell the truth on the stand."

"Exactly what I want to find out. Was there ever a secret witness at all, or was it a set up from the start? Just another elaborate piece of Amber's campaign to make herself look innocent."

Danny whistles. "If that's true, it's pretty diabolical."

"And would've required some major strokes of luck in Amber's favor." Madison is tapping her chin. "Quinn, *you* were the one who contacted Pete Diamond after he disappeared. If it was a setup from the start, how did they know you'd be so persistent in finding Pete?"

"I was thinking the same thing," Lark says. "From everything you've told us, it sounds like the secret witness was legit. But he or she simply got cold feet."

Nash and Danny are nodding along. "Maybe the same person who threatened Pete Diamond into changing his story also intimidated your anonymous witness," Nash suggests.

We all stare at one another, trying to come up with a brilliant new idea to connect these pieces.

Then Rex's phone buzzes, and he checks the screen. "It's Angela. She's got an update for us. She asked if she could call." Rex types a response, and a moment later, he answers his phone.

"Detective, you're on speaker. We've got a brain trust here

trying to puzzle out what happened with the Printz trial." Rex rattles off the names of everyone who's present. "Do you mind if they listen in?"

"Not at all," Angela says. "Wish I could be there with all of you in person, but I'm at the station. I finished up interrogating the idiot who chased you down Ocean Lane this afternoon. Good thing Leon stopped him with that fancy maneuver without getting anyone killed."

"Leon's a Bennett guy. We're all consummate professionals."

Angela barks a laugh. "There was a time I'd have my doubts, but now I've got to agree with you. Anyway. You'll want to hear this. The suspect is a twenty-year-old kid named Sam. Unemployed, living in his grandma's basement. Obsessed with Amber Printz. But unlike the others, this kid didn't stick to his story about being a loner. When he found out the kind of charges he's facing, he caved. Completely."

I take a breath, sitting forward on the couch. "Did he tell you who's pulling the strings behind the attacks?"

"He says he doesn't know the person's name. But he confirmed there *is* someone. Sam showed us the text exchanges on his phone. He met this person online through a Reddit subthread. Apparently, this mastermind has been recruiting young men to go after Quinn specifically, just as we suspected. Sam says he was promised a personal visit with Amber. *Very* personal, if you catch my meaning. But now that he's facing prison time for that car chase, Sam's realizing what a mistake he made. For what it's worth, he says he only meant to scare you."

Unbelievable, I think. He could've killed me and Rex and innocent bystanders too.

Rex grasps my hand. "How do we track down the puppet master? I want this person held accountable for *everything* that's been done to Quinn."

"I'm working on it," Angela says. "We got the person's contact info from Sam, and the number is unregistered. But we're working on getting a warrant to wiretap and track the device. The person claims to be someone very close to Amber Printz."

Who could it be? I rack my brain, but Amber doesn't have that many friends left. Not that she sees day to day, anyway.

Could it be the same person who intimidated my secret witness? Or maybe this mastermind *is* my secret witness.

I simply can't make these clues fit into a clear picture. There's something missing. A few more pieces that'll click into place and reveal what's going on.

Yet I have no idea how to find them.

26

Rex

The last of our guests leave, and I lock up the house. But Quinn's still sitting in the living room tapping away at her laptop.

"You ready to call it a night?" I ask.

She must be exhausted after the day she's had. First the verdict, then the car chase. Followed by hours of brainstorming and studying every aspect of the Printz case.

"Not yet. I've still got energy. Maybe another hour or..." She's forced to stop talking when her mouth opens wide in a yawn.

I smile down at her where she's sitting on the couch. "You were saying?"

"All right, fine." She saves her work, closes the laptop, and sets it aside. "We can go upstairs. But I'm not promising to sleep. I'm wired."

"Who said anything about sleeping?" I scoop her up, and she yelps, grabbing onto my shoulders. I take Quinn upstairs and lay her on my bed. Then I stretch out beside her. "It's been a long day. How are you feeling?"

She thinks about it. "I'm really good, actually. Not the

best day for my career. I couldn't have gotten through that part without you." Her eyes brighten, and she turns onto her side to face me. "But it's the day you said you love me, so it certainly wasn't all bad."

I play with the strands of her blond hair that have slipped across her collarbone. "I do love you. Very much."

"Feel free to keep saying it." She stretches her leg out and drapes it over my hip. "You spoke to Cliff? Did you smooth things over?"

"We did. He apologized, and I think we're in a much better place. Has he told you about going back to school?"

"For social work? Yes, he has. I didn't say anything because I thought he would want to tell you himself."

"Of course. That makes sense. I can't say I understand, but I let him know that I support him."

"I'm sure that means a lot to him." For a few minutes, we just look at each other and smile, trailing soft touches over each other's faces and arms. Then Quinn says, "It made all the difference to have my friends around me tonight. Thank you for calling them."

"Mainly I just called Cliff, and he handled the rest."

Her smile takes on a mischievous twist. "You should have invited Leon, though. I mean, everyone's talking about how he saved the day and stopped that car that was following us."

I grumble. "That again."

"Do you think you could invite him over tomorrow? Have him recount the story? I really didn't thank him enough this afternoon. Since he played my hero and all…"

Growling, I roll so I'm half on top of her, my arms caging her in. She falls onto her back below me, laughing hysterically.

"Not another word about Leon. Or any other man. Not when you're in this bed."

"Oh? Why is that?"

I drop my head to run my lips over her collarbone. My tongue caresses her neck, and then I close my mouth over the same spot and suck. Her laughs fade into whimpers.

"Because you're mine," I say.

Her fingers dig into my hair. The sweet scent of her skin, the slight hint of salt, the give of her body beneath me. All those details of her mix into an intoxicating combination.

"At times in my past, there was nothing in the world I wanted more than to be yours," she says. "I love my career, even with the headaches it can bring. I love my friends. But hearing you say that… You don't know how incredible it makes me feel. I *am* yours. I've always been yours. No other man could ever come close to you."

With every sentence she speaks, she winds me up even more. Quinn has been sleeping in my bed for weeks now, but it still astonishes me. I really get to have this woman. I get to share my days and nights with her. The happiness and the sorrow too, which isn't nearly so bad when we can lean on one another. We love each other, trust each other, based on who we are deep down. Our age difference has nothing to do with it. If I'd listened to that disapproving voice in my head that said I couldn't have her, then we'd have missed out on this.

"I'm so glad you waited for me to catch up," I say. "I love you."

"I love you too."

My cock is half hard and interested in more. But Quinn's had a rough day. I press a kiss to her temple. "What are you in the mood for?"

She stretches her arms over her head. "A nice, long shower. Want to join me?"

"I'd love to. Just let me go downstairs to set the alarm and make sure everything's locked up." I squeeze the curve of her hip. "You get started, and I'll be back soon."

"Be quick. Or I'll have all the fun without you."

If that's not an incentive to move, I don't know what is. I jog down the stairs, eager to get this chore out of the way so I can join Quinn, all naked and slippery, in the shower.

After gathering a few stray dishes from the living room, I notice we have leftover pizza. I radio my teammates in the car outside. They came in for a little while earlier, and I know they have a shift change coming up. But still, I want to see if they need anything. "Hey," I say into my phone, "anybody hungry for leftover pizza?"

"No thanks, Foxy, we're all good. You have a nice night."

Ugh, that stupid nickname is spreading.

But as I'm about to switch off the kitchen light, a car pulls into my driveway. The headlights and movement instantly make me tense. I don't recognize that car.

Within moments, one of my bodyguard teammates is out of his vehicle and closing in with a hand near his gun holster. In a flash, I unlock the hidden safe in my pantry and grab my own weapon. I head outside in my socks.

A slim, tall man is getting out of his car with his hands up. "Good Lord, don't shoot. Unless you rent-a-cops want to get sued out of existence."

It's Derek Keller. The lawyer for Amber Printz. What the *hell* is he doing at my house?

I tuck my gun away and round Derek's car. He's about to say something else. But I keep advancing and push him roughly against the side of his vehicle, my hand on the center of his chest. "What the fuck do you want? Haven't you done enough damage for one day?"

"I need to talk to Quinn."

I fist his collar. My blood boils at the sound of her name in his mouth. "Wrong answer," I snarl. "I'm not letting you anywhere near her."

"Not your decision. You're just the guard dog. You even

have a dog's name. *Rex*? That's your actual legal name? What were your parents thinking?"

Nostrils flaring, I lean in enough that he'll feel my breath in his face.

"I'll talk to him."

Derek and I both look to the side. Quinn is standing in the open doorway to the kitchen. She's wearing jeans and a Team Triumph hoodie that's big enough to swallow her.

She turns around and goes back inside.

Derek sneers at me. "Mind removing your paws from my suit?"

I step back, making a show of brushing off his lapels. "If you say anything that so much as gives her indigestion, I'm throwing you out on your ass."

"Isn't she a bit young for you, gramps?"

"Aren't you a bit young to be sassing your elders?" As if I care for one second what this asshole thinks of my relationship with Quinn. I gesture for him to follow her inside. "Remember my warning. This old dog knows plenty of tricks."

"Ha. Ha." Derek heads inside.

I lift my chin at my teammate. "Thanks. We're good for now." Then I follow Derek and Quinn into the kitchen. She's standing by the island with an icy glare on her face. I'm glad to see Derek is squirming in his rumpled suit.

I lean against the closed door and cross my arms.

"What's this about, Keller?" she asks. "If you're here to gloat—"

"I'm not. I swear. Trust me, I don't want to be here any more than you want to see me." His eyes narrow in my direction. "But I didn't feel I had a choice. Is there, uh, someplace we could sit down?"

I open my mouth to refuse, but Quinn beats me to it. "I'm

not going to make you more comfortable. Just say what you need to say. I'm tired."

Derek rubs a hand over his jaw. "Yeah, I know it's been a rough couple of days for you."

"Spit it out," Quinn snaps.

"First, you've got to believe me when I say I didn't know!" These words come out in a rush. "I swear I didn't know about what Pete Diamond had planned."

"Changing his testimony to make us look like fools? Claiming that Lana and I coerced him?"

"Yes. But also..."

I take a menacing step toward him, and he blanches.

"I'm getting to it, okay? But this isn't easy. I'm violating client confidentiality here."

"Then why are you doing it?" Quinn asks.

His eyes squeeze shut, then open again. "Because it's the right thing to do."

I'm amazed the guy knows the difference. Not because he's a defense lawyer. I know many admirable attorneys on the other side, like Jane Holt. My opinion of Keller is based solely on his past behavior toward Quinn.

"Go on," Quinn prompts. "I'm officially intrigued."

He starts to pace across the tile floor. "Okay. When I agreed to represent Amber, I interviewed all the potential witnesses in preparation for her defense. Including Pete. He said basically what he testified to in court. That Amber was in the spa the whole time on the day of the murder. Then he changed his story, and I assumed it was sour grapes because she'd rejected him. I really didn't know what he planned to do."

"Get to your point."

"I *am*. So today, after the verdict, Amber and I had our press conference with the media. Then we headed to my firm's office, which isn't far from the courthouse. Amber insisted on bringing Pete with us. He was ecstatic. Shaking hands like it was the best day of his life. But he was claiming the credit. Because, according to him, he'd tricked the prosecution and it had all worked perfectly. Pete thought the best part was that he *really saw her sneak out of the spa that day*."

Quinn's eyes bug. "You're telling me Amber is guilty? Your client?"

He looks like he wants to crawl out of his skin. "I can't believe I'm doing this either. But she's already been acquitted. It's double jeopardy. The point isn't really her guilt, okay?"

"It is to anyone who loved Thompson Hayworth," I mutter.

Quinn holds up a hand. "Wait, are you saying Pete Diamond is an accessory to Amber killing Thompson? The DA could nail him."

"I'm not in the business of putting together cases for you to prosecute. Do with Pete Diamond what you will, because he's not my client. Just let me get this out, okay? It'll make sense in the end." He takes a breath. "Amber went to another room to make some phone calls, and then Pete *really* started running his mouth. Wanted us to know exactly how smart he was. He said the day of the murder, he waited to see what Amber was up to. Eventually she came back to the spa, pretending she'd never left. But after he drove her to the Hayworth residence in the West Oaks hills, and they found Thompson's body, Pete made his move. He told Amber that he knew she'd left the spa. He asked her if she'd killed her husband. She denied it at first, sobbing, but then he pointed out the spot of blood on her ankle. She'd missed it when she was cleaning herself up and disposing of evidence. And he made her an offer."

"Let me guess," Quinn deadpans. "It involved Amber sleeping with him."

No wonder I got such sleazy vibes from Diamond that day we met with him. Thank God I didn't let him around Quinn alone.

Derek shrugs. "The way Pete told it, he offered to be her savior out of the goodness of his heart, and she accepted. Pete would pull strings to cover up her guilt and let Amber remain ignorant of whatever he did, so that she would have deniability. She was so grateful that they struck up a romantic relationship."

I snort. "Of course." What a love story. The murderess and her blackmailer.

"That makes Pete an accessory after the fact," Quinn says. "What exactly did he do to help her?"

"That's what I'm getting to. And keep in mind, Pete and Amber both swear up and down that Amber had no knowledge of anything else he did. So don't think you can bring new charges against my client."

Quinn rolls her eyes.

"Pete lied for her, to start with. He solidified Amber's alibi when the police first interviewed him. But later, when she became the main suspect in the murder, Pete came up with a new idea. Amber's accounts had already been blowing up on social media by then because of all the attention on the murder. So Pete figured, why not turn Amber's devoted followers into something more useful? A weapon."

Quinn's gaze flies to meet mine. I think I see where this is going, and I'm ready to track down Diamond right fucking now. But instead I force myself to stay still and listen.

"Pete combed Reddit subthreads about Amber for potential patsies. It took a while to find people he was sure would agree. First, he talked them into making threats against the district attorney. Then, after your role in the upcoming trial became more clear, Pete told them directly to go after you. Harass you. Make your life difficult. Maybe scare you into quitting the trial team. Pete promised them that after Amber was acquitted, she'd show her appreciation to anyone who participated in this scheme."

Quinn makes a face. "Gross."

"No kidding. I couldn't believe what I was hearing. Amber had already sworn to me that she had no idea who was harassing you, Quinn. And I suppose she didn't know directly because Pete was keeping her ignorant of the details. But if I'd had any suspicion, I would have done something to stop it."

"Sure you would have," I say, making my skepticism clear.

"It's true! Especially after Quinn got a concussion. I never would've wanted her hurt."

I cross the kitchen toward him. "Did Pete make all these admissions *before* that psycho chased us down Ocean Lane? Or after?"

Derek pales. "It was before. But I swear, I had no idea anyone was still going after Quinn. I didn't realize—"

"I don't fucking care." I keep advancing, backing him up against the kitchen table. "You should've called the police the moment you found out about Pete's goon squad. We could've been in a car accident. Quinn could've been seriously injured or worse."

"That's why I'm here now. I'm informing you both so you can take necessary steps. You're a bodyguard. It's your job to deal with this kind of thing, not mine."

"Like hell it's not your job. You're going to call West Oaks PD and tell them everything you just confessed."

Derek looks like he's about to argue with me, but Quinn interrupts. "Hold on. Just wait. Did Pete say anything about contacting me and pretending to be an anonymous witness? Was that part of his scheme?"

Derek heaves a sigh. "I'm hazy on the details. He just said you contacted him, and he decided to use the opportunity to destroy your case at trial. He thought it was hilarious that you didn't suspect he was behind the harassment. He was going on and on about his acting skills."

I clench my teeth on a growl. What I wouldn't give to have my hands around Pete Diamond's neck right now.

"And what about Christian Hayworth?" Quinn asks. "Why did he send Pete to work on that movie set in Nevada?"

"Oh, Pete did mention that." Derek rolls his eyes. "Pete hates Christian almost as much as he hates the prosecutors. He said Christian suspected him of helping Amber, so Christian tried to banish him out of state. Pete wasn't having that, so he came back to West Oaks to be close to Amber."

"But why wouldn't Christian tell the police if he suspected Pete? Or tell Quinn and the other prosecutors?"

"I don't know." He rubs the skin between his eyes. "All I know is what Pete blabbed, and I didn't memorize it. This has been an exhausting day for me too."

Quinn arches an eyebrow.

"All right, Mr. Keller." I clap a hand on his shoulder. "You said your piece. Now it's time to go."

His head snaps up. "But I was going to ask about hiring Bennett Security myself. What if Pete finds out that I snitched and sends his creepy online friends after *me* this time?"

I bark a laugh. "You're kidding, right?"

I shove Derek unceremoniously out the door and lock it behind him. When I turn around, Quinn's mouth is curved at the corner in a subtle smirk. I walk over to her. "You okay?" I ask, opening my arms.

She accepts my embrace, tucking her head beneath my chin. "It feels good to know at least part of it. I'm still pissed at myself for believing Pete. But then again, he was actually telling the truth about seeing Amber in that alley. I doubt he was the anonymous witness, though. He probably didn't even know what I was talking about, but decided to roll with it."

"He's an opportunist. That seems to be Pete Diamond's biggest asset."

"True. And if he'd kept his mouth shut today, we probably couldn't have done anything to him. He never thought Derek would rat on him. What bugs me the most is that we still have no proof that Amber was involved in the harassment campaign or manipulating the trial. Sounds like Pete kept her separate from it enough that she'll skate, once again."

"I'm sorry, sweetheart."

"I think I'll take that shower now. Still want to join me?"

"That's incredibly tempting. But I need to let Angela know what Derek told us. She can run with it from there. Combined with the progress Angela already made today with Sam, the driver of the car who chased us, I think she'll have enough for an arrest. I'd be shocked if Pete Diamond isn't in custody by the end of tomorrow. He should be held responsible for everything that was done to you since he instigated it."

"And hopefully he'll be charged as an accessory to Thompson Hayworth's murder as well. I'll talk to Lana first thing in the morning."

Quinn goes up for her shower while I draft a message for Angela. I would call, except it's getting late, and she and Matteo have a little one. I wouldn't want to wake their son.

Afterward, I make sure the house is secure and head upstairs to our bedroom. I love seeing Quinn already under the covers, hair damp and hanging over her shoulders, dressed in one of my T-shirts. She's staring intently at something on her phone.

"Anything interesting?" I ask, starting to undress.

She blinks and hits pause on whatever she was watching. "I think I've got it. The last missing piece."

"Then lay it on me."

"I was thinking again about the anonymous witness. If it wasn't Pete Diamond, I was back to my other two original suspects. Christian, Thompson's son, and Kendall, Thompson's assistant. I'd already scratched both of them off my list the day we saw them in Los Angeles. But I was wrong. It was definitely one of them."

"How do you know?"

"I think the witness found out that Pete Diamond had seen Amber leave the spa that day. The witness thought about informing the prosecutors, but wasn't ready to commit. Not until they'd explored every option. What if the witness stopped contacting me because he—or she—negotiated a more attractive deal?"

"Is this speculation? Or do you have a more specific theory in mind?"

Quinn holds up her phone. "Amber just posted a new video to her social feed, talking about what's next for her now that she's been acquitted. Take a look. See if you draw the same conclusion I did."

I watch, and as I do, I realize what Quinn's new theory must be.

A more attractive deal.

"Unbelievable," I say. "So the witness is..."

Quinn nods. "But we have to prove it. And we just might be able to lay a trap for Amber too. I've got an idea."

"I love your ideas." I shuck off my jeans and slide into bed next to her, clad in just boxers. "I'm listening."

She pulls up something else on her phone. A website. "An entertainment gossip site posted today about party planners bringing rental equipment to the Hayworth residence in the West Oaks hills. Rumor is that Amber's hosting a blowout there this weekend to celebrate the end of the trial. A black-tie affair. Invite only. Do you think Sylvie could use those hacker skills of hers to manufacture an invite for us?"

"I'll ask. I expect the answer is yes."

Quinn tells me how she's hoping this would work, and I make some suggestions and adjustments to her plan. "There's only one more thing I need," she says, "and this will be tricky. The passcode to Amber's phone. But I have some ideas for that as well. We have a few days before the event to put it all together. What do you think?"

"I think you're extraordinary." I tug her close so we're sharing the same pillow, facing one another. "Do you have *any* idea how sexy it is to watch you solve a case, counselor?"

"You get off on competency?"

"In a gorgeous woman? Hell yeah, I do. I was in the service for twenty years. There are few things I appreciate more than a job well done, and you're making me very hot and bothered."

She grins, then shifts so her leg hitches over my thigh. She takes my free hand and guides it between her legs beneath the T-shirt. She's naked. Soft and wet and oh-so-warm. "Want to show me?"

"That would be my pleasure."

I slide down the mattress until my mouth is in just the right place. My hands grasp the backs of her knees and spread them wide. And then I show her with my lips and tongue how much I appreciate her.

"Wait," Quinn gasps. "Let me suck you at the same time?"

"A team effort. I like it."

I lie on my back, pushing my boxers to my thighs, and she crawls over me on her hands and knees. I'm halfway hard already, but Quinn takes my cock into her mouth, and my length rapidly fills and stiffens against her swirling tongue.

She's still wearing my T-shirt, which brushes my stomach. I push the fabric over her hips to expose her bottom half.

Mmmm.

I lift my upper body so I've got the ideal angle, and I push my tongue inside her. She quivers. I feel the vibrations of her moans on my cock since it's filling her mouth.

We bring each other to the brink, and then over the edge. In sync, every step of the way.

27

Quinn

Our car pulls up to the gate, and Cliff buzzes down the driver's side window at the guard kiosk. The mansion beyond the high stucco wall is awash with lights, music, and voices.

"Invitation?" the guard asks.

"Ms. Ainsley?" Cliff glances back at me, and I hand him my phone. The guard scans the code on my screen. Frowns.

My heart beats rapidly at my throat.

Someone in the long line of cars behind us honks impatiently. Beside me, Rex squeezes my hand. *It's going to work,* I can feel in his gesture, as if he said it aloud.

This had better work. Because our plan will collapse if it doesn't.

We've spent the last several days prepping and avoiding the media. Interest in Amber's story has snowballed since her acquittal at trial. Lana has been making statements in writing only since she's on bed rest. I've had more requests for interviews than I can count.

I expect to be recognized tonight. But that's all part of the elaborate setup we've designed. Just like a movie.

As long as I can get inside.

My grip on Rex's hand gets tighter the longer we wait. The guard is staring at his screen.

And then, finally, he nods. "Welcome, Ms. Ainsley and Mr. Easton. Go on ahead."

I exhale. The gate slides open, and Cliff pulls us forward into a circular drive. A line of photographers and reporters peers at our tinted windows, though they can't see us inside.

"I knew Sylvie would come through on the invite," I say.

"Really?" Rex smirks. "You seemed pretty nervous there."

"Hey, it's been a stressful few days."

"I know, sweetheart." He wraps an arm around my shoulder and pulls me in for a kiss. "You've got this. I love you."

I spot Cliff looking in the rearview mirror, a hesitant smile tugging at his lips. At least that much has improved.

"Love you too," I whisper. "Always and forever." I say those words without thinking, but I truly do mean them.

His expression is soft and fond. "Let's just get through tonight and go from there."

The day of the verdict was one of the wildest roller coaster rides I've ever been on. The utter despair of losing the case. The wild adrenaline rush of the car chase, and then Rex telling me for the first time that he loves me.

And, as if that wasn't enough, Derek showing up and violating client confidentiality to inform on Pete Diamond. I certainly couldn't have predicted that. As much as Derek annoys me, he came through by making an official report to the police. Pete Diamond was arrested the next day. He failed to make bail, and he's facing a slew of charges. The charge of being an accessory to murder might not stick. But if it does, Pete could face years in prison.

I haven't been able to stop thinking about what I could've done differently at trial. For one, I wouldn't have put Pete on the stand. It's impossible to go back and correct my mistakes. Amber probably won't serve a day for killing her husband. But if the truth comes out, at least the world will know.

And the world will find out who chose to sell out their ideals and accept Amber's money instead. *My secret witness*. As the days have passed, I've only become more convinced that my theory is correct. But I've still got to prove it.

It all depends on tonight.

Cliff pulls us up to the red carpet. He's dressed up in a sharp suit to play our chauffeur, a far more honorable one than Pete Diamond ever was. Cliff pops out of his seat, rounding the car to open the back door. Cameras are already flashing.

Rex gets out first. With his muscular frame in that tux, he looks like the A-list star of an action movie. Hair slicked back, threaded with silver. His gray beard is trimmed, a lopsided smile on his handsome face. He's equal parts distinguished and devastating. The star of all my dreams.

He turns and holds out his hand to me.

I slide one leg out of the car and stand up, accepting Rex's offered hand. My dress shifts and falls into place. It's a deep sapphire, cut close to my upper body with tiny straps over my shoulders. From my waist, the skirt flares out in a generous A-line.

Rex leans close, humming appreciatively. "You look good enough to eat. Have I mentioned that?"

"Once or twice."

"Be careful," Cliff mutters, shutting the car door behind us. "Good luck."

"Thanks, son," Rex says. "We'll see you soon." He hooks my arm around his, and we start down the red carpet. I ignore shouts of my name. Questions about what I'm doing here and whether Amber invited me.

Thankfully, someone else arrives a moment after us, and the attention shifts.

When we're past the entrance, security discreetly waves a metal detector wand over us. But neither of us is armed. We make it to the wide lawn, where the party is taking place. There are tents set up. Servers carrying trays of champagne and canapes. I recognize famous faces all around. Plus banners announcing the brand names of sponsors and official photographers documenting everything. It's a cool night. Palm trees wave in a salty breeze, and flowers bloom all around the manicured garden.

"Amber's not holding the party inside the house," Rex says against my ear. "Surprised she had that much sense."

"Her guests wouldn't want to sip champs in a recent murder scene. Then again, maybe that would be a draw. You never know."

"I'm sure she's saving the murder scene party for next time."

I shake my head in disgust, forcing my smile back into place. I scan the crowd for the people I'm looking for.

Then Christian Hayworth storms in our direction. *Ah ha.* Interesting.

I assume he's headed for the exit. I don't think he's noticed me. He's scowling at something over his shoulder, and then he stops short when he gets a look at me. His expression darkens further. "Miss Ainsley. And your body-guard. What on earth are you doing at this macabre affair?"

"Shouldn't I ask you the same thing?" I say.

I lift an eyebrow at Rex, communicating silently. He keeps a tight hold on my arm.

Christian steps to the side of the walkway, lowering his voice. "Now that Amber's secured my father's fortune, she promised a large donation to the foundation I support. The only catch was that I had to appear at this…freak show. She's got corporate sponsors for a party celebrating how she got away with murder."

"She did get away with it, didn't she?"

He narrows his eyes. "I never imagined I'd see you here, considering how Pete Diamond humiliated you at the trial. I actually felt sorry for you. But here you are, stunning as a starlet at a premiere. I'd ask you again to join me for dinner, but I'm not interested in fame-seekers. I guess you've decided infamy is better than nothing? Just like Amber?"

"Watch how you speak to her," Rex warns.

"It's all right." I kiss Rex on his whiskered cheek, then turn back to Christian. "You make a fair point. But not everything is what it appears. You make movies. You should know that better than anyone."

Christian sighs, glancing around. "This is exhausting. I'm leaving."

I rest a hand on his forearm. "I just have one question. Why did you send Pete to that remote film set in Nevada?"

"Why should I tell you?"

"Because it matters. Trust me. I'm not here for the reasons you think."

Christian shrugs. "He made comments about my father that I didn't appreciate. Called him a doddering old fool who wouldn't have lived long anyway, so who cared if he was dead? I thought about firing him, but I didn't want Pete to start talking that way in the media. I didn't realize what else he was up to."

"So you care about how your father is viewed. But you've cancelled a lot of Thompson's projects. You've taken Hayworth Productions in a direction that Thompson wouldn't like."

"Says who? I've made some necessary business decisions, but I'm not completely heartless. I loved my father. Not that it's anything to you." He steps back, tugging at his lapels to straighten his jacket. "Goodnight, Miss Ainsley. I don't imagine I'll be seeing you again."

We watch him walk out the exit.

"Still holding to your theory?" Rex asks quietly.

"Yep. Christian wasn't the secret witness." He never knew Pete Diamond concealed evidence that Amber was the murderer. If he had, he'd have done far more than just shuttle Pete off to Nevada.

Murmurs spread through the crowd, and everyone turns to look at the house. Amber Printz has just emerged. Fashionably late to her own party, of course. She's wearing an off-white tea-length dress, fitted to hug every inch of her body. Stiletto heels.

She walks forward, exchanging air kisses and smiling angelically as the crowd parts around her.

"That's my cue," I say. Nerves zip through me.

"You've got this." Rex's large hand rests on my lower back, warm and reassuring. It drops when I walk toward Amber. But I hear his footsteps as he follows a couple of feet behind me.

"Hello, Ms. Printz. Freedom suits you."

Ugh. Saying that makes me throw up a little in my mouth.

Amber's smile falters when she sees me. But she recovers fast. "Quinn. I don't remember putting you on my invite list. What a...pleasant surprise."

"Must've been one of your assistants." My grin is as fake as hers. We have an audience, and several of them are probably reporters or influencers who'll repeat every word we say online.

Amber must be thinking the same thing. She grabs my hands and leans in to air-kiss my cheek. "It's wonderful to see you again. After you were *so* instrumental to the jury acquitting me."

Eyebrows raise, and I spot more than one phone recording.

"I was just doing my job. You know how it is. Win some, lose some. No hard feelings?"

Amber waves a hand. "I believe in forgiveness. Letting the past go."

"That's my attitude as well. What happened with Pete Diamond on the stand was embarrassing for me, but I'm over it." I make a show of glancing around. "Where *is* he tonight? Oh, right. Jail."

"He's not here, and that's all I care about. I had no idea he'd sent those people to harass you. You know that, don't you, Quinn?" Her tone is sickly sweet. "I don't need friends like Pete. That's not the image I'm going for. Take a selfie for my feed?"

She plucks her phone from a beaded drawstring purse and holds it up, posing as she snaps our photo. Then another. And another. "There. Had to get my angles right. I'll tag you. You'll probably have ten thousand new followers in ten minutes."

"I can only hope," I deadpan.

"I'm up to three million." She points at the tables with swag provided by her sponsors. "That's where the money is these days. There are no movie stars anymore. It's all about the influencers. Not that I *need* money after what Thompson left me."

I notice a familiar face lurking just beyond the circle of people vying for Amber's attention. It's Kendall Simms. Thompson Hayworth's former assistant. My gaze meets hers, and I give her a small nod.

There you are, I think. *Exactly where I want you.*

Just a few more pieces to get into place before my big finale.

Amber tucks her phone back into her tiny drawstring purse. I stare openly. “That bag is gorgeous.”

“Isn’t it?” She names the designer. “They sent it to me yesterday to congratulate me. The beads are all precious stones. Sapphires, emeralds, rubies. It matches your dress.” She tilts her head. “You look so *cute* in that.”

“Thanks,” I gush. “It even has pockets.” I tuck my hands into the slots, which are almost hidden in the folds of the skirt. I borrowed the dress from Lana, who attends far more black-tie affairs than I do, and had some key alterations made in the last few days.

As Amber gives my outfit a once-over, her eyes lift, and her smile turns flirtatious. “And who is this? Your bodyguard from Bennett Security, right? I saw him in the audience at the trial.”

Rex stands at my shoulder. I side-eye him like I’m annoyed. “Oh. Yes. This is Rex Easton.”

Rex steps forward and takes Amber’s hand. He brings it to his mouth and kisses her knuckles. *Yuck*. “The pleasure’s mine,” Rex says in his deepest, sexiest voice.

Amber’s large green eyes are fixed on his dark ones. A quick flash of rage makes me want to claw those pretty irises out.

Step away from my man.

But this is the exact moment of distraction I need. I lean forward, slipping my hand into the open mouth of her drawstring purse. Then back to my pocket. We’re all close together, our bodies shielding the switch from view.

Perfect.

“I’ve been looking for a new personal bodyguard,” Amber says to Rex. “Maybe we could chat about it later?”

Before he can respond, I interrupt. “Actually, I have a business proposition for you of my own. Could we discuss it? In private?”

She looks ready to dismiss me. "You'll have to call my agent."

"I promise you'll want to hear this." I nod at Rex, who's still close to my shoulder. "Then you can talk to Rex afterward. He *is* working for me tonight, but I could spare him for a few minutes."

"A one-on-one meeting?" she asks.

"Whatever you want."

I feel him shift his stance, and I swear he's trying not to laugh. *Sorry for pimping you out, Foxy,* I think. But I know he doesn't mind. I don't intend to let Amber alone with him for one second. If she tries to put her murderous hands on my guy, she'll see what happens.

Interest flares again in her eyes. "Why not? We can go inside for a bit to chat."

"Rex, could you grab Kendall too?" I ask. "She's right over there. My proposition involves her as well."

He nods. Amber looks surprised at this development, but she doesn't object. Rex goes to say a quiet word to Kendall, who follows our group into the side entrance of the mansion. As we head in, I quickly pull the phone from my pocket, enter the passcode, and pull up the app I want. It takes less than three seconds. Then I put the phone back into place in the folds of my skirt.

Amber leads us through the ornate home and into an office on the first floor. It's paneled in rich woods. Oscar statues line a shelf on the wall. She sets her purse on the massive desk, the phone inside clunking and the expensive beading tinkling.

"This used to be Thompson's office," she announces. "I thought about redecorating, but I like it, you know? It has gravitas."

Rex takes up a position by the closed door, back to playing the stoic bodyguard. But I don't miss the seductive glances Amber keeps throwing his way. Probably planning out how fast she'll get naked with him once I'm out of the room.

Kendall seems far more nervous. She's got her arms crossed over her black pantsuit. "Quinn," she says meekly. "I didn't realize you'd be here tonight."

"Ditto." I grin, and she relaxes.

She shouldn't. Because I'm lying. I had every expectation Kendall would be here tonight. In fact, we were counting on it.

"But it's nice to see you," I say. "Congrats on your news. I saw the video Amber posted after the trial verdict, when she announced it? How she'll be starring in a movie about her life, directed by *you*? That's huge for you, Kendall. Especially after Christian had you blacklisted."

Amber perches on the edge of Thompson's desk, arranging her long legs like this is a photo shoot. "Christian is part of the old guard. Men who don't want young women like us to succeed. I'm sure present company is excluded," she adds with a leer at Rex. His stoic expression betrays nothing.

"Law is the same way," I say. "I'm so tired of old men directing my career."

Amber doesn't seem to realize the irony of my statement. My boss is a woman in her thirties. But never mind that.

Amber goes on, "Women have made strides in Hollywood, but it still comes back to old men with old money. I'm turning the game on its head. Playing by my own rules now."

I laugh. "Sure, but murdering your husband to make it happen is a *little* extreme." I turn to the other woman in the room. "You know all about it, Kendall. You've known for a while that Pete Diamond saw her leave the spa that day. He made me think he was going to tell the truth, then perjured himself on the stand. Fooled me completely." I say this with a touch of admiration in my voice. But I can't fully hide the bitterness.

Amber claps. "Are the claws coming out, Quinn? Go ahead. Talk freely. No cameras here, right?"

"I'm just saying, it can't be a surprise to Kendall. She knows all about what really happened the day of Thompson's murder. In fact, she contacted me anonymously weeks ago. Claimed to have eyewitness evidence against you, Amber. And Kendall is the one who told me Christian had sent Pete Diamond off to Nevada. What I can't figure out is whether Kendall was working with Pete. Did she know Pete would set me up?"

Kendall has flushed red. She eyes the door, but Rex is blocking it.

Amber's perfectly symmetrical eyebrows have shot toward the ceiling. "*Really*? I haven't heard a word about this. You were helping Pete, Kendall?"

"Well, I…not exactly…"

"No wait, I remember now." I tap a finger on my chin. "Pete said he decided to lie to me *after* I contacted him. Pete didn't breathe a word about Kendall when he was bragging to Derek about getting you acquitted, Amber. Besides, Pete had no reason to bring her into his scheme. Kendall didn't have anything Pete could've wanted."

Kendall's jaw tightened. "I wasn't working with him, okay? I can't stand Pete. He's obnoxious and crass. And has a big mouth."

"Which is how you found out that Pete had key evidence against Amber. You both worked for Hayworth Productions, and you overheard him say something. Maybe he didn't notice you hanging around, eavesdropping? I can imagine people tended to overlook you because you were just Thompson's assistant."

Kendall huffs, glancing at the wall.

I've been spelling out my theory to check her reactions, but I think I'm on track so far. "You found out Pete had lied to the police about Amber's alibi," I say, "and that upset you. Because you really did care about Thompson. He was your mentor. One of the few industry people who saw your potential and took you seriously."

"Of course I cared," Kendall whispered, eyes on the rug. "I loved him like a father. I didn't lie about that."

Amber is watching and listening, her eyes narrowed. Rex continues to block the door.

"So you decided to contact me anonymously," I say. "You followed me the night of the lawyer gala and left that note in my purse. You wanted to tell me about Pete. But you were also nervous. Afraid of Pete or Amber retaliating against you."

"Is that true?" Amber asks.

Kendall says nothing.

"But then," I continue, "Christian fired you for sharing your opinions too loudly. You were suddenly out of a job."

"It was completely uncalled for," she snaps. "After all I'd devoted to that company."

"You were blacklisted. Terrified you'd never work in Hollywood again. So you cut off contact with me and held onto your info about Pete. You knew it could be valuable. You didn't want to burn the last bridge you had left."

"But I gave you a hint about him when you came to LA," she points out.

"I guess so. Out of guilt, I'm assuming? But I probably would've tracked Pete down anyway. He was on my list of suspects for being the anonymous witness. I was wrong, obviously." I shrug. "If you'd told me what you knew, he never would've tricked me. But then again, Amber might've been convicted. And you would've lost your shot at a job directing her life story." I grin at Amber. "Let me guess.

Kendall came to you with the idea for the movie? Convinced you that she had the right vision because she'd trained at the feet of Thompson Hayworth, yet she was a young woman rejected by Hollywood, just like you?"

"That's pretty much it, yep." Amber stands up, hands on her hips. "You're sneakier than I realized, Kendall. But you know what I say? *So fucking what.*" She sneers at me. "If you wanted to talk so you could spring that bombshell, it didn't work. I have no problem with a woman using the assets she's got. That's what I did. I'm not ashamed of anything I've had to do to make it."

Amber is triumphant, but Kendall seems to be deflating. She looks ill at having the truth spoken aloud. "You really don't feel bad at all?" she asks Amber. "Even a little? I mean, you must wish there'd been some other way. Right? Thompson was a good man."

The actress snorts. "He was a boring old man who could barely get it up anymore. It hardly took much effort to crack his skull."

Kendall flinches.

"You don't mind admitting it in front of us?" I ask. "That you really did kill him?"

"Why shouldn't I? I've already been acquitted. My lawyer Derek explained everything. It's double jeopardy. I can tell you anything I want, and it doesn't matter."

"But it's still bold of you, considering the innocent image you've created in the media," I point out. "What if I'm recording everything you say?"

"Like you'd have the balls. Recording people without their knowledge is illegal in California. And inadmissible as evidence. I know all about that. You work for the government, so you have to play by the rules."

I glance at my fingernails nonchalantly. "But I'm not the one who's recording it. You are. You're live streaming this entire conversation to your three million fans as we speak. On your own phone."

There's a pause. Rex has a tiny smile. Kendall stares at me in awe, and any trace of color drains from Amber's golden complexion.

She scrambles for her purse and tears her phone free, breaking a few expensive beads in the process. She relaxes slightly when she's holding the device, but then her thumbs keep poking at the screen. "Why isn't the facial recognition working? And it's saying my passcode is wrong. What the *hell?*"

Slowly, I reach into my pocket and remove Amber's phone from the carefully designed holster inside. There's a layer of mesh sewn into the iridescent fabric on the outside of my skirt. Hard to notice if you don't know it's there. But the mesh is placed so that the camera of a phone placed inside can see out.

This never would've worked if I didn't have Amber's code. But Derek knew it, because lawyers learn all kinds of confidential things about their clients, and he agreed to give it to me on the condition that he'd deny it to his grave.

He also told me the kind of case she uses and the image on her lock screen. It wasn't hard for me to order a similar case and put the same photo, one of Amber's modeling pics, as my wallpaper. If Amber had glanced at the phone in her purse after I switched them, she would assume it was hers. She would've gotten suspicious if she'd tried to unlock it before now. But she didn't.

"Looking for this?" I ask.

While she watches, I enter her passcode on the screen. It unlocks, revealing that the Instagram app is open.

And streaming live. Just as I said.

Amber screams.

Kendall lurches toward the door, pushing Rex aside.

Suppose I can't blame her for running. Her involvement in this was just revealed to the world. Who knows how many guests at the party were watching all this unfold in real time?

Everyone knows the truth, and Amber has no hope of spinning this.

Maybe Amber is safe from prison, but her innocent reputation is trashed. So is Kendall's. I'll bet all those corporate sponsors are already scrambling to cut ties.

I glance at Rex, feeling pretty damn proud of myself. Proud of us. Because I couldn't have done it without Rex by my side, being his foxy self and distracting Amber. He nods back at me.

"Guess we can see ourselves out," I say.

Then Rex's face blanches in horror. "*Gun*!"

Before I can react, he lunges toward me. There's a deafening pop. Rex lands on top of me on the carpet. My ears ring, and the smell of gunpowder is acrid in my nose. He rolls to one side of me, and I sit up.

A red stain is spreading on the white fabric of Rex's shirt over his chest.

"*No*!" I cry.

Amber stands by an open wooden box on Thompson's desk. She holds a gun, her mouth an O of pure shock. Like she can't believe it either. Her hand drops, and the gun clatters to the wood floor beneath the desk.

She runs for the door, and I don't try to stop her.

"I'm okay," Rex says hoarsely. He tries to get up, but I won't let him.

"No. No, no, no." That's all I can seem to say. My brain is rejecting it. This can't be happening. I push my hands to the wound, and he groans, but nods.

"Good. Put pressure." He can barely speak. Blood bubbles on his lip. He fumbles for his phone in his pocket and hands it to me.

I remember his phone code, which he told me on that day we went to Los Angeles, and I call 911. "My bodyguard, the man I *love,* has been shot. The Thompson Hayworth residence. Please hurry. *Please.*"

The operator tells me to stay on the line, but Rex says, "Quinn. Look at me." I lean over him. "I love you," he whispers. "Always and forever."

"Me too." My tears fall onto his cheeks. "Always and forever. But I promise this isn't the end." *It's not,* I repeat in my head. *It's not. It's not.* "Our forever is going to last a long damn time. You'd better fight for it."

"I am." He smiles. "I'll go to war for you. Any day."

28

Rex

We're back at the hospital. But I'm the one in the bed this time.

Not a fan.

When I wake up, I'm bandaged and stiff and sore. Groggy from pain meds. Then I look over and see Quinn asleep on the small guest couch. Instantly, I feel that much better.

Her eyes flutter open, and she sits up. "You're awake."

"We have to stop meeting like this," I croak.

"That's a terrible line."

"I've got dad jokes too."

"I know," she says. "I've heard them. I've known you a long time, and I've loved you almost as long." Tears fill her eyes. She gets up to sit beside me, gently kissing my forehead.

"I love you too, gorgeous," I say. "Tell me what I missed."

I've already been conscious several times since I had surgery yesterday. The bullet clipped my lung and broke some ribs. I lost a lot of blood. It could've been much worse. At the party, Quinn called 911, but so did a number of guests who'd heard the gunshot. The paramedics didn't take long to arrive. I'll be out of commission for a while, but the doctors expect a full recovery.

Quinn's been here every moment.

"Lana gave me an update while you were napping," she says. "Our office is working on filing charges against Amber for attempted murder and everything else they can think of. Lana said the double jeopardy on Thompson's murder is airtight. But she'll get prison time. And now that everyone knows Amber really did it, we've got a good shot at convicting Pete Diamond as an accessory to murder. For perjury too."

"What about Kendall? She concealed evidence."

"Lana's not as interested in pursuing that one. Kendall didn't know anything about the murder firsthand. It's not worth our office's time. But if Kendall thought she was done in Hollywood before, that was nothing compared to now. Public sentiment has done a one-eighty against Amber, and Kendall's tangled up in all that bad publicity. You'd think Amber was devil incarnate. She's lost two million followers since last night. Her sponsors are fleeing. Her formerly devoted fans are cursing her name. Oh, and Christian is challenging her right to inherit Thompson's money."

"And you're the heroine of the story, aren't you?"

"Ha! I was for about five minutes while the world watched that livestream."

Quinn's plan worked brilliantly. Up until the point that Amber pulled that gun from the box on Thompson's desk. Police Chief Holt stopped by my hospital room earlier, and he reported the results of their investigation so far. The gun is registered to Pete, and Amber has admitted that Pete left it there at the house after they began sleeping together. I assume Amber decided to hold on to it in case the chauffeur got too difficult to handle.

I'm angry at myself for not anticipating Amber's violent

reaction to being exposed. But after she used a sculpture to hit her husband over the head, she hadn't seemed like the gun type. I had also believed Amber wouldn't act so rashly with that many witnesses around. After all, she'd planned the previous murder so carefully.

Those oversights on my part were nearly fatal.

I think that Amber, in that moment, simply didn't care about the consequences. She wanted to punish Quinn even if it meant losing everything she'd worked so hard to preserve. Thank God I put myself in the way. I would take a hundred more bullets if it means protecting Quinn.

The irony is that if Amber had kept her temper, she most likely wouldn't be in jail right now. She could've walked having gotten away with Thompson's murder.

"Now that everyone knows you jumped in front of a bullet to save me," Quinn says, "you're getting all the glory. It's *Rex Easton* this and *Foxy* that."

I grin at her. "Please tell me you didn't share that nickname with the media."

"But it's so apt." Quinn captures my lips with hers. I stroke my tongue into her mouth. I'd love to grab her and give her the wild make-out session she deserves, but I'm not up to that yet. I need a few days to rest up.

When I'm back in action, though? Quinn had better be ready. Because while I was lying on the floor in Thompson Hayworth's office, my life flashed before my eyes. At first, it was my past. The time I shared with Lydia and Cliff. My military service and my career with Bennett Security since my retirement. And over and over again, memories of Quinn. The girl next door. My son's best friend. The intelligent young woman I considered family.

The talented, tenacious prosecutor I'm head over heels in love with. The second and equally great love of my life.

But I didn't just see my past during those moments. I saw

our future. Everything we could be. I don't intend to waste a second that I get to spend with her.

"Can't wait to get you home," I growl. "And in our bed."

"Like you're going to be in any shape to take charge. For once, I get to take care of *you*. And fulfill *all* your needs," she adds with a sexy purr.

There's a knock, and my son's voice comes from the hallway. "We're about to come in. T-minus thirty seconds. All kissing needs to cease and desist."

Snickering, Quinn gives me one last peck. "Our family's here," she murmurs. "Brace yourself for a whole lot of fussing."

Our family. I love the sound of that.

~

A MONTH AND A HALF LATER, WE'RE BACK AT THE hospital. But this time, it's a joyous occasion.

Lana had her baby.

The waiting room is packed with people from Bennett Security, West Oaks PD, and the DA's office. Aurora Whitestone, Max Bennett's younger sister, hands out sparkly blue cupcakes while her husband Devon tries to keep their energetic son from tearing up the place. Tanner Reid, who shares bodyguard co-captain duties with Devon, is here with his wife Faith, who's playing dolls with Max and Lana's older daughter Joy. Sylvie Trousseau sits with her boyfriend Nic Anderson, who's taking photos of everyone with a huge SLR camera to mark the occasion.

And then there's the cop contingent. Chase Collins is in his patrol uniform, arm around his wife Ruby, both of whom are close friends of Max and Lana. Chief of Police Sean Holt is with his wife Jane, the only other power couple in West Oaks who could rival Max and Lana themselves.

Well, maybe Quinn and I could, given our current fame. *Kidding*. I can't wait until we can walk down Ocean Lane together without being recognized. We've turned down at least a hundred requests for interviews at this point. Being famous blows. I'm over it.

But at least Quinn is back to trying cases, and before much longer I'll be back on bodyguard duty.

Quinn's also made good on her promise to take care of me. After some practice, she's become a top-notch home chef. Also I've never gotten so many blow jobs in my life. Almost worth the whole getting shot part.

Detective De Luca sidles over to us. "Where's Matteo?" Quinn asks.

"At home with Brent. Matteo's on shift tomorrow, so they're getting some daddy-kiddo time along with Matteo's niece Natalie. How are you two?"

Quinn beams up at me, and I lean down for a kiss. "We're perfect," Quinn says. "Or at least, getting there."

I nod. Each day with her is pretty much perfect. Yet our future is still less settled than I'd like.

Amber Printz and Pete Diamond are both now serving time in prison after pleading guilty. About a month ago, Christian Hayworth called Quinn to apologize for the things he said at Amber's party, and to thank her for exposing the truth to the world about his father's killer. And then he asked Quinn to have dinner with him. Again.

She declined. But after I had some choice words for the man, I don't think he'll be repeating that invitation.

But Christian isn't all bad. He's promised to donate the entirety of Thompson's fortune to charity once his lawyers finish up the process of wresting it away from Amber.

Aurora and Devon are the first guests to visit Lana's hospital room. After a while, Quinn and I get our turn to say hello to the mama and baby. When we step inside, the newest member of the Bennett family is sleeping in a bassinet. Lana looks beautiful with a shawl wrapped around her comfy sweats and tee. Max holds their daughter Joy, who's asleep with her head on her dad's shoulder.

"Meet Nicholas Bennett," Lana says.

Quinn bends over to admire the sleeping newborn. "He's precious. What a cutie pie." Nicholas opens his eyes, and Quinn lets out a little gasp.

"He might start crying any second. Do you want to hold him before that happens?" Lana asks.

"Are you kidding?" Quinn picks up Nicholas and settles onto the couch, gazing into his tiny brown eyes. "Hi, little man. You have a lot of people who already love you, you know that?"

Max puts a hand on my shoulder, and I look over at him. I've been with Max through a lot of ups and downs. Both as a Green Beret and as an employee of his company. He looked almost this happy on the day of his wedding, and again on the day he and Lana brought Joy home. But I know how each individual moment can combine and grow into something bigger. Especially when you welcome someone new into your family. The whole becomes so much more than the sum of the parts.

For just a moment, Max isn't my boss anymore, and I'm not his employee. I'm back to being his superior. The guy who used to outrank him. "You did well. Proud of you."

He grins, then nods at Quinn. "Proud of you too. Nice work."

I wink. "Just wait. I have much bigger things planned for her."

"Then I'll be right there with you, celebrating."

After we leave the hospital room, I take Quinn's hand and lead her down the hall. "You looked good holding baby

Nicholas. What do you think? Do you want one of your own? Or maybe more than one?"

Quinn sucks in a breath and stares at me.

For the past six weeks since I was shot, I've tried to bring up this topic with her. Every time, Quinn changes the subject. I'm not sure why. Cliff told me that she wants to be a mom. Maybe she doesn't want that with *me*. That would be hard for me to hear. It'll rip my heart out if she's not on the same page. But it's better that we get it out in the open now. Because I really do have plans for her, like I told Max.

She still hasn't said anything. I cup the back of her neck and rest my forehead against hers. "Sweetheart, talk to me. Cliff said you want kids. Is that... Do you not want that with me?"

I know she loves me. I've cherished every day we've spent so far. And she said *forever*. But have I somehow gotten this wrong? Does Quinn not plan on spending the rest of our lives together?

Maybe she doesn't want a guy who's almost fifty as the future father of her children.

Quinn's eyes are shining. "Of course I want that. I just didn't know if *you* wanted to have more kids. I was nervous to ask. It's not a deal breaker."

But. I hear that word in what she's not saying. *But*.

"You deserve to have everything," I say. "You shouldn't have to sacrifice to be with me. I'd never ask that of you."

She shakes her head, trying to pull away from my grip. "But this decision can't be something that's just for me."

"Hey, hold on. I didn't mean for it to sound that way." I move my hands to cradle her face, looking deep into her pale blue eyes. "After Cliff was grown, I didn't imagine I'd have another child. It didn't even occur to me. But I *do* want that with you. I want it so badly it's been taking up more and more space in my head. I want to watch your belly grow and hold our baby in my arms. Or babies, plural. And see how incredible I *know* you'll be as a mom. Let me share that with you, Quinn. Let me be the father of your children."

She shivers. "Oh wow. That's the hottest thing I've ever heard in my life. I have never been this turned on."

I laugh and kiss her nose. "Slow down, gorgeous. Give a guy a little time to prepare. And I promise, I will give you the family and the life you've been dreaming of."

"If you let me do the same for you, then you've got a deal."

EPILOGUE

Rex

Cliff clinks a fork against his beer glass. "I'd like to make a toast to my dad. Five decades. Damn. People say these days that fifty is the new forty. But Dad, you like to keep it old school, and I respect that about you."

There's laughter and cheers around the private room Cliff rented in this steakhouse for my birthday. All my friends and family have been taking turns roasting me. First my Bennett Security teammates, then some fellow Team Triumph volunteers and a few Green Beret buddies who made the trip for the occasion, and now my kid.

Yeah, I might be among the oldest guys here. But I've got the most beautiful woman by my side, so I'm not complaining. I don't think Quinn is complaining either, judging by the way she's been massaging my thigh under the table.

Or the desperate, lust-drunk moans she made when I was inside her this morning.

"But seriously, Dad," Cliff says. "You're the best. You've always supported me, even when I was too pigheaded to realize it. I've been changing a lot about my life in the last six months, and your advice has really helped."

My skin warms all over. Cliff has never said that to me, and it means more than he could know. But Quinn understands. She reaches for my hand and grips it tight.

"And while it surprised me that you fell in love with my best friend, now I couldn't be happier for the both of you. Because I see how perfect you are for one another. Your ages might be different, but your souls match up in all the ways that count. It's the best thing in the world to see two people that I love making each other so happy. Love you, Q. Love you, Dad. Cheers."

We all drink to that. Then Cliff pounds his palm on the table, shouting that it's my turn to make a speech. My other friends follow. The ruckus only dies down when I hold up my hands in a placating gesture.

"Okay, okay." I stand up and lift my glass.

Cliff gives me a small nod of encouragement. It's possible that my son and I coordinated this part. A little theatrical, sure. But it's for a good purpose.

"Thank you all so much for being here to celebrate with me. And to commiserate with me over the fact that I've reached half a century. But looking around at all of your faces, I'm blown away at how many amazing memories I've packed into that time. More than any guy could expect in a lifetime, and trust me, I'm still going strong. I'm grateful for what I've accomplished with all of you. My brothers in arms." I raise my glass to my various teammates. "My son Cliff, who's making me so damn proud. My friends from my years here in West Oaks, and friends who've stuck with me from before. Including those who can't be here today."

I pause briefly, meeting eyes around the room. Thinking of Cliff's mother, of course, but also the brothers and friends we've all lost along the way.

Then I turn to Quinn. And I set my glass on the table. "Most of all, I am grateful for you, Quinn. Most people are lucky to get one great love in life, and somehow, I get to have two. You are extraordinary. Not just in the courtroom. Or when you're famously solving cases as skillfully as any investigator." I wink, and laughter spreads quietly through the room. "You also take care of me in all the ways I didn't realize I was missing."

Quinn is gazing up at me from her seat with a sheen of tears in her eyes. *I love you,* she mouths silently. Which just makes me smile bigger, because I can't wait to see the look on her face when she hears the next part.

I dig a hand into my pants pocket. "I've been on this earth for fifty years now, as all of my friends keep reminding me. I intend to stick around for at least another fifty. And I hope to spend every single one of them with you. You are the only woman for me, and I'm honored to have you by my side."

I get down on one knee and pull the ring box from my pocket. "Quinn, will you marry me?"

She gasps, and her hands fly to her mouth. Then she jumps up and nearly tackles me as she kisses me. My beer glass knocks over on the table. We're laughing and maybe crying—I'll admit it—and for a brief second, time seems to freeze.

This is where our life truly begins, I think. *So long as she says yes.*

Of course she said yes.

Six months later, I'm standing behind the beach house in a tuxedo, a brand-new one bought just for this occasion. Waves crash onto the sand beyond, and a cool breeze drifts over, caressing the back of my neck. A violin soloist plays while our friends and family talk quietly, taking their seats.

The sun is just sinking beneath the horizon, painting the sky with broad strokes of color.

And then the music swells and Quinn appears. She steps out through the patio doors in layers of ivory silk, like a goddess come to life. An image straight out of my dreams.

She holds Cliff's arm, and they walk down the aisle toward me. We've kept things simple. No other wedding party members except the three of us. But really, I consider everyone here with us today to be part of the ceremony. They're lending their support and love as we start this next step of our lives together.

Even Quinn's parents. They were surprised to find out she planned to marry the man who used to be their next-door neighbor. The father of her friend. But they've been polite about it, not outwardly showing any disapproval. Because they've rarely had a strong opinion on anything Quinn does. This is one moment that I don't mind their indifference as parents. I wouldn't want any damper on her smile today.

But it speaks volumes that she asked Cliff to walk her down the aisle.

Quinn reaches me, her lips trembling. "Hi," she whispers.

"Hey, gorgeous." My voice is thick with all I'm feeling.

"Love you, Quinn. Take care of the old man." Cliff gives her a kiss on the cheek and then opens his arms to give me a hug. "Take care of her, Dad. Love you." Then he stands beside me to act as my best man.

I reach for Quinn's hand, and together we face the officiant. Electricity zings between us where we touch. A reminder of the promises we've already made. And the promises we're making now in front of all the people we care about. Friends old and new.

But when we kiss, everyone else disappears, and it's just us. My girl and me. My wife.

This moment adds to all the good memories that have come before, and I can honestly say I have never been this happy.

And it's only getting better from here.

Quinn

We kept our ceremony short and sweet. By the time the sun is completely down, we're hugging and kissing our friends and family, and the band is starting up under the rental tent. Even though we decided on the beach house as the venue, I still wanted to make this a swanky party. If only because Rex looks so dang good when he's dressed to the nines.

I briefly considered pink tulle for my dress, just like prom night ten years ago. But that would've been a lot of effort for a silly inside joke between Rex and me. And more importantly, I'm not eighteen anymore. I'm not that sad girl pining after a man she can never have.

I got my man. And today is about celebrating the love we have right now. We're soulmates. It just took us both a while to become the people, inside and out, that we are today.

I did go with white and yellow roses for my bouquet,

though. As a reference to the first night Rex and I spent in bed together. That sexy massage he gave me was hot, and I wouldn't mind a repeat.

As we greet our guests, I notice two faces I hadn't expected to be here. "Aiden," I say, rushing over to give him a hug. "You made it!"

"We weren't sure with the restaurant and our other responsibilities in Hartley. But it worked out." My former roommate is here with his girlfriend, Jessi. Aiden looks good in his suit, even though I suspect he'd be far more comfortable in jeans and no shirt.

Jessi leans closer to me. "He pulled a bunch of strings to make sure we could be here. My brother and his wife are covering for us at the tavern."

"Tell them thanks for me." I hug her. Jessi's a tall brunette with a pretty, kind face. I've only met her once before, the last time she and Aiden came to West Oaks to move his belongings permanently to Colorado. But she's a sweetheart and a perfect match for my grumpy ex-roommate.

Danny and Lark come up behind us. "It's a Pink House reunion," Danny says, snagging Cliff by the jacket and dragging him and Lia over too.

"Missed you all," I say.

Aiden gives me a look. "You sure about that?"

"Well, I miss your cooking, Aiden. And Danny's sunny personality."

"What do you miss about me?" Cliff asks.

The rest of us stare at him, saying nothing. He flips us off. "You're all assholes. Bride included."

We crack up. I hook my best friend around the neck, pulling him down to kiss his cheek. "I barely have time to miss you because I see you all the time. I wouldn't want it any other way."

"Thanks, Stepmom," he quips.

"I'm okay with that title now. I'm ready to own it."

Lark pulls me aside because we haven't had a hug yet. "Congrats, Mrs. Easton. I'm so happy for you. Also, I called it."

"You just had to say it."

"Yep. And now, we can party."

We've rented a big white tent for the reception. Fairy lights are strung all around the rafters, and moonlight reflects on the waves. Tonight is a mix of formal and casual. Elegant centerpieces and dressy clothes paired with burgers and beer. Rex confessed that he hates champagne, and the truth is, I'm indifferent. We do what's right for *us*, and we don't care what anyone else thinks because we know our loved ones have our backs. Just like we have theirs.

I wanted tonight to be all about celebrating with our friends and family. And they do us proud, keeping the party going on the dance floor until late.

But finally, the guests trickle to their ride-shares to stay at a nearby hotel. As for Rex and me, we're spending the night here at the beach house.

Our first night as husband and wife. I get giddy every time I think those words.

"You ready, Mrs. Easton?" Rex asks me. He's even sexier with his bowtie undone and hair disheveled.

"I've been ready since…" I think about it. "The night of the gala about a year ago. When I saw you in your tux."

"Only then? Not before?"

I shake my head. "No. Because that's the first night I really started getting to know you as *Rex*. I thought I loved you before that, but I had no idea." I reach up to run my fingers through his hair. "The real you is so much better than anything I could dream up."

He scoops me into his arms and carries me through the patio doors. But he makes a detour, setting me down in the place I least expect.

We're in the garage. His workshop.

"I want to show you what I've been working on." Rex takes my hand and pulls me to his worktable. There are wooden boards laid out in various sizes, including a lot of long, thin ones. Definitely a complex project underway. "This is what I started when you first visited the beach house. When you were healing from your concussion. I didn't know what it was at the beginning, just that it was for you. Well, *us*."

"And what is it now?"

He puts his arms around my waist. "A crib. Or I should say, it will be. Once it's finished. Good thing we have time."

"Oh, Rex." I turn and kiss him, my ribcage nowhere near big enough to contain the muscle inside it. I have so much love for this man.

And I get to be with him. Get to call him my husband and soon, I hope, the father of my children. How did I ever get so lucky?

"I've been picturing this night for a while," he says, voice deep and low. "How it's going to feel to have nothing between us."

"Me too. I can't wait."

"Should we get started?"

"I'm not stopping you."

Rex picks me up again and carries me to the main bedroom, where he lowers me to the edge of the bed.

I suck in a breath. There are vases of white and yellow roses *everywhere*. And candles, though tonight they're LED ones. Smart move. Neither of us wants any interruptions if a stray flame ignites something.

The scents of rose and salt perfume the air, and I can just

make out the crash of the waves into the shore from our backyard.

Rex goes down on one knee, lifting my gown just enough to slide my flip-flops off my feet. No heels for me. This was a beach wedding after all, even if we went with fancy attire.

He brushes a few grains of sand from my skin, his calloused hands so gentle. An eager shiver runs down my spine.

"Ready to make a baby with me?" he asks.

That shiver cascades into a lightning storm, dancing along my nerve endings. "*Please*."

He leans forward, still on his knees, and palms the back of my neck. He guides my mouth to his.

We've been planning this part of our honeymoon for months. We're going to stay right here in the beach house and, if all goes well, start a new addition to our family. We both got checked out, and Rex's swimmers are working fine. I'm fertile too. I haven't gone so far as to nail down my ovulation schedule, because we didn't want to stress ourselves out unless that's needed. We had all the details we could handle just with planning the wedding.

But this'll be our first time making love without any protection. Another level of intimacy I can't wait to enjoy on the way to growing our family.

Rex's lips tease mine. Kissing softly. Then a sharper nip of teeth. "Might not get it right the first time. We'll need to keep trying. A *lot*. My cock will be inside you more often than not the next several days. I plan to take you whenever and however I want you. Make you mine in every possible way, Quinn Easton. Sure you can handle that?"

I rub my thighs together as my clit pulses with heady arousal. "I'm up for the challenge if you are." I cast a meaningful glance at the bulge in his tailored pants.

There's a predatory gleam in his dark eyes. A devilish smirk on his full lips. "Take off your panties."

"I'm not wearing any."

He groans, chewing his lower lip. "Then get up and bend over the bed."

I do as he says, bending at the waist and draping my upper body over the mattress. Still kneeling behind me, Rex's palms start at the backs of my calves, then slowly drag upward along my legs, lifting my wedding gown as they go. Until finally, I'm exposed to him. He trails kisses over the backs of my legs. My bare butt.

"So precious," he whispers. "My beautiful wife."

When his tongue meets my center, I cry out, grabbing fistfuls of the blankets.

Rex's mouth works me over. His tongue slides into me, but it's not enough.

"Need you," I pant.

"Need your husband inside you?"

"I can't wait anymore."

"Okay, gorgeous. You've been patient enough." He stands, and I hear his belt buckle loosening. The zipper on his fly. His cock fills me up in a single, smooth motion, so hot and thick and more *there* than I've ever felt before. No barriers.

I turn my head to look back at him. Every stroke feels so good, it's almost unbearable. He's still mostly in his tux, and I'm in my bridal gown, and this is the sweetest torture. The slowest build.

But eventually, we get there. Together. I come undone at the same time I feel the hot pulse of his release inside me.

Then we both wind up sprawled on the mattress, our wedding clothes rumpled and the widest grins on our faces.

"I love you, Quinn," my husband says. "I'm so glad you're mine."

"I love you too. You're it for me. Always and forever."

The End.

I hope you've enjoyed Rex and Quinn's story, and the West Oaks Heroes series!

Don't miss Aiden's spin-off story in *Hard Knock Hero*.

A NOTE FROM HANNAH

I can't believe this is my last book (at least for now) set in West Oaks, California! This imaginary town has become real to me over the twelve books I've set here, both in the Bennett Security series and West Oaks Heroes. Hopefully you noticed that nearly every past couple from those series made an appearance here, however small. It's hard to say goodbye.

The great thing is, though, that no goodbye is forever. I have a new series, Last Refuge Protectors, which is set in Colorado and features Aiden Shelborne in Book 1. Plus, other folks from West Oaks turn up on occasion, like Aiden and Madison's brother Jake.

A big thank you to my advance reviewers and loyal fans. And extra love to my prosecutor husband, who dutifully helped me with trial details and pointed out inaccuracies. I had to use poetic license in a few spots for the story's sake, so please forgive me!

Until next time,

-Hannah

ALSO BY HANNAH SHIELD

LAST REFUGE PROTECTORS

Hard Knock Hero (Aiden & Jessi)

Bent Winged Angel (Trace & Scarlett)

Home Town Knight (Owen & Genevieve)

- And more coming soon -

WEST OAKS HEROES

The Six Night Truce (Janie & Sean)

The Five Minute Mistake (Madison & Nash)

The Four Day Fakeout (Jake & Harper)

The Three Week Deal (Matteo & Angela)

The Two Last Moments (Danny & Lark)

The One for Forever (Rex & Quinn)

Bennett Security

Hands Off (Aurora & Devon)

Head First (Lana & Max)

Hard Wired (Sylvie & Dominic)

Hold Tight (Faith & Tanner)

Hung Up (Danica & Noah)

Have Mercy (Ruby & Chase)

ABOUT THE AUTHOR

Hannah Shield writes steamy, suspenseful romance with pulse-pounding action, fun & flirty banter, and tons of heart. She lives in the Colorado mountains with her family.

Visit her website at www.hannahshield.com.

Made in the USA
Coppell, TX
20 February 2024

29217981R00194